PENGUIN BOOKS

FELIX IN THE UNDERWORLD

John Mortimer is a playwright, novelist, and former prac-
ticing barrister. During the Second World War he worked
with the Crown Film Unit and also published a number of
novels before turning to theater. He has written many film
scripts as well as stage, radio, and television plays, including
A Voyage Round My Father, the Rumpole plays—which
won him the British Academy of the Year Award—and the
adaptation of Evelyn Waugh's *Brideshead Revisited*. He is
the author of ten collections of Rumpole stories and two
volumes of autobiography—*Clinging to the Wreckage* and
Murderers and Other Friends. Among his novels are *Summer's
Lease*; *Paradise Postponed* and its sequel, *Titmuss Regained* (all
of which have been made into successful television series);
and *Dunster*. John Mortimer lives with his wife and two
daughters in Oxfordshire, England.

FELIX
in the
UNDERWORLD

John Mortimer

PENGUIN BOOKS

PENGUIN BOOKS

Published by the Penguin Group
Penguin Putnam Inc., 375 Hudson Street,
New York, New York 10014, U.S.A.
Penguin Books Ltd, 27 Wrights Lane,
London W8 5TZ, England
Penguin Books Australia Ltd, Ringwood,
Victoria, Australia
Penguin Books Canada Ltd, 10 Alcorn Avenue,
Toronto, Ontario, Canada M4V 3B2
Penguin Books (N.Z.) Ltd, 182–190 Wairau Road,
Auckland 10, New Zealand
Penguin India, 210 Chiranjiv Tower, 43 Nehru Place,
New Delhi 11009, India

Penguin Books Ltd, Registered Offices:
Harmondsworth, Middlesex, England

First published in Great Britain by Penguin Books Ltd 1997
First published in the United States of America by Viking Penguin,
a member of Penguin Putnam Inc. 1997
Published in Penguin Books 1998

1 3 5 7 9 10 8 6 4 2

Copyright © Advanpress Ltd., 1997
All rights reserved

PUBLISHER'S NOTE
This is a work of fiction. Names, characters, places, and incidents either are the
product of the author's imagination or are used fictitiously, and any resemblance
to actual persons, living or dead, events, or locales is entirely coincidental.

THE LIBRARY OF CONGRESS HAS CATALOGUED THE AMERICAN
HARDCOVER EDITION AS FOLLOWS:
Mortimer, John Clifford, 1923–
Felix in the underworld/John Mortimer.
p. cm.
ISBN 0-670-86079-4 (hc.)
ISBN 0 14 02.7496 0 (pbk.)
I. Title.
PR6025.07552F44 1997
823′.914—dc21   97–16562

Printed in the United States of America

For Emily and Rosie

Facilis descensus Averno:
Noctes atque dies patet atri ianua Ditis;
Sed revocare gradum superasque evadare ad auras,
Hoc opus, hic labor est.

Light is the descent to Avernus!
Night and day the portals of gloomy Dis stand wide:
But to recall thy step and issue to the upper air
– There is the toil and there the task!

Virgil, *Aeneid*, VI, 126

Chapter One

The voice said: 'They told me to get in the motor. I would describe their manner as peremptory. They were hostile. You might say unpleasant. They alleged I had given rise to a whole mountain of paperwork and wasted time they might have spent on ODC, which one of them translated as Ordinary Decent Crime and laughed unpleasantly. I told them frankly I had little or no idea what they were talking about.'

Felix Morsom wasn't paying attention. He was staring at a long sheet of paper, hoping to fill it with his neat, handwritten words. Writing had never been the difficulty but stories now came to him as rarely and unexpectedly as sex. The voice from his elaborate sound system was an unnoticed accompaniment, like the distant murmuring of the sea. It continued: 'At the station my request for legal advice and assistance was met with laughter and a question from the smaller one who was dressed casual: "What've you got against kids?" I said I had nothing against kids. At least, nothing in particular. Then I was banged up without further ceremony.'

Then it occurred to Felix that he was no longer listening to Mahler's *Des Knaben Wunderhorn*.

'The police cell was by no means spacious and a great deal of room in it was taken up by a man wearing a crumpled blue suit and a number of heavy rings. One of them I noticed was a sphinx's head which might have come into use as a knuckleduster. I do not exaggerate when I say that he smelt like a bar parlour on the morning after. I noticed in particular that his hands were not clean and his fingernails were what my mother used to call "in mourning for the cat's mother". By this time I was in considerable distress and I asked if he objected to my making use of the inadequate toilet facilities provided. His words to me, spoken in a slurred voice, were, "Be my guest, sunshine."'

Felix was not writing. A large part of his day, when he came to think of it, was spent not writing. He was looking at the objects on his desk and admiring their neatness. He couldn't start work until the metal duck which contained his paper-clips was directly in front of the clock presented to him by the public libraries of Sussex, until the framed photograph of Chekhov was properly aligned with the glass paperweight with its view of the old Coldsands, until a small plaster model of a sailor, roughly painted and constantly breaking and having to be mended with Uhu, was in its place in the centre of these nick-nacks. He bit the end of his pen and looked out over the sullen, gunmetal sea. He had been full of confidence when he woke up but now ideas seemed to drain away as the waves are sucked back across the pebbles. With nothing else to think about he could hear the voice more clearly.

'It was while I was relieving myself that my cell mate approached, pulled down my clothing and bent me over the toilet. The next thing I was aware of was a sharp pain in my rear passage and a feeling of resentment.'

Bloody wireless! Felix thought. Nothing on it, from morning till night, except people suffering from various complaints: 'Me and my erysipelas', 'How I faced colostomy'. The halt, the aurally challenged, the sexually abused, the partially sighted, and those who had undergone unfair dismissal and false, or perhaps not so false, imprisonment were queuing up at the studio doors. Pale, deprived and sinned-against figures were cramming into the lift and being escorted down the endless corridors of Broadcasting House to flood the airwaves with their quiet, deliberately uncomplaining voices. The trouble with his Orpheus digital sound system, bought with the advance from the novel which was ebbing away from his mind, was that the controls were only labelled with symbols: here an arrow, there a triangle, in another place a couple of mysterious dots. He thought he had pressed the CD button and his first chapter would be coloured by sounds of unearthly beauty, music scarcely heard on land or sea. He had clearly touched the wrong nipple and got Radio Moanalot. He squatted to inspect the device more closely. He pressed the button which he believed silenced the radio but the voice spoke to him again.

'After the incident described above my cell mate started a conversation on the subject of the ordination of women priests saying that the "dog-collared bitches" should be burned at the stake. I was unable to join in owing to embarrassment, and it's no exaggeration to say that I passed a sleepless night. Owing to various pressures I will have to sign off now. When my story is complete, I just hope you will understand the responsibility you bear for all that happened to me.'

Behind a small window of smoked glass Felix now noticed that wheels were turning. What he had set in motion was a tape. 'I shall watch your future career with interest,' the tape said, and then fell silent.

Chekhov is lolling on the steps of a verandah. He is wearing a peaked cap and a long overcoat buttoned to his neck, with its collar up round his ears. He has clear, sharp features and his eyes are half closed, not from weariness but to focus on the world more clearly, for he is not wearing his usual pince-nez. His legs are crossed. His left hand holds a crook-handled walking-stick as though it were a long pen. His right arm is round a floppy-eared dog, which snuggles against him, no doubt for warmth.

Felix looked at the photograph on his desk with envy. When he wrote his first novel he had been called, by one reviewer, 'the Chekhov of Coldsands' and had never been quite sure if this were intended as a joke. He envied the man on the verandah steps not because Chekhov had genius, instead of a certain talent, but because he was a doctor and Felix would always have turned his eyes away from suppurating sores and retreated from evil-smelling bedclothes and sour underwear. He kept the photograph on his desk, among the shells and the curiously coloured stones picked up on the beach, because he had been pleased by the review, which had described his world as one of 'rain-soaked promenades and white paint flaking off the doors of seaside boarding-houses, of dogs shitting on windswept shingle, dried seaweed, tapped barometers and frustrated middle-class lives'. There are things that you and I understand, Felix communicated silently with the picture of the writer leaning back on the verandah steps (plenty of white paint and an ancient wicker chair). Then he wondered how Chekhov would have reacted to the unexpected tape that had spoken to him when, thinking he was about to receive a poignant dose of Gustav Mahler, he had pressed the wrong nipple.

The tape, when he got it out and examined it, played on one side only. There was nothing written on it, no label, no hint of its origin. Although his approach to all machines was tentative, he wound it back to the few sentences which had been spoken while his thoughts were elsewhere. There was a slight hissing noise and then the voice started again with no preamble. 'What happened to me came out of a clear blue sky, although, truth to tell, it was overcast at the time. I had got home from work and noticed an unmarked car waiting in the road in front of my address. I had my latchkey out and ready when they spoke. They told me to get in the motor. I would describe their manner as peremptory. They were hostile. You might say unpleasant.' It was during this action replay that the telephone rang.

'Felix? Hi! It's Brenda.'

'Brenda Bodkin?' He usually asked this, although he knew the answer perfectly well.

'The very one. You all set for tomorrow?'

'Absolutely.' He switched off the tape which was now repeating itself in a way he no longer found interesting.

'Gravesend, London, Winchester and Bath,' Brenda reminded him.

'It sounds marvellous.' It did, to Felix.

'Oh, and I've had Denny Densher's office on. They want you desperately for "Good Morning, Thames Estuary".'

'It still sounds OK.'

'Denny wants you for seven thirty. I'm getting Terry, the rep, to drive us. Could you be ready by six?'

'Without the slightest difficulty.'

'That's great. All your fans will be waiting for you.' And Ms Bodkin rang off.

Left alone Felix thought his fans, a diminishing and ageing group, well scattered. Letters would come in spidery handwriting, written on thin paper, from Canada, New Zealand, Birmingham or, occasionally, Japan, asking for a signature, a photograph or, if his luck were out, heralding the arrival of a bulky manuscript to be submitted for his opinion. Sometimes there were presents: a sprig of heather, a snap of an unknown family in an unvisited garden, perhaps a slice of cake wrapped in silver foil, once a packet of contraceptives marked 'To my literary sperm-bag from Carol Jenks of Cape Town'. He had dropped them wistfully into the waste-paper basket but sent back his usual letter: 'Your kind appreciation of my work gave me enormous pleasure.' Quite often people sent him tapes.

He was burrowing in a wooden box which had once contained wine sent by his publisher when a Morsom novel touched the list of bestsellers. Now it was the depository for unanswered, unanswerable letters. Then he found what he was looking for, a Jiffy bag with the covering note in it, uncertainly typed, unsigned and short: 'I have read every word you have written and always admired your character-drawing and subtle technique. I am wondering if the story I have put on tape for convenient listening would be of interest. Does it seem to you to have television possibilities? Yours truly, An Admirer.'

Felix felt an unusual lift in his spirits. Looking out over the rooftops he saw a crack in the ceiling of grey cloud through which a shaft of sunlight fell and glittered on the sea. The trip he was about to take with Brenda Bodkin should bring him as near to happiness as he got these days. And the tape which had seemed threatening when he heard it was no more than an idea for television; he could dismiss all its unpleasant details from his mind.

Chapter Two

'Just one more schlocky record and a bit of travel, then it's Felix.' The host of 'Good Morning, Thames Estuary' had red curls, a high-bridged nose and the general appearance of an irritable dowager compelled to suffer the boredom of the village fête. The headphones were clamped on his ears like a cloche hat, his T-shirt, bearing the logo 'Good Morning, Thames Estuary' and his own face, was stretched over a capacious bosom and a swelling stomach. He wore gold-rimmed spectacles which he balanced on the end of his nose while he stared with disapproval at the world. He didn't seem to approve of the record which was finishing either, although Brenda Bodkin, privileged to sit in on the author chats during the Denny Densher show, was moving her slender hands in a delicate little dance to the thump of the music. As she did so, Denny smiled at her. She was popular at Radio Thames Estuary because she brought authors in to fill up the gaps between the records and the advertisements.

'His book going well, is it?' Denny asked Brenda the question as though Felix were deaf or a child.

'Melting off the shelves . . .' Ms Bodkin, now lying, was what is known as a strawberry blonde. She was of the pale golden colour that strawberries take on in early summer before they ripen. She was beautiful enough not to have to worry about her clothes, wearing a striped football shirt, much too large for her, baggy tartan trousers and trainers. Felix knew that she carried, stuffed into her handbag, a long green dress for formal wear. He was surprised by the facility with which she lied. Terry, the rep, had, after all, told her the truth in the car: '*Out of Season,*' Terry had said, 'not really moving yet.'

Felix had been sitting beside the rep, blue-suited Terry, in the Vauxhall Astra. Brenda was in the back among the boxes of books and beside the cardboard cut-out of her author which would be part of the display at the literary lunch. As she leant forward to speak to Terry, Felix could feel her breath on his cheek, see the short, silvery hairs on her forearm and enjoy the clean smell of fruit not yet ripe. 'Mind you,' Terry was consoling her, 'you couldn't get Charles Dickens to shift. Not in the present climate, you couldn't.'

'Nothing moving then, Terry?'

'The new Tantamount's selling on well.'

Felix felt something roll against his foot and then emit a mechanical bleep. He stooped and picked up a small, space-age Genghis Khan with a flashing gun on his head. Terry took it from him and said, 'Bloody kids! They leave their stuff everywhere,' and threw the invader over his shoulder where it lay beside Brenda and was immediately silent. Brenda said, 'Is that *Grandslam*?'

'What?' Terry asked her.

'The new Sandra Tantamount.'

'Yes. Right. Sex and shenanigans in the international world of contract bridge. You can say what you like about Tantamount. She certainly does her research.'

Felix wondered about his research, confined, as it was, to his life in the seaside town where he was born, a few love affairs and a marriage ended when Anne committed the final infidelity and died. Should he have explored some unknown country? Should he have learned to play bridge?

'*Out of Season* starting slowly?' Sometimes Felix took a melancholy pleasure in repeating bad news.

'It's a bit of luck Brenda's fixed you up to do the Denny Densher.' Terry was trying to be kind. 'He's got a huge audience and a few of them actually read books.' They had arrived in front of a building, gaunt as a disused warehouse, on which Radio Thames Estuary was written in broken letters. 'Why don't I let you off here, sunshine?' Terry twisted in his seat to speak to Brenda. 'And I'll go park.'

'My special guest this morning, for those of you who are awake, is Felix Morsom. He's here with a new novel. Good morning, Felix.'

'Good morning!' Felix said in a loud and cheerful voice which he hoped would appeal to those countless inhabitants of the Thames Estuary who were yawning, stretching, scratching their stomachs or attempting, with sleep-blurred eyes, to plug in their kettles. 'It says here' – Denny was holding a press-cutting at arm's length, as though it had an offensive smell, and squinting at it over his glasses – 'that you're the Chekhov of Coldsands-on-Sea.'

Taking in his ornamented T-shirt, his Diet Coke drunk from the tin and the fag-end of his Danish pastry balanced on the top of a pile of compact discs, Felix had put Denny down as some sort of local radio yob. Beware of stereotypes. This Densher was clearly a man of sensitivity with wide cultural interests. When the record had thumped to its ungainly end he had said to Brenda, while a disembodied female voice was describing the tailback round Gravesend, 'After that sort of garbage I feel I want to wash my mouth out with a Haydn

9

quartet.' And then he opened the subject of the great Anton Pavlovich himself.

'That review gave me enormous pleasure. Of course I wouldn't dream of comparing myself to Chekhov,' Felix said modestly.

'I don't suppose you would.' The reply, sharp and unexpected as a knee in the groin at a literary luncheon, renewed Felix's faith in stereotypes. Was he not face to face with a genuine yob after all? 'Chekhov wrote about the cholera wards, the prison colony on Sakhalin Island. Know what I mean? *In Season* hasn't got much of the gritty side of life in it, has it?'

'*Out of Season.*'

'Oh, I beg its pardon. I mean, nobody shoots themselves. In Chekhov they do shoot themselves.'

'Offstage.'

'All right, offstage. What I'm getting at is, what's your novel got to offer a young kid brought up on *Pulp Fiction*?'

'What I'm interested in' – Felix began a speech which had seen him through dozens of interviews and guest appearances on 'Start the Week' – 'are those unguarded moments which allow us to see, through the smallest crack in the door, the tragedy of a lifetime. If you know Chekhov (he restrained himself from saying 'If you know so bloody much about Chekhov!'), you'll remember the moment when Uncle Vanya comes into the room with a few late roses for the woman he loves and finds her kissing another man. So he simply drops the roses on the sofa and –'

'Goes out to get a loaded revolver, from what I can remember. Which he fires.'

Once again Felix felt the boot put in by the literature course his interviewer had taken but he fought back with, 'All right, he fires. But he misses.'

'So it's all right if he misses, is it?' Denny, clearly not in the best of moods, decided to end the game. 'Let's turn you over to the punters. Tania from Tunbridge Wells, good morning. What's your question to my breakfast guest?'

'Good morning, Denny. Good morning, Felix.' The voice, quiet and motherly, came out of a loudspeaker fixed to the wall.

'Good morning, Tania!' Felix called out with an unexpected heartiness and Brenda studied her fingernails in embarrassment.

'What I want to know about your writing, Felix,' Tania asked anxiously, 'is whether you use a word processor?'

Felix confessed that he had no mechanical skills or time for many inventions since the introduction of the ring-binder.

'So, Felix, could you please tell me, do you write with a pen or a pencil?'

Tania asked the question as though her life depended on it, and the right answer would enable her to finish a book which would get a mention on 'Good Morning, Thames Estuary'. Felix, not wanting to pursue the secrets of his modi-fied success, played a defensive stroke. 'If you want to know what I write with,' he said, 'I must be honest and tell you that I write with difficulty.' This was a saying which he had used at more literary lunches than Brenda Bodkin cared to remember. He punctuated it with an encouraging chuckle but there was no laugh from the loudspeaker. Brenda was groping into the depths of her handbag for a cigarette and Denny Densher looked increasingly grumpy.

'All right, Tania. That seems to be all the information you're going to get out of my breakfast-time celebrity. So you can get on with the ironing, darling. Now, who's next?' There was a moment's awkward silence. Then Denny muttered, 'What do you write with? Bloody Tania! I know her sort.

Probably writes with a poison pen. Nothing better to do in sodding Gravesend.' With which he bit savagely into what was left of his Danish and glared at the microphone when it said 'My name's Gavin.'

'Where are you from, Gavin?' Denny managed to splutter through the *crème pâtissèrie*.

'Good morning, Denny. As a matter of fact, and to be honest, I'm from the contraflow. And, I'll tell you something else, Denny.'

'Get on with it!'

'I'm a first-time caller.' The voice was ostentatiously modest, as though its owner had just won the lottery or got the OBE for services to animals injured on the motorway.

'I don't give a damn if you're a thousandth-time caller! I'm not going to treat you with kid gloves, Gavin. I'm not going to send you a commemorative card and a slice of cake. I'm going to treat you just as I would any other caller. No better. No worse. Is that clearly understood?' Denny Densher sounded as though he wished to God the breakfast show would come to an end and he could get on with lunch.

The voice said, 'I get the message, Denny.'

'OK. So what's your question to Mr Felix Morsom? And keep it short.'

'Thank you. Good morning, Felix.'

'Good morning, Gavin.' At least this first-time caller would be easier to deal with than the distinctly stroppy Denny Densher.

'I just wanted to ask you one question, Felix.'

'Ask it for God's sake! We can't spend all day with you stuck in the contraflow.' Denny sighed heavily and searched for another record.

'Let me first say I am a terrific admirer of your books,

12

having gone through each and every one of them, page by page. I love your work, Felix.'

'Well, thank you very much, Gavin.' Felix was starting to enjoy the breakfast show but Denny's finger was on the switch and his voice rose in a warning, 'Your time's running out, first-time caller.'

'I'm coming to my point, Felix. And my point is this. Denny put it to you very straight when he said your books don't have sensational events. No shooting or violence, or happenings of such description. Didn't you put that to him, Denny?'

'Yes, I did,' Mr Densher had to admit. 'And now your question to my celebrity guest, *please*!'

'Very well. Understood. Now here's my question, Felix. You must have had dramatic events in your own life. Not shooting perhaps. Not guns. But highly dramatic events. Of great importance. Moments of passion. Times when you lost your usual self-control. Why don't you write about some of these times, Felix? I feel sure they would be of interest to your readers.'

'I think a writer has to make a choice. I suppose I'm not one for the big moments. I just hint at them through glimpses of everyday life in a seaside town.' Felix ended with another small laugh, a nervous one this time. The disembodied voice of the first-time caller spoke again.

'Or do you rely on other people to have the big, dramatic moments for you?'

The question hung in the air of the shabby little studio, unanswered. Denny had switched off Gavin and was slipping a CD into its slot as he announced his verdict to the entire Thames Estuary area. 'Damn cheek! Asking that sort of kinky question to my celebrity guest! It'll be a time before he calls here again, *I'll* tell you. Kinky callers. At breakfast time! I ask you. Now let's get back to something serious . . .'

'Price and publisher!' Brenda, bolt upright and pale with anger, hissed in a whisper that would be audible from the Isle of Dogs to the Goodwin Sands.

'I am reminded' – Mr Densher lowered his head in mock contrition – 'the work we have been discussing is *Out of Season* by Felix Morsom, published by Llama Books for a mere sixteen pounds ninety-nine p.' Then further conversation was submerged by the Stone Roses performing *I Wanna Be Adored*.

In the car Brenda lit a cigarette and held it by one end, waving it vaguely about like a blind man's stick. 'I thought,' she said, 'Denny gave you a bit of a hard time this morning.'

Felix didn't answer her. He remembered where he had heard the voice of the first-time caller. It had come, unexpectedly, out of his Orpheus sound system and had seemed to deal, exclusively, with the big, dramatic moments.

Chapter Three

It was not that Felix's life had been without drama. There was a story that he had folded up, sealed in an envelope and locked in a drawer of his mind. He had never used any part of it in the books he had written and hardly allowed himself to remember it at all. When the memory came it was of the sweet, sickening smell of hospital corridors as he walked away from the sight of a woman dying. Perhaps he had given up thinking about Anne because, like most of science, computer technology and higher mathematics, she was something that existed outside the field of his understanding. She was an occurrence he couldn't explain.

They met during her first term at the University of the South Coast (in those days the Coldsands Polytechnic) where he taught English, where he lived in his parents' house on Imperial Parade, where he had turned his childhood bedroom into a writer's workplace, so that he could still look out of the window and see the seagulls circling and the distant blur of ships passing, where sky and sea became indistinguishable. It was the year his third novel had been compared to Chekhov and its success, like some strong medication, had numbed the ache of anxiety which usually troubled him. Anne came regularly to his lectures but he hardly noticed her.

With her sandy clothes, hair and eyebrows she was, he thought, even after they had got to know each other, as hard to pick out against the beige of the Poly walls as the flat, colourless fish that lay on the bottom of the tank in the aquarium. Perhaps he would have gone on not noticing Anne if she hadn't, suddenly and unexpectedly, sent him a Valentine's Day card, in which she had, breaking all the rules governing such communications, ostentatiously signed her name.

Feeling that he owed her something (he had received no other Valentines), he invited her to come with him to a performance of *Endgame* by the Saltsea Strolling Players. After it they bought fish and chips and went back to the room at the top of his mother's house. He was talking to her about ambiguity in literature, hinting at greater mysteries which don't necessarily have to be understood by the audience, or indeed by the writer, when she moved to unzip his trousers. She had seemed so colourless and yet he was astonished by the vitality with which she made love. Locked away in that store of memories not to be visited was the sound of the sea, the smell of fish and chip paper, and the sharpness of her small and even teeth.

Five years after they were married, she told him she no longer loved him and was to go away with Huw Hotchkiss who was head of Media Studies and had been offered a job in Singapore. Then three months later she said that she couldn't leave because the result of a test she had undergone showed that she had little time left to live and 'It wouldn't be fair on Huw.' Felix had taken her in his arms and promised to look after her, and they continued to make love while she still had the strength. After he had walked away from her for the last time, down the corridor which smelled of rubber and sickly sweet disinfectant, his life became uneventful and he locked away these memories.

His longing for Ms Brenda Bodkin remained comfortingly unfulfilled.

'What I really admire about you, Mr Morsom, is your deep understanding of women.'

'Of women?' Felix, who had failed to fathom his wife Anne from the first to the very last, was taken by surprise.

'I mean the women characters in your books.'

'Oh, yes. Of course. Them.'

Felix looked round at the crowd, predominantly women, who filled the seats at the *Sentinel* lunch in the ballroom of the Rubicon Hotel. They had come, he admitted reluctantly, to hear a woman. Sandra Tantamount, her hair frozen into position, her wrists jangling with gold bracelets and dangling charms, was sitting at the top table. She had brought her own champagne and a small pot of caviar which she was spooning on to toast whilst the editor, who had arrived at the *Sentinel* from the *Newcastle Echo*, was giving her the benefit of his no nonsense, north country, one hundred per cent sincere admiration. As Sandra raised the black, glittering pile to her carmine mouth, Felix stared down at his unyielding slice of unripe melon and the scarlet cherry planted in it like a sign of danger.

'So many male novelists undervalue women.'

'Yes.'

'And turn them into fantasy figures. Dreams to jerk off to.'

Felix, who had been watching Ms Bodkin in animated conversation at one of the less than top tables, turned back to his neighbour. The woman beside him was tall and grey-haired, with a delicate nose and a porcelain complexion. She wore a black suit with a brooch in the lapel. She might have

been an excellent aunt or a sensible grandmother to very
young children. 'Women don't do that?'

'Jerk off? Oh, certainly. From time to time. But at least
they live in the real world. Men won't face up to their
responsibilities.'

'All men?' Felix felt one of the outcasts, having fallen below
the standards of the handsome grandmother.

'Not you, of course.' She smiled at him in a forgiving way.
'You live up to your responsibilities as a writer. And such a
successful one.'

'Well, not all that successful.'

'Yes, surely?'

'I've been criticized lately.'

'Who criticized you?'

'A man on the radio. He thought more should happen in
my books. More violent events. Murders, probably.'

'You should have told that man on the radio he was being
very silly.'

'Should I?'

'Everyone thinks murder's interesting. When I was a gel I
thought murder was strange and exotic and really rather glamorous. My head was full of Sherlock Holmes and Dorothy Sayers
and Father Brown stories. I was as excited by murder as the other
gels were by thoughts of sex. When they were marking passages
like "He slid gently into her and her world exploded", I was
reading about the Malay dagger he slid into her or of the single
shot that rang out. Now, I know that murder's a pretty mundane
business, really. About as glamorous as washing-up.'

'You know that now?' Felix asked her in some surprise.

'Of course. Now that I've done so many.'

'Done? You mean written about them?'

'Oh, no! I don't write about murder at all. Although I am

into a novel at the moment. I call it *Here on This Molehill*. You know *Henry VI*?'

Felix was not sure he did.

'The king's sitting on a molehill, looking at the distant battle. Isn't that what novelists do? Sit on molehills and look at events? By the way, I must find a decent publisher. Who's yours?'

Felix told her about Llama Books. Then she turned away from him as the sharp-faced man on her other side, wearing the chain of some civic dignitary, said on a high note of complaint, 'Appalling way little sods from North Kensington are putting paid to civilization as we know it.'

'What can we do?' She had her hand on the man's sleeve and was speaking as gently as she had been on the subject of murder. 'Except wait until they get bored with violence. In the good old days, I suppose, we would have packed them all off to the colonies.'

'No respect for authority,' the man was saying. 'They don't stop short of vandalizing the mayoral Daimler.'

'I think you'll find they do us a very acceptable coq au vin at the Rubicon.' The editor had felt it his duty to tear himself away from Sandra Tantamount and speak to Felix with north country candour. 'I've not actually *read* your book. But my wife's got through it and praise from her doesn't come easily, I can tell you that.'

'So, did she praise it?' Felix was foolish enough to ask.

'I can't remember if it was yours she praised. Not if I'm honest. Of course, she couldn't put down Sandra's effort.' The editor turned back to Mrs Tantamount, who was opening a plastic box which contained her own goat's cheese and wild mushrooms, nestling on a salad of radicchio.

★

After the lunch came the signing. Felix stood by the life-size cut-out picture of himself, a person, he felt, who looked nothing like him. He thought he looked quizzical, detached and as amused as Chekhov on the verandah steps with his dog. The cardboard *doppelgänger* who stood beside him had an apologetic, furtive look and an unconvincing smile, as though he were concealing some guilty secret. He did his best to ignore it and looked across at Sandra Tantamount whose cardboard cut-out looked as well-groomed as the original.

Felix had to admit that the Tantamount queue was longer but his was, at least, respectable. He engaged his readers in chat about their holiday plans, their children, what the weather was doing and the M20 contraflow – the sort of questions that hairdressers ask. So his line moved more slowly than Sandra's because she scribbled her name with no questions asked and with the quick mirthless smile of an air-hostess. He wasn't humiliated. In his speech he had done the one about writing with difficulty and the handsome Grandma had let out a laugh like a chime of bells. Now she held out the copy of *Out of Season* she had bought and said, 'Do go on writing this marvellous stuff. Don't waste your time on murder.'

'A book signed is a book sold' was Brenda Bodkin's philosophy of life, and Felix remembered it as the handsome would-be authoress moved away, leaving behind her a faint, perfectly healthy smell of lavender talcum powder, a card with her name and address and the hope that they might meet again.

When the signing was over Felix took Brenda and Terry down to the Island in the Sun saloon in the Rubicon Hotel and there, to the tune of piped calypsos, he bought them Margaritas which he only drank on book tours. As Ms Bodkin put out a pink tongue to taste the salt rim on the edge of the glass, a macho feeling came over Felix and, for an enjoyable moment, he felt more a Hemingway than a Chekhov.

'Fantastic ring!' Brenda, making conversation with Terry, was looking at his hand as it clutched the margarita glass. A silver-plated sphinx stared up at her from Terry's middle finger. 'Magnus Merryweather gave me that . . .' Terry seemed proud of it. 'Remember when we did the tour of his *Nearer God's Heart*?' Felix wasn't paying attention to this exchange. He had dug in his back pocket for money and brought out, among the five pound notes, his lunchtime neighbour's card. She was, he was surprised to discover, Detective Chief Inspector Elizabeth Cowling, OBE, attached to Paddington Green police station.

Chapter Four

'The *Sunday Telegraph* was good.'

'Did you really think so?'

'I'd count that as a good review.'

'"Those who enjoy Felix Morsom's work may like his new seaside portrait in pastel shades."'

'Well, you can't say that's bad.'

'I suppose not. What about the *Guardian*?'

'I strongly advise you not to look at the *Guardian*.'

'Well, all right then.'

'Don't think about it. Try and think about something else.'

They were having the full afternoon tea in the Beau Nash room of the Bath Hotel. Brenda dissected a scone, shovelled on a dollop of clotted cream with her knife and surmounted it with a neat cairn of strawberry jam.

'All right, I'll try.' Felix admired her dexterity. He was afraid that, undertaking the same operation, he would drop jam on his voracious pullover. There was a silence between them and then she asked, 'Well, what else are you thinking about?' She had, he was pleased to see, a small blob of cream hanging from her upper lip.

'My bathroom,' he told her.

'I told them you were a famous author.'

'Thanks.'

'No problem. So they gave you the Aquae Sulis suite. It's the one usually kept for Sandra Tantamount.'

'I was thinking about the jacuzzi.'

'Oh, yes?' She sounded, he thought, insufficiently interested. 'What were you thinking about it?'

'Well, it's huge. With marble steps leading up to it. And golden lions' heads with open mouths spouting hot and cold. And soap on a rope. And a glass shelf for pot-pourri and cotton-wool balls. And every sort of fragrancy by courtesy of the management.'

'So?'

'I was just thinking' – he put his cards face upwards on the table – 'we might possibly twiddle round in the jacuzzi together?'

She looked at him and seemed to be smiling. He thought he might clinch the argument by adopting a literary approach as he always found writing about life easier than living it. 'It would help me enormously in my work.'

'Your work?'

'I mean, I can't go on writing for ever about the view from Coldsands pier. I do need some sort of drama in my life.'

'What sort of drama?'

'You and I in the bathroom,' he told her. 'It'd be an experience.'

'Something for you to write about?'

'Well . . . yes,' Felix had to admit it and felt he was losing any advantage he might have had.

'That's all you want me for, isn't it?' She looked pained. 'To bung me into a book?'

'No, it isn't. Honestly, it isn't.' Not for the first time he noticed that the introduction of the word 'honestly' robbed the sentence of all conviction. Brenda added hot water to the pot, stirred it and poured out tea in an alarmingly maternal fashion.

'Felix, I really like you . . .'

'Well, that's a start.'

'And we get on extremely well together.'

'Of course we do.' Felix was encouraged.

'So, it's just as though we'd already done it!'

'Done what?' Felix was surprised.

'All that sex stuff!'

'Have we?' Felix was puzzled. 'I never noticed.'

'I mean, we did it in our heads. In our imagination. That's where all the important things in your life go on, isn't it?'

'Of course not!' He denied it more vehemently because he recognized the truth of what she'd said. At least, in so far as it related to him.

'So let's keep it that way, shall we?' She was holding her cup with both pale hands to warm them and looking at him across the little lake of almost colourless tea, as though she were doing him a huge favour. 'Don't let's spoil it all by struggling around naked in a bath or anything revolting like that.'

Felix wouldn't have minded spoiling it all but he didn't like to say so.

Millstream's were undoubtedly the best booksellers. Their dark, panelled shops tinkled with baroque music and were staffed by knowledgeable graduates. The young men, often shaven-headed and pierced in various parts of their bodies, were supervised by girls who peered out from under their fringes or over their spectacles, both sexes being dressed in the black clothing favoured by stagehands changing scenery when the curtain is not lowered. The shops were always open late and on Sundays. Each month Millstream's in Bath staged an author event. Felix, introducing his new book, was that month's attraction.

He stood with his notes resting on a high pile of Sandra Tantamount's novel, facing an audience of about fifty on folding-chairs. 'Not standing or sitting on the stairs as they did when we had Sandra,' the manageress had murmured from under her fringe. 'But not a total humiliation.' Behind them tables were laid with refreshments for the meet-the-author session. Bottles of Carafino white, jugs of orange juice, samosas and sausages on sticks, sausage rolls and slices of quiche nestled among the bestsellers and piles of paper table napkins. The audience, turned towards Felix, couldn't see this spread or the glass doors and the rain-soaked, palely lit street.

As Felix talked he could see these doors open and the little cluster of doorway sleepers, the homeless and dispossessed, silently enter. They wore layers of clothing, scarves and bala-clavas or bobble hats. Felix had seen them, or some like them, under a line of eighteenth-century arches on a windswept pavement they had furnished with bundles and boxes and sleeping-bags. Now they advanced, slowly, remorselessly, on the food, less like locusts than blundering bumble-bees, and stretched out for it with mittened fingers reddened from the cold.

They didn't clear every plate, which would have exposed their theft, but picked a few sausages, a sandwich here and there, a selection of samosas, and a modest swig from a bottle of white wine. Felix wished them well and tried to hold the attention of his audience, and the staff of the bookshop, while they ate. By the time he had finished his speech, to a gentle shower of applause, the swarm had vanished and the plates, though depleted, looked undisturbed.

When the queue formed for booksignings, however, an alarming smell approached him. That part of life which Felix feared most came first to him by way of his nose, which was now filled with a cocktail of stale urine, dirty feet, bad breath, fried food and, somewhere in the background, the dry, musty all-enveloping smell of shit. Standing in front of him, parcelled into a collection of wrappings fastened with binder twine, was a dumpy woman of unfathomable age.

'Put your name on there, Felix. Sorry I can't afford a book.' The woman was holding out a sheet, yellowing with age and brittle, of the *Western Mail*.

'What name is it?' Felix was trying to speak whilst holding his breath so that he sounded like a ventriloquist's doll.

'Evangeline. And you can put "With love from Felix" and I shan't mind.'

He put that and watched her go. What should he have given her? Money, a bottle of the Carafino, a free copy of *Out of Season*? Whatever he should have done, he had missed his chance. She was on her way to the door and another book, opened at the flyleaf, was being pushed in front of him. He asked, as he always did, 'What name shall I write?'

'Just your signature would be an honour, Mr Morsom. Dated, of course, if you'd care to oblige.'

It was the voice he had come to recognize. The voice he was hearing for the third time. 'You're sure you don't want me to write your name?'

'It's *your* name that's important, Mr Morsom. Your name and your book. I'm quite simply a member of the public. No more and no less.'

Felix's signing of the book produced a small flash of light. The member of the public had handed a camera to the next person in the queue, who had snapped author and fan chatting at a literary event. This member of the public looked younger than Felix. Perhaps he was not yet thirty but his hair was already receding. He had a pale face and a delicate turned-up nose. Although young he had the look, both anxious and resigned, of middle age. He wore a blue suit and a tie with a crest on it. Felix thought it might have been the tie of a Rotary club or the rowing club of a bank. Watching him recover his camera, Felix said, 'You're a member of the public who seems to have been in some terrible trouble. Didn't you send me a tape?'

'A tape? You think I'd send you a tape?' The member of the public looked at Felix with sympathetic concern.

'I'm sure you did. And you spoke to me on "Good Morning, Thames Estuary".'

'Good morning, what?'

'Thames Estuary.'

The member of the public shook his head, still apparently bewildered.

'The Denny Densher show. You were a first-time caller,' Felix reminded him.

'It puzzles me' – the member of the public frowned – 'that a writer of your stamp, sir, should be listening to such a programme.'

'I wasn't *listening* to it!' Felix was losing patience with this lugubrious person who spoke extremely slowly. 'I was *on* it!'

'Oh, of course. I should have remembered that you were the star. As you are here, tonight.'

'I recognize your voice.' Felix had no doubt about it. 'You sent me a tape describing a terrible experience! You were arrested.'

'You mean *someone* sent you a tape. I expect they thought it might be useful to you. It might give you some idea of what goes on in the real world. Writers have to learn from somewhere, don't they? Oh, by the way, I've brought an old friend to see you.'

'I'm sorry' – Felix signed his name hurriedly on the proffered book to end a dialogue which seemed to be getting nowhere – 'there are a few more people who want books.'

'Oh, she can wait. Heaven knows, she's waited long enough already. But, of course, your many admirers must come first.'

So the member of the public stood, palely at attention, while Felix signed books for grey-haired men in anoraks and grey-haired women in trousers, school teachers, civil servants and social workers – and an occasional lawyer. As they gave him their names he wrote to Carol or William, or Annette or even Justin, and when the last book had been signed the silent watcher said, 'I did so admire the courteous way you treated your public, Mr Morsom. Even those who came in from sleeping rough. I noticed your courtesy to them. I speak as one who knows what it is to doss down in a doorway. I have been reduced to that, Mr Morsom, in the ups and downs of my own past.'

'I'm sorry,' Felix felt he ought to say.

'No, you're not, Mr Morsom. Why should you be sorry? You hardly know me as yet. Now, let me take you over to Miriam. I well know what a busy man you are but I think you owe her five minutes of your valuable time.'

Felix looked round for Brenda's help but he saw her far away in Gender Studies, wearing her long green dress and laughing with the darkly clothed bookselling staff. So, alone and defenceless, he allowed himself to be led to an alcove where, beneath a notice which read Foreign Travel, a woman sat fast asleep.

'Miriam.' The member of the public spoke in the firm but

gentle voice of someone who's taken a long journey to visit a friend in hospital. 'Wake up, Mirry. Felix is here to see you.'

Nothing stirred, then the woman dragged open heavy lids shadowed with blue make-up. 'Felix,' she murmured. 'At last! Such a long, long time no see.' Then she smiled and he noticed that her quite seriously protruding teeth were coloured with scarlet lipstick.

'So,' she said, 'Gavin's brought you to see me at last?'

'You remember her, don't you?' said the hitherto anonymous man she had called Gavin. 'Surely you remember Miriam Bowker?'

'Well, yes,' Felix lied politely. 'Yes, of course. When was it exactly?' His way of dealing with such situations, which happened frequently on book tours, was to feign total recall and keep the conversation going until some dropped hint, some lightly touched reminiscence, focused his memory and a clear picture emerged.

'When? I should've thought *you'd* remember when. Ten years ago, Felix. Can you believe it! How time flies.'

'Ten years ago,' Gavin agreed. 'Isn't it a birthday, Miriam?'

'Your birthday?' Felix tried to think back ten years but all was confusion. He had always been hopeless at dates.

'Not *my* birthday. You should know when my birthday is. Although I'm not admitting to a day over thirty!' She laughed then, nervously, shaking her shoulders, and he blinked, dazzled by the colours that she wore. When she was still, her clothes were less obtrusive, but when she moved, it was like staring at a brilliantly lit asymmetrical kaleidoscope. A red high-heeled shoe, half off, hung at the end of pink tights decorated with a hole exposing a circle of pale thigh. He took in the purple mini, electric green shirt and blue velvet jacket sewn with sequins. Her hair, dyed a deep, chemical red, was stiff and brittle, as though made of spun sugar, and her face was pale and weary. Her bright clothes were crumpled, stained and grubby, so that she looked like a court jester who had been made to sleep in the straw above a cold stable and was still suffering from it. Her voice was curiously high and full of breath like the voice of a child. 'I hope you're happy, Felix,' she said. 'I think of you so often and I hope you're happy.'

'I'm fairly happy.' Felix felt he had to say this because she looked genuinely concerned. It would be hard to say that shut in the safety of his room, staring at the sea, tracing in black ink, when he was lucky, a thousand words a day, he was either spectacularly joyful or unbearably miserable. But with the distraction of a book tour and the possibility of Ms Brenda Bodkin, it would be hard to pretend he wasn't content. 'And you?' he was polite enough to ask her.

'I have my moments,' she said. 'I'm proud to say I still have my moments. Now that we've found each other again, stay in touch. Will you promise me that?'

'If he doesn't stay in touch with you,' Gavin said, Felix thought quite unhelpfully, 'I'm sure you'll stay in touch with him.'

'Well . . .' Felix had decided to wind up the conversation. 'Great meeting you again and I hope you enjoyed the talk.'

'Oh, I wasn't listening to the talk!' He had the uneasy feeling that she was laughing again. 'I was too busy looking at you. And as you stood there, so serious, I couldn't help mentioning it to Gavin, you looked exactly like Ian.'

Who on earth was Ian? Felix felt panic stirring, faced with yet another character he couldn't remember. He looked round for Brenda and there she was at last, dependable and ready to rescue him. 'I'm so sorry,' she said, 'I must tear him away. We're going to dinner with the Millstream's people.'

'Goodbye,' Gavin said. 'And thank you for your time.'

'Goodbye.' Felix remembered the tape, the slow, unperturbed voice describing suffering. 'I'm glad your troubles are over.'

'Oh, my troubles are quite over now. Thank you, Mr Morsom.'

'Goodbye, Felix. Don't let it be so long next time. Oh and I want you to have this.' Miriam delved into a multi-coloured velvet handbag and produced a brown envelope. 'At least it'll help you remember.' He took it, relieved that it couldn't be a novel or even a short story – at worst a lyric poem. He found himself thanking her as he slipped it into his pocket.

'Who on earth were that Gothic couple?' Brenda asked as she led him away. 'Extraordinary friends you have!' Felix had to admit that he hadn't the remotest idea who they were, except that the man had been in some sort of trouble with the police.

'And the woman looked like trouble for everybody. What a complete mess she was! Offputting.' Beauty, Felix thought, is handed out far more unfairly than talent or money and those, like Brenda, who are blessed with it, condescend to the overweight, long-nosed, hairy-handed, pinch-mouthed and less attractive majority. 'It's a horrible thought but do you think they're an item?' He said he didn't know what they were and didn't care if he never found out.

The Millstream's workers drove them to a bistro, where they ate grilled monkfish, the pale, black-clad manager opted for the vegetarian platter, and Brenda ordered more and more bottles of Australian Long Flat Red on Llama expenses. She was particularly sparkling, as though to underline the horror of the Gothic fans from whom she had rescued Felix, and amused the table with the adventures she and her author had on their many book tours. She told them how she pinned the Booker winner's name on Felix at a sales conference and assured the half-intoxicated reps that the prizewinning author had changed her sex; how she had been bursting for a pee while they were marooned round Spaghetti Junction and Felix had nobly drunk up the Méthode Champenoise presented to them by a Writers' Circle in Stoke-on-Trent. Felix remembered with a stab of lust that she had held the bottle decorously under her skirt and he had heard the splash and little gasp of relief above the sullen murmur of traffic. She told them that Felix had stood signing books in Harrods with his zip undone, and later he had shown an unsavoury interest in an insolent girl with pert breasts from the *Godalming Times* until she had ordered him, with the full authority of a publicist from Llama Books, to 'put her down because you never know where she's been'. At all these literary anecdotes the table laughed, another bottle of the Long Flat Red was uncorked, and Felix revelled in the legend that his life had contained a strange and exciting number of events.

Later, as they went up in the hotel lift together, a contraption lined and quilted like the inside of a sedan chair, Brenda was still giggling at the memory of some incident in the course of their invasion of the country's bookshops. Felix found the courage to say, 'You've told them all the things we did. What about the things we haven't done?'

'You're not inviting me to your jacuzzi again?'

'Why not?'

'Because I'm exhausted.' She put the back of one slim-fingered hand to her mouth and acted an enormous yawn. 'Do you think I'm being unfair?'

'We can't just leave it in our imagination.' He fell back, as usual, on a literary argument. 'I mean, my books have to get written. They just can't float about in my brain for ever.'

'But isn't it hard work writing them?' They'd reached the third floor. His arm was round her waist and she wasn't altogether steady on her feet.

'Sometimes it is. Sometimes it's quite enjoyable.'

'Sometimes?' She gave him her wistful look, as though gazing back at a distant and ever-receding point.

'You don't think we ever will?' They had reached her door and she fumbled in her bag for the key which was no longer a key but a piece of plastic which caused lights to flash and the door to buzz open. She said, 'It's against Llama Books' policy for publicists to sleep with authors. In England, anyway.'

'We shan't always be in England.'

'Shan't we?'

'If we ever went abroad for the book that'd be all right, wouldn't it?'

'I suppose it would.'

'We've got a date then?'

'Yes. We've got a date.'

She put her small mouth to his and her lips seemed dry and brittle, like the body of an exotic insect. Then a green light glowed on her door and she left him in a mood of unusual triumph. The lonely days and solitary nights, the hours of staring at the grey sea and white paper, the arranging of objects on his desk, the walks to the end of the pier in search of stories – all these aspects of his working-life seemed gloriously worthwhile to Felix when he thought of abroad and the joke he would one day dare to tell Brenda, quoting Hamlet, about making his 'quietus with a bare bodkin'.

This high mood stayed with him as he started to undress. He emptied his pockets and found the brown envelope Miriam Bowker had given him and opened it, expecting a fan letter or a request for literary advice. What he found was the photograph of a child, a small boy, perhaps nine or ten years old. Felix had little experience of children. The boy in question was standing on a beach under a grey and threatening sky. If he was on holiday, the child didn't seem to be extracting much pleasure from it. He peered at the world from behind spectacles which were too large for his face and looked as though he had seen a great deal in his short life and didn't expect much good to come of it.

Felix only puzzled over the photograph for a moment and then put it back in its envelope. But when he closed his eyes that night, strangely enough it wasn't Brenda Bodkin in her eagerly anticipated nakedness that he saw but the myopic child standing on the beach by the sea, where he didn't seem to be playing.

Chapter Five

Felix had boxes for everything and he had three big files full of photographs. After his book tour he should have been catching up with the new novel but he was wasting time in his room shuffling through his memories. His dead father stared up at him, a man caught on holiday, wearing a small moustache, a white open-necked shirt and a blazer decorated with the crest of the South Coast Bank golfing society: crossed clubs on a tee argent and the motto *Mens sana in corpore sano*. He was squinting angrily at the sun as though hating it for being so bloody cheerful when he was filled with disgust at the boredom of his life as manager of the Coldsands branch. He had urged Felix to get a secure job with a bank, not wishing his son to escape what he had endured so painfully. When Felix chose a writer's life he was as resentful as those fathers, tied to an ageing and unsympathetic spouse, who watch, with horror and envy, their children revelling in transitory romances with beautiful and interesting girls from Sussex University. His father's job turned out to be less safe than Felix's. Many employees of the Coldsands branch were sacked in a 'slimming-down operation' and replaced by stacks of machines and computers which bleeped messages, ate people's bank cards, confused the accounts, charged them usurious rates of interest and stole their money without any human supervision. Felix, who had adopted the risky life of an author, had to keep his father in pink gins, subscriptions to the golf club and Spanish holidays until the Guvnor, or Guv as he liked to be called ('I always gave my father that title and what was good enough for the old man's good enough for me'), died of terminal disappointment at the age of sixty-three.

He was looking at his mother now, standing at his father's side with her arm through his and making the best of it. When the Guv died she was released from all anxiety and, proud of her son's career, adopted a strange *vie de bohème* – or as much of it as could be had in the environment of Coldsands. She took to wearing large and improbable hats, many-coloured shawls and enrolled as a mature student at the Coldsands university. There she flowered considerably, became an important member of the Union and had a circle of admirers among the gay and lesbian students whom she entertained in the local wine bar, where they enjoyed her increasingly ruthless jokes at the expense of the faculty. Although Felix was no longer teaching, he felt bound, from a bewildered love for his mother and a feeling of respect for the extent to which she had benefited from his father's death, to accept her constant invitations to speak to the Fiction Club or the Creative Writing Society, and he would stand, embarrassed, in some sparsely attended lecture hall with his mother spread out in the front row, flanked by her supercilious circle, taking copious notes and calling him Felix when she asked him questions about authors of whom he had scarcely heard.

He saw his father laughing at Felix's wedding-party at the golf club, and Anne joining him, her head bowed, her hand on the arm of his Moss Bros tailed coat to steady herself. He could remember none of this and wondered what they had both found so comical about his marriage. And then there were a number of uncommunicative pictures of a night barbecue on the beach when Anne was still a student. He recognized Huw Hotchkiss, with whom she had fallen in love, wearing a pair of swimming trunks and a chef's hat, and his wife with a string of sausages round her neck, waving a wooden spoon. He saw faces he no longer remembered, lit from below like devils by the driftwood fire and a blurred woman, brightly dressed and shadowy in the background, with a bottle raised to her lips. It might have been his mother.

And then came a black and white picture of a boy, perhaps ten years old, a solemn child wearing spectacles, standing on the sand under a cloudy sky and not looking as though he were enjoying it. For a moment he thought it was the photograph Miriam Bowker had handed him in the bookshop but then he remembered that was in colour and the child was wearing jeans. The boy in the picture he held was wearing longish shorts, kept up by an S-buckled belt. Peering at it more closely, he realized that it was himself.

He heard the front-door flap rattle and the thud of letters falling into the hallway. He came downstairs, as always half hopeful, half in dread, to confront his post. It didn't look particularly promising. There were two invitations to parties for other people's books, a letter from someone called Kurt in Hamburg who wanted the Herr Doktor's autograph, and a sheaf of poems from prison which he had agreed to judge for a competition.

He opened the long brown envelope with the letters PROD and the official stamp last. He had hoped it might be a cheque from some public library at which he had spoken. He read its contents, at first with amazement, then with laughter and finally with rage. It had been a long while since he had gone through so many emotions in half a minute. The letter was short and the names and the amount of money filled in on some sort of printed form. The Parental Rights and Obligations Department required the immediate payment by Felix Morsom of the sum of twenty thousand pounds for the maintenance, over the last ten years, of the infant Ian Bowker. Cheques were to be made out to the Ministry of Social Welfare and crossed PROD Account. Failure to pay would result in the immediate commencement of legal proceedings.

Chapter Six

'Young Morsom's my guest at luncheon.'

Septimus Roache stood in the hall of the Sheridan Club on that square island of carpet which is reserved for the feet of members only and shouted up an immense staircase. Above him dangled a figure with one hand gripping the balustrade, another in charge of a walking-stick which splayed out like a third and spindly leg, motionless on the white marble stair like a dark spider in its web. Sir Ernest Thessaley, the distinguished author of *The Light of Evening*, a trilogy dealing with the life and times from wistful boyhood up to his present state of near immobility of a character indistinguishable from himself, called back without turning his head, 'Is he a member here?'

'He's in your line of business, Ernest.'

'What business is that?' The great man appeared to have forgotten.

'Storyteller. Wordsmith. Mythmaker. Oh, for God's sake! He's a bloody novelist.'

'What was his name again?'

'Felix Morsom.'

'I thought that was it. Never heard of him. Anyway, I can't stand the stuff he writes. Friend of yours, is he?'

'No, he's come to me for a bit of advice.'

'I should think he needs it. Writing like that. Virginia Woolf and piss.'

'Read him then?'

'Read him? Of course I don't read him! Life's too short to read Morsom. Why on earth are you having him to lunch?'

'I told you,' Septimus Roache shouted gleefully, 'he's in a spot of trouble!'

Members were struggling up to the bar for drinks. Other members came clattering down on their way to lunch while others stood in the entrance hall, warming themselves in front of the fire, reading the evening paper or the news on the tickertape, and waiting for their guests. Some of them may not have known who Felix Morsom was but now they all knew he was in a spot of trouble.

'Don't step on this bit of carpet.' Septimus Roache's voice was deep and somehow disembodied, so it was difficult to associate his warning rumble with his rare smile of welcome. 'Members only!' Felix, who had advanced with an outstretched hand and a polite 'Mr Roache, isn't it?', skipped back from the minefield the members' carpet no doubt represented.

'Yes, I'm Seppy Roache.' The rumble was more gentle now, as though the explosive device had been temporarily defused.

Felix said, 'Simon Tubal-Smith at Llama told me you specialize in authors' troubles?'

Septimus Roache's grandfather had been articled to the firm of C. O. Humphries, Son & Kershaw, which acted for Oscar Wilde when he took his disastrous journey through three trials to Reading Gaol. Young Artemus Roache had been no more than a silent spectator at these proceedings, having been sent out of the office to fetch hock and seltzer to quench the thirst of the nervous literary martyr. However, it gave him the idea that artists, particularly literary artists, were vulnerable creatures, usually with secrets to hide, who might be lured into costly and unwise litigation. He started his own firm, Roache, Pertwee & Musselbaum, in which he was succeeded by his son and grandson. Writers as diverse as Somerset Maugham, Mrs Radcliffe-Hall, Agatha Christie, Henry Miller and Edgar Wallace would wander casually, and as though they never quite meant to, into the old house in Bedford Square and discuss everything from infringement of copyright and wills to blackmail, gross indecency contrary to the Criminal Law Amendment Act and, on one or two surprising occasions, murder.

So Septimus (he was so called not because he was the seventh son but because he was seventh in a long line of frustrated hopes, imaginary pregnancies, miscarriages and other disappointments – and the only child to fight, argue and cheat his way into existence with an aggression to which he owed his success in the law) carried on the family tradition and managed to grab from his partners (the descendants of Pertwee and Musselbaum) all the exotic cases arising from the aberrant behaviour of poets, novelists, playwrights and the occasional painter or composer. He was already an Honorary Fellow of the Royal Society of Literature and was shortly to be knighted for services to the arts. He was a short-legged, square man with wide shoulders, the face of a discontented Pekinese and wiry grey hair which sprouted, not only around his bald patch, but from his nostrils, his ears and on the backs of his fingers. He wore a bow-tie, a black suit with a wide chalk line, and a monocle dangled round his neck like a foreign order.

'Well, young fellow,' he said to his prospective client as they sat together at a table by the high window, 'what've you been up to exactly?'

'As a matter of fact I've just got a new book out, *Out of Season*.'

'You'll have the brains?'

'Well, I'm not sure that writing a novel requires brains exactly. I mean, as I'm sure you'll know, you've got to find a theme. Something you can get a feeling about and then, well, just hope a story can sort of grow out of it.'

'No, I meant *brains*. I hope you're going to eat them?'

Felix looked round the room as though searching for a way of escape. Was eating brains a rule of this mysterious club, like not standing on the carpet? Several elderly men were crouched over a white mess on their plates. The voice of Septimus boomed in his ear. 'At last, I've persuaded chef to do offal. Or would you prefer liver, sweetbreads, black pudding? Next month we're going to introduce members and guests to chitterlings dressed up as *andouillettes*. Charlie!'

An alarmed Indian waiter, whose short white jacket revealed the ends of his braces, stepped forward and smiled nervously.

'Yes, Mr Ross?'

'*Roache*. Septimus Roache. Try and get it right, Charlie. I will have the brains, please.'

'Brains?'

'Yes, brains!' Septimus roared. 'And my guest will take . . .What will you take, Morsom?'

'Perhaps,' Felix hesitated, in search of the least disgusting parts of the menu, 'pasta.'

'Pasta!' Septimus spat out the word as though it were a shameful disease. 'With meat sauce?'

'Perhaps tomato.'

'I suppose you can drink a carafe of the club's burgundy without going green about the gills?' Septimus Roache opened one eye wide to allow the monocle to drop to the end of its string, put away the menu and said, 'Now what particular skylarking have you been up to, my lad? I understand you're

42

in a bit of a scrape?' At which Felix started to pull the letter from P R O D from his pocket and was greeted by the horrified look an unreconstructed bishop might give to a couple of choirboys he found comparing sizes behind the high altar. 'Put that away at once!' was exactly what Septimus said.

'Really? Why?'

'Because you can't give me papers in this club.'

'Oh, I see. Why is that?'

'Because we're not allowed to conduct business in this club.'

Felix wondered what they were going to talk about for the next hour. 'I thought you wanted to know what sort of trouble . . .'

'We can *talk* about that, of course. We can *talk* about anything. Charlie's knowledge of the English language is strictly limited and, if we can keep our voices down, I can make a date to bugger you on the snooker table and no one'll be any the wiser. But pull out papers and we'll be drummed out of this club and that's all there is to it. Now then. Who did you prod?'

'Nobody. I had a letter.'

'Shut up about the letter!'

'I heard from the Parental Rights and Obligations Department. They want me to pay twenty thousand pounds for a child.'

'Seems steep! There must be parts of the world where you can pick up a child for a fraction of that money.' Felix had a horrible suspicion that this appalling lawyer, who was now leaning too close to him for comfort, one hand cupped round a hairy ear so that he might miss none of Felix's secrets, was not joking.

'It's meant to be my maintenance for a child.'

'The child's a big spender?'

'Over ten years.'

'Whose child is it?'

'They say it's mine.'

Septimus let out a loud and unexpected laugh. 'Your little bastard, your by-blow, your wrong side of the blanket?'

Felix's nature was such that he felt immediately protective of this unseen child who seemed likely to cause him so much trouble. 'I know nothing of the child,' he said. 'And I only met the mother last week.'

'Hardly time to produce a ten-year-old child.'

'Hardly.'

'But who was this mother?'

'She said her name was Miriam Bowker. She gave me a photograph of a small boy.'

'Your boy?'

'Certainly not mine.'

'A boy you didn't recognize?'

Felix hesitated for a moment, remembering the picture of himself, and then opted for 'Yes.'

'You don't sound too sure about it.'

'I'm sure that extraordinary woman isn't the mother of my child.'

'Extraordinary?'

'Dressed like a sort of clown.'

'All women are extraordinary if you want my opinion.' Septimus was lapping up his brains with a spoon. Felix turned from this spectacle as firmly as he looked away from poverty. 'Anyway, this one has some sort of financial claim against you?'

'So she says.'

'What do you want me to do about it?'

'My publisher thought you might give me legal advice.'

'Legal advice? For a little scrap in the Magistrates' Court? What did Tubal-Smith want me to do? Engage counsel at vast expense? Call experts on the medical side? Have the woman watched by some professional dickhead at two hundred pounds an hour to find out who the real father is? Use your common sense! It'd be cheaper to pay it. Cheaper still to hire a contract killer.'

'You mean' – Felix froze, a forkful of dripping tagliatelle poised in the air – 'kill the child?'

'Both. Mother and child. You could get a contract for two at around five hundred. Yes, what do you want, Charlie?' The waiter, whose name was Aziz and not Charlie, had come up to tell Septimus that he was wanted on the telephone.

'If you don't want to go to that expense' – Septimus was laboriously pushing his way out of his chair – 'take her out to a rattling good lunch and say, "Look here, darling. Tell me who's the real father of the little bastard." Poke her if you have to, or whatever you do to women. Distasteful business from all I've heard of it.'

'Extraordinary!' Felix said aloud, his mouth full of pasta, to Septimus's retreating back.

'What's extraordinary?' Sir Ernest Thessaley had arrived at the table and, rearranging his leg and walking-stick, folded himself like a lanky insect into a vacant chair.

'That you can arrange to kill two people for five hundred pounds.'

'Can you, by jove?' Sir Ernest laughed, a sound like a dry gargle. 'I might get that done to Pikestaff on the *Indy*. He gave a horrible notice to my memoir. Called me an old snob. Typical of someone who went to a minor place like Oundle. And who are *you* planning to do in?' Felix, feeling inexplicably guilty, said, 'No one, really. No one at all . . .' He thought his voice lacked all conviction.

'Well, keep your nose out of trouble, my boy. I happen to be a fan.'

'A what?'

'A great admirer of your work.'

'Well, that *is* a compliment, coming from you.' In fact Felix had read as little of Ernest Thessaley as Sir Ernest had of Morsom but he felt that one kind word deserved another.

'So why don't you order a bottle of the club's champagne? To celebrate our mutual admiration.'

'I'm only a guest here.'

'Put it on Seppy's bill. He can afford it.'

'You're sure?'

'Absolutely sure.'

'All right then. Charlie, a bottle of the club's champagne.'

'Bubbly coming up right away, sirs.' The waiter was more relaxed with Septimus out of the way.

'I'll tell you what,' Sir Ernest said before the cork popped, 'they don't make enough fuss of you. I thought that was a pretty dire notice you got in the *Guardian*.'

'Was it?' Felix took a hurried gulp of champagne. 'I didn't read it.'

'Did you not? "Virginia Woolf and piss", I think that was the expression. I may have a copy at home. I'll send you a photostat.'

'Please. Don't trouble.'

'No trouble at all. I believe the fellow who wrote that review went to Winchester.'

'Did he?'

'Perfectly decent school. You know what you need to do if you want good notices?'

46

'What?'

'Die. Get increasingly poor notices, or no notice at all, as you grow old. But you've only got to die and poof! You're a bloody genius. That's what I intend to do. Die. That'll make them change their bloody tune!'

When Septimus came back he said, 'Hullo, Ernest. I see you've ordered champagne.'

'No, you have. I've been chewing the fat with young Morsom here.'

'Oh, yes? And what have you two literary giants been talking about? "Whither the novel?"?'

'Not at all! Morsom here was discussing murder.'

'Were you, by God!' Septimus raised his glass to Felix. 'If you ever think of doing anything like that, just give us a ring. We'll put out the red carpet and get you the best silk in England.'

Chapter Seven

Ken Savage, Senior Collection Officer
Parental Rights and Obligations Department
St Anthony's Tower
Lambeth
London SE1 7JU

Your ref: 0149638924 BIB 472
            re: Ian Bowker, infant

25th May

Dear Mr Savage
I received your letter suggesting that I owe arrears of
maintenance for the above child. Since I have never met
the mother and know nothing of her or her son, and
have never been responsible for his maintenance, I feel
sure that this request was caused by some clerical error
in your department. I hope this mistake will be rectified
and I will hear no more of the matter.
Your sincerely
Felix Morsom

It was three weeks since he had posted this letter and he was
encouraged by the prolonged silence. It was something, like the
death of his wife, which he could file away in a never-opened
drawer. When he was writing the letter he knew that, in
saying he had never met Miriam Bowker, he was slipping

from fact into fiction. But he decided that a casual encounter at Millstream's, Bath, hardly counted as a meeting.

Since Felix wrote his letter to Mr Savage the weather had changed. At the end of August, a ferocious late summer had set in. Standing at his window, he watched the seagulls float lazily down to settle on the sluggish green sea. Even the pier, half boarded up and in desperate need of paint (the palmist and the summer shows had long since deserted it and the ghost train was permanently out of order), looked inviting and romantic in the sunshine. Girls in bikinis lay on towels spread on the damp sand, as though they were in an advertisement for Caribbean holidays. Fat couples in shorts wobbled as they jogged down the promenade, or panted as they stood in a queue for ice-cream. The roadmenders had stripped off their shirts and, bent over a spade or electric drill, displayed half their buttocks to the great amusement of a small group undergoing care in the community. Watching all this, knowing that he should sit down and start to drip words from the top of his pen, Felix noticed a smart, businesslike woman with scraped back hair. She walked as though preceded by some sort of herald in the shape of a pale child, a boy wearing spectacles.

Felix saw the woman hesitate on the pavement opposite while the boy strode recklessly and relentlessly on to the crossing, causing a bus to brake so suddenly a party of senior citizens lurched in their seats. A small red car skidded to a standstill and a cyclist swerved and fell. The child marched on and found a place on the bench next to a grey-haired man who was conducting an invisible orchestra in a silent performance of Tchaikovsky's *1812 Overture*. Now the woman, safely across the road, was trying to persuade the child to get up and continue their journey but her pleas and eventual frustrated anger failed to dislodge him. She moved away, nearer to the houses in Imperial Parade. And then Felix heard a ring at his doorbell.

'You don't remember me?' The woman was standing on his doorstep. Behind her Felix saw the boy on the bench watching them with what looked like contempt.

'Not exactly.'

'Millstream's bookshop. With Gavin. I'm sure you remember. And before that, long before. I'm Miriam. Miriam Bowker.'

'I didn't recognize you.'

'You've got a short memory, Felix. Of course I was dressed different. Gavin likes to see me in something bright. He doesn't get much brightness in his life, poor bugger.'

Felix looked again at the woman who might have been a solicitor or a PA in a firm of mortgage brokers in her grey suit and with her hair, now brown, gathered in a scrunchy. (He was careful to learn such words to help with his writing.) Perhaps distracted by the brightness of her clothes, he hadn't noticed her face in detail. He remembered the forward-looking teeth but not the large eyes that also protruded slightly, the statuesque chin that gave her the look of a Victorian heroine, and the lines of laughter or exhaustion. She said, 'This respectable outfit's quite new. I only stole it yesterday. I'm joking, of course. I put it on to come and see you.'

'I'm afraid I'm terribly busy. I'm writing.'

'No, you're not. I saw you. You were staring out of the window.'

'I know. I have got to get on with it. So . . .'

'Don't shut the door in our faces, Felix. Ian's been eagerly looking forward to today.'

'Ian?'

'Your son Ian. He's sat there on the bench with a mind of his own.'

Felix looked at the child who sat with his hands folded, staring out to sea and pretending that he had no connection with the persistent woman on the doorstep or her outrageous requests. All the same, he felt they had both come to undermine his stability, to throw his life into confusion, to prevent him for ever from doing the only thing he knew how to do, which was to sit alone and write. The twenty-thousand-pound demand was ridiculous and when he thought that he could get rid of both of them for ever for five hundred pounds he was, for a moment, sorely tempted. And then he remembered Septimus Roache's second, less daring solution and plumped for it.

'It's a quarter to one,' he said. 'Why don't I take you out to a rattling good lunch?'

'Well, Felix!' The woman smiled. 'I can see we're going to get on ever so well.'

'Will he come too?'

She turned towards the child on the bench who refused to look at her. 'I suppose,' she said, and her smile turned to a look of fear, 'he might condescend.'

'I do like a nice lunch set out with a silver service,' Miriam said.

'Don't say that, Mum.' The child sounded severe.

'Why ever not? I'm sure Felix wants us to appreciate the treat.'

'It's embarrassing.'

Felix thought the boy had a point but his mother apologized for him. 'Ian's changed school so many times,' she said, 'he learnt no manners, really. You see, we've always been on the move. Never been able to settle, worse luck!'

'Look here, darling.' Felix remembered how Septimus had instructed him to start. Then, thinking he had gone too far too soon, changed rapidly to 'Look here, Miriam.'

'Darling's OK by me, but I'm Mirry.'

'Well, then. Look here, Mirry. Do you know, do you have any idea, that I've just been sent a bill for twenty thousand pounds by PROD?'

'*Prod*?' Mirry started to laugh. It seemed to Felix that he had hit on a subject she greatly enjoyed. 'Rather an appropriate name, if you come to think about it. Ian, do Mummy a favour won't you?'

'What?' The child's loud question was full of suspicion.

'Just go and sit at one of those empty tables and draw a nice picture. You don't know that he can draw really well, do you, Felix?'

The Princess Beatrice Hotel, Coldsands-on-Sea, had been, Felix had thought in his childhood, a place of unbelievable luxury and splendour. It was where his father's golf club held its annual dinner-dance, to which he was allowed to come, wearing a small, rented dinner-jacket that smelled of mothballs. Once a year, on his summertime birthday, his parents took him to lunch there, after which they went to a performance given by the Airy Nothings who did an annual summer show on the end of the pier. He remembered a short-haired, blonde girl who slipped off her pierrette costume to reveal a spangled bikini and who did a dance during which she was thrown about like a tennis ball by two men dressed in caps and baggy trousers, billed as Les Apaches. At the end of the dance, Les Apaches appeared to toss the girl into the audience and for a moment she came flying towards the lap of the twelve-year-old

Felix until she was caught by the wrist and ankles and restored to her low-life lovers. As a result of this theatrical moment Felix achieved a surprising and prolonged erection and was afraid to stand up for 'God Save the Queen' in case his mother noticed.

At that time the Princess Beatrice was full, prosperous and smelt of floor polish, brown Windsor soup, brandy and cigars. Members of the Rotary Club slapped each other on the back in the bar, laughed loudly and stood rounds. Honeymoon couples held hands at breakfast and only looked at each other a little less passionately than those on illicit weekends. A pianist in a white dinner-jacket played selections from *South Pacific* during the cocktail hour and there were always cucumber sandwiches and scones and cream at teatime. Now the town had fallen on evil days. The holidaymakers, fleeing from the rain, preferred Torremolinos and Lanzarote. The businessmen no longer supported the Rotary Club. McDonald's and the Thai takeaways did good business but the tables in the Princess Beatrice dining-room stood white and empty as ice floes in a polar sea. In an effort to attract some new and classy custom the food had become elaborate without being good. Gone was the comforting brown Windsor soup, the roast beef and Yorkshire, the fried plaice and chips. Mirry and Felix started with 'grilled goat's cheese de Coldsands avec son salade verte'. After this Ian had called for chicken nuggets but, these delicacies being unavailable, he joined his mother and Felix in 'pintade à la mode paysanne avec son vin rouge' – a stringy fowl in a slightly vinous gravy, accompanied by a side plate of barely cooked string beans, carrots and bulletlike potatoes. 'It's a real treat,' Mirry had said, 'eating out *à la Française.*'

'All that PROD stuff,' Felix said. 'You know it's nonsense?'

'Ian, I said, will you please go to an empty table and draw a picture?' Mirry gave this order with surprising firmness and, even more surprisingly, Ian went.

'You see,' she said when the child had gone, 'I've changed my hair colour since Bath.'

'Yes, I noticed that.'

'You notice quite a lot of things, don't you, Felix?'

'It's my job.'

'I thought you found the Titian Russet a bit startling.'

'A bit.'

'So now it's the colour it was when we first met. All those years ago.'

'Miriam,' he said, trying to smile and refilling her glass with the champagne he had ordered to carry out Septimus Roache's idea of a rattling good meal, 'you know we never met at all those years ago. We first met at Millstream's all those weeks ago.'

She looked at him, smiling kindly, and said, 'You're a liar, aren't you, Felix?'

'That's not altogether true!' Felix did lie a little.

'Oh, but you are. When we met at Bath . . .'

'Yes. We met then.'

'Gavin said, "Surely you remember Miriam Bowker?" Didn't Gavin say that? Weren't they his very words?'

'Well, yes, I think they were.' Felix had the feeling that he was walking, blindfold, towards some deep and bottomless pit.

'And what did you say to that?'

He became deliberately vague. 'I can't quite remember.'

'Let me remind you, Felix. You said, "Well, yes. Yes, of course." Those were your very words. So you're a liar, aren't you, darling?'

SEVEN

'I was a liar *then*,' he admitted, 'when I said, "Yes, I remember you."'

'Why did you say it?'

'To be polite.'

'What?'

'Not to hurt your feelings.'

'Very considerate, I must say.'

'And because I *might* have met you. At some bookshop or lecture.'

'Or party?'

'I suppose it might've been a party. So, I thought I'd say yes I'd remembered you, just until we talked a bit and then you'd remind me exactly when it was.'

She put the back of her hand to her mouth to block laughter. 'That is the most ridiculous story.'

'I often do it.' Felix agreed with her that it did sound unconvincing, as the truth usually does.

'And were you just being polite when you wrote to PROD three weeks ago and said you'd never met me and you knew damn well we'd had that little chat at Bath?'

'You saw the letter?' Being without a defence he took refuge in an accusation. '*You're* behind this ridiculous demand?'

'Of course I saw it. I keep in close touch with Ken.'

'Ken?'

'Ken Savage. The bloke you wrote to. He's been very helpful.'

'Oh, I'm glad he's helpful!'

'I'm glad you're glad.'

'You put him up to this!'

'I was very hurt when I saw what you wrote to Ken. You know what he said? Ken said, "There now. He's told you another porky. We've got him down as 'liar' in our computer

55

system." I defended you. I said your job was making up stories. I said you're not a habitual liar. Only sometimes.'

'I'm not a liar!' Felix looked over at the child who was drawing quietly on the back of a menu, his head down and his tongue out in concentration. 'He's nothing,' he whispered, 'to do with me.'

'There's *two* lies we've nailed down already. Now what about the third?'

'What's that?'

'Where we first met?'

'First?'

'Here. At Coldsands. Right here.'

'In this hotel?' He wondered what she would invent.

'Course not. We couldn't afford hotels like this. Not in those days. Not when we're that much younger. It was at a party. An outdoor party. On the beach.'

The barbecue. The dark photograph. His wife with a string of sausages around her neck, waving a wooden spoon. A shadowy figure in the background which couldn't possibly have been the woman who sat in front of him, crinkling her nose as she drank unaccustomed champagne. Huw Hotchkiss, a man with a deep chest and sturdy, athletic legs, wearing black swimming trunks and a chef's hat. 'Who gave the party?' he asked, hoping she wouldn't know. 'Who gave it?'

'Huw, of course. He gave all the parties.' She smiled and he felt something like despair and asked, with only a glimmer of hope that she wouldn't know the answer, 'Huw what?'

'Hotchkiss. You should remember his name, considering his relationship with your wife, which they didn't bother to hide particularly.'

'Where?'

'What?'

'Where did we do it?'

'Ssh, Felix! Not in front of *him*,' Miriam said in a piercing whisper, which Ian disregarded.

'*Well*?'

'Beside a breakwater, so far as I remember. On a lilo someone had brought.'

'And after that?'

'It's up to you to remember.'

'I told you, I don't remember any of it.'

'I'd never have had a chance to remind you, would I? Not if Gavin hadn't brought us together.' She laid her hand on his and looked as though she were profoundly amused.

'Who is this Gavin, anyway?' Felix withdrew his hand.

'Gavin Piercey. Don't you remember *anything*?'

'Nothing much that you tell me, I have to admit. Piercey, you say?'

'He used to hang round Media Studies at the university. Trying a part-time course. We've kept in touch, Gavin and I have. He believes in keeping in touch more than you do, I must say.'

'Odd way of keeping in touch. He sent me an extraordinary tape and then he kept turning up like the voice of doom uttering vague threats.'

'I think he wanted to warn you.'

'Warn me?'

'Gavin had a bad experience.'

'So I believe.'

'Got in wrong with PROD about a child. You see, he didn't answer their letters. Just didn't open the envelopes. So they got a court order. Threw him in the slammer!' Miriam covered her mouth with her hand again to trap laughter, which was exploding as though she had just said something both comic and obscene.

'Whose child was it?'

'Not Gavin's.'

'Not?'

'No. That was the whole point of it. It turned out not to be his child at all!'

'Sounds familiar.'

'So PROD stopped chasing him and he's in the clear now and he's got his job back. He's in your business, actually.'

'You mean he's a novelist?'

'Not as grand as you. He drives around selling books. Well, delivering them to bookshops. For Epsilon Books. I think people have to pay to be published by them.' She looked at him, deeply concerned. 'You did answer PROD's letter, didn't you? It doesn't do not to answer.'

'I told you I wrote and said it wasn't my child either.'

'Of course. You told them a few more porkies.'

'Miriam,' he started.

'Mirry.'

'All right. Mirry, I don't know what you've told PROD, but now you've got to tell them you've made a mistake. You are utterly and completely mistaken. Of course, if you're really in trouble, I could help you out. To a certain extent. I wouldn't mind doing that. What do you say?'

'I'm not in trouble, Felix, and I don't want you to be either. But you've got to face up to the truth. You've only got to look at Ian to tell you what that is.'

He looked at Ian. The child had finished drawing and returned to his mother. She looked at the menu he had decorated and handed it to Felix. It was a distorted child's vision of himself, his hair standing on end, his spectacles askew and his shoelaces undone. Under it was a single word, Dad.

Chapter Eight

'Is this where it was?'

The summer had vanished ten days after it arrived. Now the wind whipped up froth on the heavy sea, loaded with rubbish. The beach was empty except for elderly couples, their raincoats blown flat against their bodies, calling after wet dogs who bounded off to sniff and clamber on each other. The mess of the short summer – bottles, Coke cans, cardboard plates from takeaways, and the wrapping of contraceptives – lingered among the hillocks of sand. Two men walked along the beach: one with thinning hair disturbed by the wind, lifting to expose bald patches; the other square, short and dark, broad-shouldered and Celtic. They were Felix and Huw Hotchkiss, head of Media Studies and one-time county player of rugby football. Huw was a man who smelled, Felix remembered, of old leather chairs. With his fingers he made a square like a viewfinder and squinted through it, as though planning a shot of the damp breakwater and the litter-strewn sand.

'"Exterior. Empty beach. Day. Grey sky. Rain. Sound. Laughter. Party chatter. Dissolve to exterior breakwater and beach. Night. There is a party in progress. Huw is barbecuing a chop. Anne Morsom is wearing a necklace of sausages. Assorted students and hangers on are eating, laying out food or getting laid behind the breakwater." It's all visual. You can do that sort of thing on film. Caxton's dead and buried. The age of the book is over.'

'Do you remember that party?'

'Of course I remember.'

'Was there a lilo put there, do you remember?'

'A lilo? Oh, you mean an *airbed*.' The Welshman in Media Studies sometimes pretended he could only understand American – the language of the visual arts. 'Oh, loads of them. Those that didn't bring a steak, or a bottle of red, brought an airbed. It's good to see you, boyo!' Huw put his arm around Felix and squeezed his shoulder painfully. They hadn't met since Anne's funeral and when Huw was embarrassed he became very Welsh, called people boyo and either embraced them or punched them hard in the ribs. In moments of extreme embarrassment he had been known to bring even women down with a flying rugby tackle.

'It's good to see you too.' Felix was lying again; he had avoided all contact with Huw for years. The strange Miriam had forced him into a meeting with the man who now said, 'We both lost her, didn't we?'

'I don't want to talk about Anne.'

'I understand that, Felix. I understand that completely. She was a beautiful girl and we couldn't keep her.'

'I want to ask you about another woman.'

'You've found someone new? Oh, I'm sincerely happy. From the bottom of my heart I'm happy for you, boyo. I won't take this one from you, I promise.'

'I haven't found her. She's found me. And, as far as I'm concerned, you're welcome to her.'

'You're bitter about me, boyo.' Huw looked hurt. 'I can hear the note of bitterness in your voice. But I say this from the bottom of my heart. I wish you every happiness.'

'Do you remember anyone called Miriam? Or Mirry?' Felix was determined to concentrate on the question he had to ask.

'There were so many girls about. Students. Friends of students. Wannabe students. We had a whole crowd from central casting. It was a big scene, Felix. A big, vibrant scene in the picture. What was she like?'

'I'm not sure.'

'What's she like now?'

'Either someone from a travelling circus or a quiet, serene-looking secretary.'

'Make up your mind!' Huw laughed.

'Whatever she looks like, her name's Miriam Bowker. What I want to know is, was I on a – whatever you call it – an airbed with her at any time during the party?'

'I don't know. Do you think you were?'

'From what I remember I was on an airbed making love.'

'With this circus person?'

'No, with my wife.'

'You couldn't have been, I'm sorry to have to tell you.'

'Why not?'

'Because I was. There now. Bloody hell, I've hurt your feelings!' Huw punched Felix on the upper arm.

'It doesn't matter. Do you remember anyone called Gavin Piercey?'

'Piercey? Bloody pain in the backside!'

'You remember him?'

'Extra-mural. He used to turn up at my class on the Moving Image until I discovered he only wanted to be an accountant on a film unit and I chucked him out. Have you come across him lately?'

'Quite lately, yes.'

Gavin had rung him the evening of Miriam's lunch. She

and Ian had left without trouble when he had given them money for their fare and a 'spot of cash for gas bills and boring things like that'. She had promised to have a word with Ken Savage at PROD and calm him down: 'I think he fancies me just a little does our Ken.' When Felix put them in a taxi for the station, Ian had looked at him and said, 'Thanks for a great meal, Dad.'

Gavin's call came while Felix was watching an adaptation of *Vanity Fair*. The persistent, always slightly hurt voice said, 'I'm so glad you hit it off with Mirry and Ian. I hear you gave them lunch and helped them out. It'll be a new interest in life for you, won't it, Felix? See you at your next event.' Felix was about to say he didn't want to see or hear from Gavin again, ever, when the phone clicked and he was left alone with Becky Sharp. Now he stood on the beach with Hotchkiss, staring at the scene of whatever crime he had committed. 'She says I gave her a child.'

'Who says that?'

'This woman, Miriam.' And Felix winced as his arm was punched again. 'I'm happy for you, boyo! It's great news.'

'Is it?'

'It's the future, Felix. You'll push yourself out into the years to come.'

'It couldn't have been done at the party. Not with anyone except Anne, that is. Dammit, my mother was there.'

'So far as I remember your mother was paddling in the sea with a couple of queens. Later on she was dancing with both of them. How can you be sure what happened?'

'I suppose I can't.'

'We were drunk on youth and love and Carafino red. That's what we were, boyo. You know, come to think of it, Anne never gave either of us a child.'

'No.' Felix had a horrible suspicion that there were tears in the Welshman's eyes. Then Huw burst out laughing, punched him in the stomach this time, and shouted, 'I'm happy for you, Felix. Sincerely happy.' Then he vaulted over the breakwater and ran away fast across the sand as though he were carrying a ball and scoring a try at Cardiff Arms Park.

It was a sunny day and Felix smelled once again the sickly sweet, disinfected air of hospital corridors. But this time he was in the Evening Star Rest and Retirement Home, seven miles to the west of Coldsands. He was following Miss Iona Wellbeloved, the perpetually anxious head of the establishment, down a corridor in which the sunlight dappled the linoleum and burnished a vase of plastic daffodils. Miss Wellbeloved knocked and opened the door to a small bright room where his mother lay, propping up the mountain of bedclothes and smiling perpetually. 'I'll leave you two alone together, although I'm afraid, Felix, you still won't find her exactly chatty.'

He sat by the bed and took his mother's hand but got no answering squeeze.

'Well,' he said, as usual hopelessly, 'how are you, Mum?

'Treating you reasonably, are they? I believe *Out of Season*'s doing quite well. I've been on a book tour. Did I tell you that?

'Mum, I've been meaning to ask you this. You remember being at a barbecue on the beach? A party given by Huw Hotchkiss? Please listen, Mum. Do your best. It's important. Do you remember a girl hanging about there called Miriam Bowker? Please can you hear what I'm saying?'

There was still no reply, but Felix tried anyway. 'I need to know. Urgently. Was I ever on a lilo with Miriam Bowker?'

Mrs Morsom smiled and kept her counsel, as she had for

six years. On the way out Miss Wellbeloved asked Felix if he had ever considered termination.

'For me?'

'For your mother. We don't see much hope of a change. Of course I'd have to have a word with Dr Cheeseman.'

'Please don't!' Felix was positive. 'I get the feeling that, most of the time, she's secretly happy.'

Later he travelled to London for a book signing in Millstream's, Covent Garden. In his pocket was a letter he had received that morning from PROD. It ran:

Dear Mr Morsom

Your letter dated 25th May has been noted and will be dealt with by our Mr Savage on his return from paternity leave. Meanwhile, I have to inform you that your liability for the infant Ian Bowker has been reassessed at £25,000. I should warn you that failure to pay any sum due to PROD will result in immediate court proceedings.

With all good wishes

Yours sincerely

Placidity Jones pp. K. Savage

Brenda Bodkin, driven by Terry, the rep, met Felix at Victoria. She was, he thought, looking radiantly beautiful that morning and smelling of freshly baked bread. Her nails were less bitten than usual and her hair lit up Terry's dingy car like sunshine. However she was in a brisk and businesslike mood which forbade any reference to the distant prospect of abroad or of translating his desire from fiction to fact. Instead he sat brooding on the evil Gavin, the scheming Mirry and the senseless injustice of PROD.

'You're not listening!' Brenda had been giving him the *Out of Season* sales figures.

'No. Are they good?'

'All right, that's what they are. Perfectly all right. Anyway, what are you looking so miserable about?'

Terry was listening to a Meatloaf tape and Felix lowered his voice under the sound of the music. He needed someone to confide in.

'About a woman.'

'What did you say?' Brenda shouted above the music.

'A woman's causing me terrible trouble.'

'I'm not causing you trouble. I'm telling you your sales figures and you're not even listening! You're not going on about our getting out of the country to do it, are you? Because if you do, I probably shan't.'

'It's not you. It's another woman.'

'Oh, really?' Brenda's voice was like a chill blast of winter. 'I thought I was the only woman in your life.'

'Well, you're not, worse luck.'

'What's this other woman done to you then?' Brenda was looking out of the window, making it clear that she had very little interest in the matter.

'She claims to have had my child.'

'She *what*?' Brenda turned to look at him.

'She says this solemn little boy she has is mine.'

'So naturally you did it with her?'

'It's just possible. Years ago. On the beach. Well, there was a lilo under the breakwater. The trouble is I simply can't remember.'

Winter had given way to spring and now Brenda was smiling. 'You mean,' she said, 'there've been so many?'

'Well' – he decided there was no harm in letting her think so – 'perhaps.'

'Bloody hell! You old devil.' Terry cornered with panache,

the Astra bucked and rocked and they were thrown together. He felt the warmth of her tartan-trousered thigh against his and she didn't move away. 'At least we've got something we can grab hold of, publicity-wise.'

'You think I need this sort of publicity?'

'Of course you do! You know, the trouble with you, Felix, as a promotable author, you're not colourful. That's why your sales figures are all right but not spectacular. You're a nice chap, Felix. As an author you're perfectly acceptable. You don't smell. You don't get drunk. You don't chase your publicist round the room. You ask politely. You talk nicely to punters at book signings. But let's face it, Felix, you are monochrome. It seems that nothing has ever happened to you.'

'People have been saying that lately.'

'People are right. Take Helena Corduroy.'

'I'd rather not!' Felix remembered the formidable historical novelist with whom he'd once shared a literary lunch where she read from her *Age of the Troubadors* for forty-five minutes.

'Wicked, Felix. Wicked!' Brenda was laughing now, her hand on his thigh. 'When Helena's husband went off with another man she got the centrespread in the *Meteor* and bang on to the bestseller list.'

'Nothing to do with her book?'

'Of course not! Her books are terrible. And Tim Gosshawk. Remember him? *Gosshawk's Gardening* was dull as ditch-water. Had up for gross indecency on Wimbledon Common and he made it to number five in the non-fiction.'

'It sounds like a hard path to success.'

'You betcha! But worth the slog. "Famous Novelist's Love-Child": I think Lucasta Frisby on the *Meteor* would be *very* interested.'

'I'm not sure that it was love exactly.'

'Novelist's child of lust. Even better. And I'll tell you what –'

'What?'

'When we've got the *Meteor*, we'll go to Dublin. Together.'

'I thought we were going anyway?'

'Well, perhaps, yes. Perhaps we are.' She lit a cigarette holding it, as always, like a magic wand with the tips of her bitten fingers. 'Seeing that you've become more colourful, I'll ring Lucasta.'

'Just hold on a minute' – Felix, like Queen Elizabeth I, was a strong believer in the politics of prevarication – 'just till I get a few things sorted out.'

'All right then.' Brenda smiled at him. 'Tell me when you're ready.' And they held hands all the way round Trafalgar Square.

When he came up, as Felix knew he would, in the queue outside Millstream's in Covent Garden, Gavin wasn't carrying a book. Instead he was holding a brown envelope which contained, he said, a message Miriam had asked him to deliver. Felix took it, stuffed it into his pocket and said, with extremely hard feelings, 'Do you want a book signed?'

'No thanks, Felix. I've bought one of yours already. I'm afraid I can't sub you any more although I do realize that you need the money.'

'Then, if you'd just move along. There are other people waiting.'

In fact Felix's customers were standing patiently. Behind them, at the end of a row of shops, a pale girl was collecting money in a bowler hat for a man who stood in chains and was only prepared to liberate himself when the hat was loaded. Gavin spoke to Felix as though they were alone in a room.

'I wanted to warn you. Be careful of those bloodsuckers at PROD. They're not fools, those bloodsuckers aren't.' Gavin was smiling. 'And they'll chase you without mercy, they will. Unforgiving, they are, if they think you let down a child. Also they duff you up in custody.'

'As you know to your cost.'

'To my cost. Yes. Indeed.'

'Don't worry. I've got no intention of being banged up in a cell.'

'I wouldn't advise it.'

'Which child was it you failed to support?' As Felix asked the question he suspected what the answer must be.

'It was young Ian. I'm sure you know that by now?' Gavin's attention had been caught by the chained man. 'If he gets out of that lot I'll suspect some sort of trickery.'

'Of course. You're Ian's father.'

'Oh no, I'm not. Mirry *thought* I was. She thought that for a long time until I went through it with her. Then she agreed it must have been you. It was the only answer.'

'The only answer for *you*!' In his anger Felix felt a wild moment of relief, as at the climax of love. Unaccustomed to rage, he found the sensation intoxicating and heard his voice as though it were someone else calling in the distance, 'You bastard! I'm going through all this just to get you off the hook? Is that what you're saying? Let me tell you something. Prison's too good for you! Get out of my life, do you hear me? You can drop dead, Gavin, for all I care. Drop bloody well dead!'

Gavin, smiling, turned to join the crowd round the chained man and Felix heard a sharp command, 'Sign this, will you, with some message of respect for an older wordsmith. *Il miglior fabbro* or some such brown-nosing inscription.' Gavin's place had been taken by that uncoordinated daddy-long-legs of an elderly author, Sir Ernest Thessaley, who had paused outside the bookshop on his way to the Sheridan Club and was interested enough to ask, 'Was *that* the fellow you're planning to kill?' and, as he took the signed copy of *Out of Season*, 'Have I contributed, in some small way, to the price put upon his head?'

On his way home in the train Felix opened the brown envelope. In it he found further photographs of Ian, his latest school report, and a sprig of brown seaweed. Such a piece, he remembered, used to hang outside the back door of his parents' house at Coldsands in order, by its occasional dampness, to foretell the state of the weather. As a bored child he would pinch and pop its dried pimples. This present of seaweed was attached to a card which showed the silhouettes of a pierrot and pierrette kissing in front of a yellow dinner-plate of a moon. On it Miriam had scrawled in green ink 'A memento of our great occasion. I took it home from the breakwater.'

Felix put everything back into the brown envelope and, being alone in the compartment, threw it out of the train window as they approached Guildford.

Chapter Nine

In the crime stories Felix had read, in the films he had seen, the central character returns to find his house in total disorder, drawers pulled out, desk rifled and cupboards emptied, in the search for some clue or treasure he didn't know he possessed. Feeling that an undeserved and fraudulent mystery had been dumped upon him, he was not surprised, some days later, to find that a window-pane next to the front door and giving on to a downstairs lavatory had been broken and the window was swinging open. By the seat a small table, carrying a pile of literary magazines and a useful work called *The World's Most Popular Plots*, had been upset and an entrance clearly effected. After a thorough and prolonged search of his home he found nothing missing or apparently disturbed. What housebreaker would enter merely for the pleasure of looking at his ornaments, reading the half-covered sheet of paper on his desk, or taking in the view of the sea from his workroom window?

A week later he gave himself a day off to go to London, having invited Ms Bodkin to lunch in the wine bar opposite Llama Books in the Fulham Road. As usual he looked forward eagerly to such an encounter but this time it went badly from the start. Brenda arrived twenty-five minutes late and apparently triumphant.

'I've been speaking to Lucasta,' she told him. 'She's all set to do a piece in the *Meteor*.'

'About my book?'

'About your baby!'

'No!'

'Of course she'll give the book a passing mensh.'

'It's not a baby. It's ten. And it's certainly not mine!'

'Oh, go on, Felix!' Brenda was laughing happily. 'You know how keen you are on doing it. You hardly talk about anything else.'

'Well, I didn't do it with her. Not with the child's mother. Not on a lilo on the beach.'

'Is *that* where it happened?'

'I don't know who she is. That is to say, I hardly know who she is.'

'Make up your mind.'

'I had no idea who she was when this unfortunate child was conceived.'

'Unfortunate? Why do you say he's unfortunate? I should think he's quite lucky if he's got you for a father. A person in the public eye.'

'Listen, Brenda' – Felix tried to sound firm, clear-headed and determined – 'I have no children. Nothing ever happened. We've got to kill it.'

'The child?'

'Of course not! The story.'

'Too late. Lucasta's getting all the details.'

'How?'

'Someone's rung her who knows you quite well and, incidentally, he's a tremendous admirer of your work.'

'Oh, my God! Gavin!' Felix shouted, causing the copy-editors at the next table to look up in alarm.

'Who the hell's Gavin?'

'He's been following me. Dogging my footsteps. Persecuting me! Actually you met him at Millstream's.'

'The Gothic couple? And that woman . . . ?'

'Ian's mother.'

'Felix, you must have shut your eyes *very* tightly indeed. Hadn't you better tell me the whole story?'

Telling it was a relief to Felix. He went through it all from the first-time caller on the Denny Densher show, the tape-recorded message, the lunch with Miriam, the meeting with Huw Hotchkiss and the letter from PROD. She listened attentively and he felt, as he didn't always feel with Brenda, whom he loved, that he was being interesting. At the end of it she put her hand on his and said, 'So PROD are after you?'

'Twenty thousand and growing steadily.'

'That's a hell of a lot of money!' Brenda gave a respectful whistle.

'So I don't really want a story in the papers,' he told her. 'Not till the whole thing's settled.'

'When's that going to be?'

'I'm not sure. I'm going to find Gavin and have it out with him finally. He started all this. So can you hold Lucasta off?'

'I'll see what I can do.'

'We'll have a wonderful time, won't we, when we go abroad?' Felix did his best to turn the conversation to happier subjects.

'I'm afraid,' Ms Bodkin smiled at him, 'abroad is likely to be postponed. You've got too much on your plate.'

'Isn't it the Basingstoke Literary Circle next week? I know that's not exactly abroad but . . .'

'No, Basingstoke is *not* abroad.' Ms Bodkin was quite firmly of the opinion. 'Anyway, I'm not sure how you'll get there. I've got so much on I don't think I'll be able to drive you to Basingstoke.'

'What about Terry, the rep?'

'Terry's away.' Brenda slid up the cuff of her footballing shirt and stared closely at her Mickey Mouse watch. 'It's half past already! I'll be late for the meeting with Tubal-Smith. Goodbye, Felix. I've really got to scoot.' So she gulped the rest of her glass of Fleurie and scooted with her game pie hardly touched. And Felix, filled with hardly bearable loneliness, went off to find a telephone directory and the address of Epsilon Books.

'Mr Morsom, sir. This is indeed an honour. If you have anything in your "bottom drawer", sir. Anything which may have given Tubal-Smith of Llama "cold feet". Something not for the "general reader". Shall we say, "flagellation", "bestiality", "necrophilia", "socialism"? We would issue it for you, sir. Cloth-bound. A "luxury presentation". Copies for private circulation among a "few close friends". On the most "reasonable terms".'

'I just dropped in . . .'

'And I'm so glad you did, Mr Morsom. So delighted you did. We could, of course, publish you under a "suitable pseudonym", "confidentiality guaranteed". A well-known male sportswriter, who shall be entirely nameless, does the Sadie at School series under the name of Petunia d'Aquitaine. We could cloak you, Mr Morsom, under some such similar disguise.'

'I just called in here to see one of your staff.'

'Staff, Mr Morsom? We are a "slender outfit", sir. Very "slimmed down" indeed.' The chairman of Epsilon Books, who had introduced himself as Jasper Kettering – a name which sounded to Felix as spurious as Petunia d'Aquitaine – was a tall, florid man, dressed in a tweed jacket and spotted bow-tie, whose hands trembled and whose hair looked as though it had been dyed with boot polish. He spoke largely in inverted commas as he stood in the middle of the basement room in Gordon Square, among piles of cardboard boxes and forgotten manuscripts, and waved a large, shaky hand at his secretary who, wrapped in a plaid shawl, grinned at them from behind her typewriter.

'And Gavin Piercey?'

'Gavin?' Jasper Kettering looked doubtful for a moment, as though he had been spoken to in a foreign language.

'Piercey.'

'Oh, Gavin Piercey!' Kettering beamed in delighted recognition. 'Epsilon, as I always say, stands on "twin pillars". Miss Trigg is one and Gavin Piercey's the other. "Tireless on the road". Much loved in the bookshops which deal with "specialized and selective reading". Gavin is the sort that "won't take no for an answer". Without Gavin, Epsilon would long ago have been on "queer street". And without Miss Trigg too, of course. The only "fly in our own little brand of ointment" is . . .'

'Gavin seems to have vanished.' The secretary was smiling broadly, as though Gavin's disappearance was an irresistible joke.

'Not vanished, Miss Trigg. It's far too soon to say he's vanished. Let's say a "strange silence" has fallen over him.'

'Silence?' Felix was puzzled. 'From all I've heard Gavin's been far from silent.'

'He has favoured us' – Mr Kettering looked solemn – 'with a quite unusual silence. When he's "on the road" Gavin usually "calls in" two or three times a day to "touch base". Isn't that so, Miss Trigg?'

'Oh, more often than that, Mr Kettering.' Miss Trigg sighed patiently. 'Considerably more often than that.'

'But for the last three days "not a squeak". Am I right, Miss Trigg?'

'Entirely right, Mr Kettering.'

'And we have telephoned his home number?'

'Repeatedly. All I've listened to for the last three days is Gavin on his answering machine.' Miss Trigg indulged in a little light laughter as though Gavin's repeated message was in every way more enjoyable than Gavin direct.

'Could you possibly give me his address?'

'Could we give Mr Morsom Gavin's address, Miss Trigg? Can you see "any objections"? I don't believe there could be any "serious objection" if you were to "scribble it down".'

Miss Trigg scribbled it down on a small square of yellow paper and gave it to Felix as though she were glad of being shot of something distasteful. Mr Kettering said, 'Is there any message we should pass on, Mr Morsom, when Gavin "puts in an appearance"?'

'Just tell him to shut up! That's all. Just tell him I came to shut him up.' Something about the stuffy basement office and Mr Kettering's oleaginous presence had restored to Felix the delightful feeling of being about to lose his temper. He slipped the yellow paper into his jacket pocket and said goodbye to Epsilon Books.

The next day, when he was about to take his secretary for a large gin and tonic in a pub near the British Museum, Mr Kettering received a call which filled him with horror and surprise, so he almost dropped the phone. Miss Trigg, when it was relayed to her, received the news with amazing calm.

After he had left the Epsilon offices Felix grew tired of hearing, from various phone boxes, Gavin's flat monotone announcement that he was unavailable to come to the phone at the

moment and would the caller please leave a message after the
bleep. He had left messages after the bleeps, ranging from the
conciliatory 'Can't we have lunch and discuss the whole thing
sensibly?' to the threatening 'If you won't withdraw your story
at once, I shall be compelled to take steps to silence you!'
Then he had persuaded himself that Gavin was at home, hiding
behind his answering machine. He took the tube to Bayswater
and sat in an empty carriage, solitary between rush hours,
thinking of the endless combinations of threats and promises
which he might use to extricate his life from Gavin's plotting
and return to the safety of his loneliness.

A sudden dry wind had sprung up, rattling the privet and
untended laurels in the garden of the Bayswater square which
had not yet been gentrified, where the stucco on the tall
buildings was peeling, where there was no white paint or
window-boxes or brightly coloured front doors and where a
multitude of bells showed that no house was occupied by a
single family.

Cars were parked outside the address Felix had in his pocket,
among them a battered van with Epsilon Books painted on
the back door. Suddenly convinced that Gavin had just driven
up and was sitting in the van, Felix, the low afternoon sun in
his eyes, stepped off the pavement and pulled at the handle of
the driver's door. Stumbling on the edge of the pavement, he
steadied himself with his other hand on the side window.
Then he saw that the van was empty and he looked up at the
gaunt façade of 9 Carisbrooke Terrace, the home of the man
whose single leisure-time activity seemed to be the persecution
of Felix Morsom. A woman in a sari, loaded with plastic
supermarket bags, was trudging up the cracked steps to the
front door and Felix followed her up to the fourth floor. He
watched her go into her flat and then found himself alone on

the landing, the wind blowing through an open window. He heard a creak and turned to see that the door of number 5 had been left open. He walked into Gavin's flat.

What struck him was the sad tidiness of the place. A couch and two armchairs covered in imitation leather were set at perfect right angles. There was a table on which four magazines – the *Bookseller*, *Publishers Weekly*, *Exchange and Mart* and *Hello!* – were in similar order. Beside them, on a lace doily, stood a small glass version of Hans Andersen's mermaid. The DIY bookshelves, assembled with rigorous efficiency, held telephone directories, a wide selection of The World's Hundred Best-known Titles in their uniform green bindings, and hardback copies of Felix Morsom's books including *Out of Season*. On the mantelpiece stood a pink china shepherdess, a box of matches in an embroidered cover and a framed studio photograph of Miriam, softened and slightly blurred, looking, in this instance, like someone who used to introduce children's programmes on television.

The door to the bedroom was also open, the bed neatly made: the only sign of carelessness being a cupboard door open to show a tweed jacket, a number of anoraks, odd trousers and a blue suit swinging on a wire coathanger. In the kitchen the sparse equipment was in place except for a mug decorated with the god Pan sporting a huge erection and the inscription EPSILON'S HISTORY OF EROTICA, which had been left half full of milky tea on the draining-board. Influenced by the order of the kitchen, or with nothing better to do, he poured the cold tea away down the sink, rinsed out the cup and put it in the plate-rack beside the taps.

Felix went back to the sitting-room, where he sat for a long time. The phone rang once and he expected a message which was not delivered. Then he wrote an angry note on the back of Miss Trigg's yellow paper: 'Don't think you can get away with this. I'll be back. Felix Morsom.' He left the note between the pink shepherdess and the portrait photograph of Miriam Bowker.

Down in the entrance hall the woman in the sari was seeing off a visitor, a grey-haired man carrying a briefcase. She looked up for a moment with large brown eyes from under a wide brow with a caste mark. He was struck by her beauty and then left Carisbrooke Terrace. Much later, when at home, he checked his answering machine but nobody had called him, nor did Gavin Piercey ever ring him back.

It was almost midnight when a woman's scream could be heard in Carisbrooke Terrace. Cries and the shrill call of burglar alarms were so common in that part of London that no lights went on, nor were windows opened. A little later, in answer to a 999 call made from the box on the corner, a police car arrived with its blue lights flashing. Miriam Bowker was standing beside the Epsilon van in which the driver had clearly been struck about the head and face with a heavy object, which was found to have fractured his skull, broken his nose and reduced his features to pulp. The weapon used, which might have been a heavy spanner or jack handle, was never recovered.

Chapter Ten

'It's down to the kids in my opinion. It's a little-known fact that 69 per cent of violent crime in this area is down to the under-twelves. Make our job a whole lot easier if they went to school in cuffs and were locked up at night!' The speaker was Detective Sergeant Wathen, a lean, hatchet-faced, balding man who spoke in complaining tones and would tell anyone at Paddington Green nick who cared to listen that some daft, homosexual judge in the family division had given custody of his three children to his mentally defective wife. His own kids, who calmly walked off with more than half his wages, were no doubt mixed up with other under-twelves who spent their days doing drugs and their nights mugging old ladies.

'I don't believe an under-twelve battered a publisher's rep to death in a Ford van in Bayswater. I hardly believe that's possible.' Detective Chief Inspector Elizabeth Cowling, who was examining police photographs, smiled tolerantly. She knew that Detective Sergeant Wathen hated and resented her, not only because she was his superior officer but because she was a woman and, as such, capable of gaining the custody of children and robbing innocent and unsuspecting police officers of their money.

'Well, now, Chief.' Wathen flicked through the pages of his notebook, using the word 'Chief' with patronizing contempt as a man might call his wife 'Blue Eyes' when he thought she wasn't very bright. 'The deceased has been identified as Gavin Piercey, male, white, five foot eight inches. Papers on the body show him to have been a publisher's representative, flat 5, 9 Carisbrooke Terrace, Bayswater.'

'I know all that, Frank,' Elizabeth Cowling said.

'Death discovered by a Miss Miriam Bowker who had an engagement to meet the deceased and, getting no answer to his bell, looked casually into the van. Appeared to be genuinely horrified by what she saw and was able to identify the deceased in spite of considerable facial injuries. Unless further inquiries show otherwise, there seems no reason to regard Miss Bowker as a suspect. In any case this is not a crime of the type likely to be committed by a woman.'

'Or a twelve-year-old child.'

'Some of those twelve year olds are bloody strong, Chief. Believe you me. Some of those fucking twelve year olds have highly developed minds, which they get through living on the fat of some poor bugger's alimony.'

At this point Detective Constable Newbury entered the room, a small, sandy-haired and eager man dressed in a tweed jacket, jeans and an open-necked shirt. He brought with him the tapes from Gavin's answering machine, which he fitted up for the Chief to hear. She was going over the notes made by the scene of the crime officer as Detective Sergeant Wathen droned on: '"It has been revealed that a custodial sentence was once passed on the deceased by the West London Magistrates for non-payment of maintenance due to Miss Bowker's infant son Ian." Vultures, some women when they get a court order behind them! "But the matter has since been resolved when it was established that the deceased was not, in fact, the father of said infant." I wish I knew his bloody lawyer! "And

Miss Bowker states that she and the deceased were now the best of friends and put all that behind them!"'

'Do be quiet a minute, Frank.' The Chief gave him her beaming schoolmistress smile and seemed about to add, 'There's a good little boy.' Instead she said, 'I do want to listen to this.' Detective Constable Newbury pressed a switch and a voice filled the room with messages ranging from the conciliatory 'Can't we have lunch and discuss this whole thing sensibly?' to the distinctly threatening 'If you won't withdraw your story at once, I shall be compelled to take steps to silence you!' When the machine had been switched off the Chief said, 'I just can't believe it.'

'What can't you believe now, my dear?' Detective Sergeant Wathen was at his least bearable.

'He simply doesn't write like that.'

'Who doesn't write like what?'

'I mean, his books are all about sensitive people in situations which are only, well, just hinted at. I can't believe he'd ever write a sentence like "I shall be compelled to take steps to silence you!"'

'You know who that is?'

'Oh yes, I'm sure I do. We had an extremely agreeable lunch together.'

Felix didn't take the *Meteor*. In fact he had given up opening newspapers altogether in case he should trip over an unexpected and adverse review of *Out of Season*. He did, however, buy the *Meteor* at the sweetshop by the entrance to the pier because he feared that WELL-KNOWN AUTHOR'S LOVE-CHILD might be the morning's feature. He didn't open it at once but carried it to the end of the pier as someone charged with defusing a bomb might first move it to a remote place believing that there the explosion would do less damage.

So he sat staring down at the yellowish water slurping against the supports of the pier, in the company of a single fisherman who seemed to have been long ago resigned to catching nothing, holding the unopened *Meteor* in some considerable anxiety. And then he heard a sound like approaching cavalry and the boards shook as Huw Hotchkiss came round the corner wearing trainers, a purple tracksuit and a white baseball cap. He thundered to a stop, grabbed the *Meteor* and said, 'My God, Felix! Have you seen the paper?'

'You mean' – Felix's mouth was dry and his voice filled with apprehension – 'about my love-child?'

'No.' Huw was turning the pages which, buffeted by the wind, were trying to escape from his hands. 'Why should it be about your love-child? We're all glad about your love-child. I told Sheena, my present partner whom you've never met, and she was really chuffed you'd got a love-child. We all rejoice with you, boyo, from the bottom of our hearts. But one love-child more or less in the world is hardly earth-shaking news, is it?'

'That's exactly what I think.'

'And you're hardly the sort of chap that's always in the papers. Sorry about that review in the *Guardian*, by the way. Sheena wanted me to make it clear our hearts went out to you. No, nothing about you in the paper today. Not even a stinking review. It's about –'

'About what?'

'Well, that weird character that tried to muscle into my course of lectures on the Moving Image. What was his name? I remembered when I saw it in the paper. Here you are. Piercey!' And Huw slapped the *Meteor* so that a small paragraph of home news could be pushed in front of Felix's eyes: PUBLISHER'S REP FOUND DEAD IN LONDON SQUARE. Gavin

Piercey, 31, was found with severe head injuries in his van it said and added, after very little further information, that the police were looking for a man who might be able to help with their inquiries. 'It must be the same chap, mustn't it?' Huw said. 'The right age and all that?'

'Yes,' Felix told him, 'it must be the same chap.'

'I thought he was extremely weird, but you can't help feeling sorry for the bloke. These sort of ghosts' – Huw was unexpectedly poetical – 'come looming up at you out of the past.'

'I suppose so.'

'Take you, for instance.'

'What about me?'

'I thought you'd never want to speak to me again. The years went by and I never heard a word. And then you sought me out. It did my heart good, boyo, that you should seek me out and offer me your forgiveness.'

'I wanted to ask you about Miriam Bowker.'

'So you did! I well remember that that was the reason you gave but I read the message in your eyes, old son, and they spelled out very clearly "I forgive you, Huw. Shake hands on it and no hard feelings."'

'Did they?'

'And that Miriam girl. She came looming up out of the past, also. Called in, she did, at the private address of me and Sheena.'

'She *what*?'

'Like you she was asking about that barbecue on the beach. Wanted to know if I had kept any photographs of the occasion. Particularly interested in who might have been in occupation of the airbed. I told her very frankly that it was all lost in the mists of time. But I promised to look for snaps.'

'Did she leave you' – Felix was almost afraid to ask – 'with any sort of an address?'

'This is Sheena, my partner. Felix Morsom, a very old friend. Sheena's been dying to meet you. I've told her so much about you. I'm always talking about Felix, aren't I, Sheena?'

'So far as I remember you've never mentioned his name.' A gigantic girl, at least a foot taller than the squat Huw, stood by the window in his house in Coldsands Old Town with a comb in her hand, searching for split ends. She was blonde and looked like a goddess in an over-life-sized statue which had suffered from the passage of time. 'Huw's such a bloody liar! Aren't you, Huw?'

'I knew you two would get on like a house on fire!' Huw was smiling as though he had been paid the highest compliment. 'Felix is interested in that girl, Miriam Bowker.'

'Just if you've got an address,' Felix reminded him.

'Here somewhere.' Huw was searching on a desk piled high with letters, bills, books, video tapes and other visual aids to the study of the cinema. 'You remember Miriam, the girl who came here, don't you, Sheena?'

'It's none of my business who comes and goes.' Sheena turned to look, with great interest, on to an empty street where nothing in particular was going on.

'She wanted to know if I had any pictures of a party I gave on the beach. Years ago. A party where Felix was definitely the star.'

'It was such a relief to us all,' Sheena spoke loudly to the street below, 'when you gave up having parties.'

'Got it!' Huw, who had been burrowing among his possessions, announced the find.

'Thank God for that! Now perhaps we can have a moment's

peace.' And Sheena went on with the close examination of her hair.

So Felix started to walk home with Miriam's address and phone number in his pocket, hoping that calling on her wouldn't reach such a terrible and unlooked for conclusion as his visit to her friend Gavin. And he walked along the promenade towards Imperial Parade, past the small hotels boarded up and bankrupt for lack of business, and the souvenir shops with their postcards, Union Jacks, baseball caps and COLDSANDS WARM HEARTS T-shirts, past the small, smelly aquarium and the plump statue of King Edward VII, past the sea sucking away at the dark sand and the gulls screaming as they battled against the wind – the permanent backdrop to his life and novels. He thought he should be relieved that his unaccountable enemy was silenced at last and, in that awful and dramatic way, had done what Felix wanted. But as he walked into the wind he couldn't help feeling sorry for Gavin.

His father and his wife had long been the only dead people he'd known well and now they were joined, inexplicably, by Gavin Piercey. Gavin had forced himself into his life, dogged him, badgered him, bothered him, puzzled him and persecuted him. There had been moments, perhaps too many moments, when he felt like killing Gavin himself. Yet condemnation came hard to Felix. Perhaps this strange, over-serious, lonely figure who had been ill-treated and misjudged genuinely thought he had found Ian's father? Felix remembered the too tidy pathetic flat in Bayswater. He remembered, almost with gratitude, the line of Morsom hardbacks, starting with his first, *The End of the Pier*, which had been so well received that his father, overcome with envy and regret, had refused to read it. As he reached Imperial Parade, and the point where he had watched the arrival of Miriam Bowker and Ian, he was doing his best to think well of Gavin.

And then he saw, parked outside his front door, an unmarked car driven by a policewoman in uniform. On the front step, ringing at his bell, he saw a tall, bald, hatchet-faced man accompanied by a smaller assistant who was – and the phrase came back to him like a punch in the stomach – 'dressed casual'. He walked quickly back across the road and, almost running down a number of side-streets, made his way to the railway station and caught a slow train to London.

Chapter Eleven

Felix saw Ian Bowker trudging towards him, carrying a small, purple games bag, apparently just home from school. He said, 'Hullo, Ian,' but the boy didn't answer. He said, 'School's over, then?' which was a question he agreed might not call for any further comment. He said, 'I've just come to see your mother.'

'That lift hasn't worked for weeks,' Ian told him.

The tower block was behind the dwindling pubs and shops at the World's End, the last gasp of the King's Road. The concrete stairs had been littered, peed on and seemed to Felix, who took little exercise, almost terminally exhausting. The stained walls were liberally decorated with graffiti, among which swastikas and other advertisements for racism predominated. When they got to a door on the fifth floor, Ian opened it with a key which he kept hanging round his neck under his navy-blue pullover.

They walked into what seemed to be a single, all-purpose room which couldn't have been a greater contrast to the demented tidiness of the late Gavin Piercey's home. There was a bed which might have been no more than a mattress on the floor; it was so covered with clothes, shoes, shirts, stockings, a huge plastic bucket of dirty washing and the remains of a takeaway meal for two that it couldn't be identified. Other clothes were on hangers dangling from a broom

handle fixed between the end of a curtain rail and a corner
wall. There was a sink with a bowl full of unwashed dishes, a
stained cooker and a green glass vase in which a lavish bouquet
of roses and lilies had long since died. The dirty plates on the
draining-board seemed to be stuck together. Yellowing magazines and newspapers were stacked against a wall which was
otherwise decorated with Ian's school reports, pinned up, and
a long, school photograph in which he could, no doubt, be
identified by anyone with the time and patience to look. The
surprising thing about this tip was that it didn't smell disgusting.

Miriam Bowker was wearing a high-necked sweater and
jeans. Her hair was cut in a fringe and combed straight down,
so that she looked like a French café singer of the sixties. She
was watching a blurred quiz show on a portable television set
propped on a pile of clothing on the bed. Its aerial had been
adapted from a wire coathanger. When she turned and saw
Felix, she looked terrified.

Later she said, 'It was the most horrible thing that ever happened. I've never seen anyone dead before.'

Ian said, 'Quiet, Mum! I'm doing my homework.' He was
reading a book, his head pillowed on one arm, his spectacled
eyes very near the page. Miriam said, 'If you don't want to
listen to us, Ian, please go to your room.'

'What are you reading, Ian?' Felix felt sorry for the boy
who had been ordered out.

'A book called *Where's My Left Sock?*'

'I don't believe it!'

'It's by Sonia Foot.'

There was a moment's stunned silence. Miriam looked
unforgiving. Then Felix laughed. In fact he thought it was
quite funny.

'I read another one.' Ian gazed solemnly at their visitor. '*How to Make Easy Money*.'

'Who wrote that, then?'

'Robin Banks! And *Falling off the Cliff* by . . .'

'That's *quite* enough of that.' Miriam was running out of patience. 'Please go to your room. I won't ask again.'

'. . . Eileen Dover. I'm bored with my room.' Felix had seen it and knew what he meant. Ian had been given the only bedroom but, apart from a single bed, it looked unfurnished. Stuck to the wall was a small author photograph cut from the dust-jacket of *Out of Season*. The sight of it filled Felix with fear and embarrassment but also a strange gratitude. Miriam had found the remains of a bottle of white Rioja in her fridge and he was given what seemed to be the only glass. She was drinking out of a cup and had become calm. He asked, 'You went to see Gavin?'

'He'd asked me round.'

'What for?'

'You're as bad as the police!' When she smiled he thought she looked momentarily attractive. He didn't mind the forward-looking teeth; her top lip no longer seemed to be pulled back in any kind of sneer. 'He wanted to talk.'

'What about?'

'He said about you being after him all the time. Trying to get at him.'

'I thought it was the other way round. He was always after me. Did you tell the police that?'

'He said you went after him at his work. Yes, I had to tell them the truth.'

'I suppose you did.' He took a gulp of the cold white wine which did little to steady his nerves. 'I was there a few nights ago. I couldn't find him. I kept on ringing . . .'

'I was there the night before last. I'm afraid I did find him.'

'How?'

'Ian? Please, darling. Will you finish your homework in your room?'

'*All right*!' Ian shouted with unexpected rage. He slapped his books together, took a long time filling his pencil-case and then banged the door as he left them. Miriam said, 'He didn't answer the bell so, for some reason, I thought I'd look inside the van.'

'What time was this?'

'Oh, late. Past eleven o'clock.'

'So it was dark?'

'Yes. I suppose that's why no one noticed him before.'

'You were out at eleven?'

'Yes.'

'Who was looking after Ian?'

'Ian looks after himself. Why are you asking me all these questions?'

'Someone killed Gavin. I just wondered who.'

She was looking at him, no longer smiling. 'Yes. I wonder who it was.'

'The van wasn't locked?'

'No. But I could see inside it. He'd fallen over the steering-wheel. There was blood. I could see so much blood.' She said it calmly, still looking at him. 'I went to a call-box and rang the police.'

'It must have been terrible for you.'

'Pretty terrible. Particularly when I had to go with them to identify Gavin. I don't know why they needed that. It was his van. He had his driving licence, all his stuff in his pockets. I don't know why they had to put me through that at all.' She got up and searched the room for a cigarette, found the last Marlboro in a jacket swinging from the broom handle and lit it by switching on the gas cooker, holding back her hair to save it from the flame. As she straightened up, she said, 'Are you hungry at all, Felix?'

He didn't answer but said, 'Who could have done that to him? Did Gavin have enemies?'

'I don't know. I didn't know him all that well.'

'You didn't know him all that well and you said he was the father of your child?' It was, as he had suspected, an accusation she flung at the merest acquaintances.

'I knew him. Of course I knew him. When we were all young. When we all hung round the university.'

'And you slept with him?'

'If you call it sleeping. He was enthusiastic, Gavin was.' She laughed. 'You could say that for him. Over-enthusiastic at times.'

Felix felt a moment of embarrassment for the dead Gavin and was angered at Miriam's laughter. 'Made up in enthusiasm for what he lacked in experience. You could put it like that,' she said.

'And afterwards?'

'He kept in touch. I didn't want him to particularly. Christmas. Always remembered my birthday and Ian's. Helped me out from time to time, I've got to admit it.'

'So you shopped him to PROD?'

'Did Gavin tell you that?'

'As good as.'

'They were on at me to name a father. On and on. Remorseless. I had to give them a name. I gave them his.'

'Not mine?'

'I didn't want to cause you trouble.'

'But you changed your mind?'

'Because of what they did to Gavin. Locking him up. That wasn't fair.'

'So you lied to get him out of trouble?'

'I had Ian to consider. So I told them the truth.'

'Even if it happened. Even if anything like that happened' – he was standing up, but keeping his voice down, remembering the silent boy behind the door – 'on a lilo. On the beach. Once. Why should that mean . . . ?'

'Because I knew. I knew as soon as it was over. That's it, I thought. Women always know.'

'Women don't!'

'In your books they might not. I know what I felt. None better.'

'And all these years. You've never said a word.'

'Like I said I didn't want to worry you.'

'Worry me? Do you know what I saw? Today? Policemen. Two of them at my front door. Remember what happened to Gavin? Two men came to arrest me. Because of Ian.'

There was a long silence and then she said, 'I don't think it was because of Ian.'

'What do you mean?'

'I think it was because of Gavin. You want to stay and talk about it? Why don't you buy your little family a Chinese meal?'

His mind raced through the past weeks. Sometimes it seemed like days, sometimes years, since he had listened to Gavin's tape. As he talked, Miriam became gentler and he found it harder to maintain his anger. It had, after all, she explained, been Gavin's idea to finger Felix to PROD. She had gone along with it, she said, but always reluctantly and with Ian's best interests at heart. And, once the suggestion was made, of

93

course, she understood why he denied it. Anyone would have wanted to meet Gavin, to have it out with him, to come, perhaps, to some sensible compromise. That wasn't suspicious. In Miriam's opinion that wasn't enough to make him a suspect in the matter of Gavin's unusual and sudden death.

Soothed after a while by the new and reasonable Miriam, Felix gave her money to go out and buy a Chinese takeaway for three, in which might be included six cans of beer and a bottle of sake. He stifled a phrase which floated disconcertingly into his mind: 'The condemned man ate a hearty breakfast.'

The light faded outside the uncurtained windows; Mirry switched on two lamps with plastic, art-deco patterned shades which gave the chaotic room an almost festive appearance. She lit joss-sticks in a jam jar on the mantelpiece which wafted Felix back to his first days at university. The television was taken off the bed and turned on in a corner of the room, where it glowed and burbled, a meaninglessly talking light. The food in the silvery cardboard dishes gave off a strong smell of monosodium glutamate. Ian, dressed in striped pyjamas, said the Chinese dinner was cool and ate solidly. Felix drank three beers and most of the bottle of sake as his anxieties dwindled. After a while Ian went to bed. Mirry followed to say good night to him and when she came back Felix stood and said he ought to be going.

'It's late,' she said. 'And you're a bit pissed, quite honestly. Also, those coppers might be waiting for you.'

'I suppose they might.'

'Why not stay? You can decide what to do in the morning.'

'No room.' He looked down at the pile of jumble which was her bed.

'I'll make some room.'

She worked at it, moving armfuls of her clothes and dumping

them on chairs or beside the television. He lay down in surprising comfort and she lay beside him. He closed his eyes and felt he was back, years before Huw Hotchkiss's beach party, to the time when he had smelled incense and tried to stretch out in too small, inconvenient beds, in lodgings or halls of residence, and stumbled on unforgettable excitement and suddenly revealed happiness. Miriam was undressing him with the efficiency of a nurse and then she changed character as she pulled the sweater over her head. He had expected, even feared, dirty bra straps but her small breasts were free, her body was white, without any individual smell to it. Her face was near his, her eyes full of what seemed to be genuine concern. Deliberately and with unexpected pleasure, he did what he might or might not ever have done before. Then they both fell asleep.

An hour later he was awake with a dry mouth and a headache. He turned over, disentangling himself from the embrace of the sleeping Miriam, and looked at his watch, surprised to see it was only a quarter past ten. He found himself staring at the bright light of the portable television. A grey-haired, handsome woman he recognized was standing outside Paddington Green police station talking to reporters: 'Our inquiries have led us to believe that Gavin Piercey was receiving death threats,' she said in the gentle but enthusiastic tones of a headmistress announcing the results of the sixth form relay races. 'We are still looking out for a man we believe can help us with our inquiries. We should be able to name him shortly. No further questions!'

Felix crawled out of the floor-level bed and switched off the television, causing Miriam to turn over, almost woken by the sudden silence. He stood motionless until she was sleeping securely again and then dressed and let himself out of the flat, stifling the feeling that he ought, in some way, to have said goodbye to Ian.

As he turned the dark corner to reach the last flight of stairs, he could see, lit by a weak bulb in a clouded glass, a tall, bald-headed man with a shorter companion. The shorter had his finger on the lift button and the taller was angrily telling the empty space that fucking twelve-year-old yob vandals had fucked up the lift. On the dark stairway Felix froze again like one of Sleeping Beauty's attendants. And then with a furious rattle and a jolt the lift unexpectedly arrived and yawned open, as though to disprove the charge of criminal damage against minors. As soon as the men had been carried away, Felix left the building and, setting off towards the World's End, broke into an unaccustomed trot.

If the Furies were after him; if, at the whim of the Gods, the bald man and the man, as Gavin would have said, casually dressed, had gone to search for him at the World's End, they couldn't be in Coldsands. So surely, at least, he was safe to go home, to make plans, to collect his thoughts. In the house where he had been a child, where he could have a bath and sleep in his own bed, get up early and look out as the sun rose over the unconcerned sea, he would be able to discover a sensible course of action, as he found consistent behaviour for the characters in his books. The worst that could happen to him would be that he'd have to lose a pile of cash to satisfy PROD – the advance on a new novel perhaps. If he was really up against it, he could find money for Ian as he'd had to find it to keep his mother, silent and smiling, in the Evening Star Rest and Retirement Home.

But then, as he sat on top of a bus creeping along the King's Road on a late summer evening, where crowds were standing outside the pubs, drinking, laughing, quarrelling and sitting on walls, where drivers were trying to back into impossible parking spaces outside bistros and a man with a shaven head was leading a taller man on a chain and dog-collar, Felix remembered that his present difficulties couldn't be solved by a hefty slice of a publisher's advance. 'I don't think it was because of Ian,' Miriam had said when he told her about the Furies, 'I think it was because of Gavin.'

Gavin. Everything started and ended with Gavin. Gavin had sent him the tape and dogged his footsteps on his book tour. Gavin, found dead in a car with his head battered in, was still pursuing him. The police were looking for a man who could help them with their inquiries, and men from whom the police sought assistance were soon, Felix knew, in serious trouble. What had the policewoman with literary leanings said on the television news? 'Our inquiries have led us to believe that Gavin Piercey was receiving death threats . . .' Could she believe that a novelist without a stain on his character, once described as the Chekhov of Coldsands-on-Sea, would utter death threats to a publisher's rep who was, as he had constantly shown, a devoted admirer of that novelist's work? The idea was absurd. Did it become less absurd because the novelist, after drinking champagne in a London club, had been led into a fatuous conversation about a contract killing with an elderly solicitor who fed himself on brains?

For a moment he wondered if he shouldn't go straight to Paddington Green police station and seek an interview with the headmistress. But then his thoughts, straying irresponsibly, wandered to his message on Gavin's answering machine: 'If you won't withdraw your story at once, I shall be compelled to take steps to silence you.'

He hadn't said that, had he? That wasn't an accurate

quotation. But then he was afraid he had said *exactly* that. Well, if he had, could such words be construed as a death threat by the porcelain-faced Chief Inspector? When he asked himself this question the disloyal voice within him answered, Let's face it, that's exactly what she thinks. Looking round, he thought the woman with beads and a long nose, sitting on the other side of the aisle, was staring at him curiously. He picked up the sports page of the paper which had been left on the next seat and held it to hide his face all the way to Victoria Station.

The lights seemed unnecessarily bright when he stood waiting to buy a ticket for Coldsands. He slapped what he thought was the breast-pocket of his jacket to make sure he had money and realized that he had no jacket, no wallet and no credit cards. He was wearing the clothes he wrote in, dressed as he was when he left the house, it seemed a lifetime ago, to buy the *Meteor* – blue shirt and sweater, suede shoes and grey corduroy trousers. It was his habit to keep his credit cards in his wallet, his bank notes in the back pocket of his trousers, his change in his trouser pocket and his cheque book in the top left-hand drawer of his desk. He now remembered that he had paid for his ticket to London with money because entrance to his house was barred by the Furies. He had given his last wadge of notes to Miriam for spare ribs, seaweed and beer, Peking duck, sweet and sour pork, mixed vegetables and sake. Now all he had in his trousers were four pound coins and two fifty ps.

Felix's father had a minimal influence on his son. He failed to pass on to the young Morsom his reverence for golf, bridge, cricket commentaries, the Conservative Party and the South Coast Bank. He did, however, give him one piece of advice

Felix respected: 'If you want to telephone or pee while out, always go to the best hotel. Don't use the same facilities as the great unwashed. Telephone kiosks and urinals are much the same to them. When in need slip into the Princess Beatrice Hotel or somewhere similar. Treat yourself to the best. The hall porter will respect you for it.' Felix came up the black marble stairs that led to the Station Hotel, keeping as far as possible in the shadows and walking quickly with his face turned to the wall. He chose a stall far away from the only other inhabitant of the Gents and then slipped quickly into the telephone box in the hall. He put in fifty p, because he didn't want to ask the hall porter for change, and rang Brenda Bodkin's number.

It rang five times and Felix was about to put the phone down when a voice, male and Australian said, 'Yep?'

'Oh, is Brenda there?'

'Brenda's shot through. What can I do for you?'

'Well . . . It's Felix Morsom.'

'Bloody hell! Not *the* Felix Morsom?'

'Well . . . *A* Felix Morsom.'

'Not Felix Morsom, the novelist *extraordinaire*?'

'I'm a novelist. Yes.'

'Not Felix Morsom, well-known pen-pusher who does book signings?'

'I do. Yes. Sometimes.'

'And shoots off round the country with Brenda?'

'That's right. You could say.'

'Just tell me one thing, Mr Morsom.'

'What's that?'

'Is Brenda Bodkin a good fuck?'

His instinct was to try to laugh it off but his laughter sounded hollow. He said, 'I honestly wouldn't know.'

'No, I didn't think you would.' The phone was disconnected and purred loudly.

Felix sat in an armchair in the corner of the lounge. A waiter came up to him and he ordered a large brandy which cost him four pounds. He drank it, fingering the last coin in his pocket, and then, unusually exhausted by fear, alcohol and love, fell asleep.

He dreamed that the bald policeman was standing over him, wearing some kind of ornate uniform and shaking him by the shoulder, and then he saw, more clearly, that it was the hall porter saying, 'I'm sure you don't want to stay here all night, sir. We can't have that, you know.'

'No, of course not. Thank you for waking me.' Felix wondered if this were all part of his dream.

'You're travelling, are you, sir?' The porter was not completely bald but had strands of black hair fixed across his skull. He had small, beady eyes and, Felix thought, a cruel mouth. He smelled of boiled sweets.

'Yes, of course, I'm travelling. Thank you. Thank you very much.' He didn't believe he was completely awake when he walked back down the stairs, although he could hear his footsteps echoing across the station and the rumble and clatter of a distant truck. Far away in the shadows someone was whistling.

He stumbled over a pile of newspapers stacked outside a shuttered bookshop and looked down to see his own face peering over the title of the *Meteor* and read: 'NOVELIST'S LOVE-CHILD. SEE CENTRE PAGES'. He pulled until he extricated a copy from the tight string and, still unsure if he wasn't half-asleep, crossed to a table in front of a dark café and opened the paper, the first thing he had ever stolen in his life. The faces stared up at him as though in a dream: Ian and Miriam, himself as a boy, himself ten years ago and himself now – the author portrait from the back of his book. There was even the barbecue snap, dark and blurred, reproduced and captioned THE BEACH LOVE-IN WHERE THEY MET. He remembered the broken downstairs window of his house and that he had never looked to see if anything was missing from his box of photographs. He read:

> Prestigious novelist Felix Morsom, once nominated for the Booker Prize, refuses to acknowledge and support his love-child. 'When will Daddy come to see me?' ten-year-old Ian asks mum, Miriam Bowker, 30, who is desperately trying to make ends meet on National Assistance and part-time waitressing. The truth in Felix's life is a great deal more colourful, it seems, than his highbrow fiction.

Felix didn't feel called on to read further. Lucasta's story seemed no longer important. What turned his dream into a nightmare was the face of the man Detective Chief Inspector Cowling wanted to help her and this would be pushed through the country's letter-boxes and seen by millions on their way to work. He folded the paper neatly and went in search of the nearest rubbish bin.

He got rid of the *Meteor* and straightened up. About fifty yards away a man was standing in a pool of light by an empty platform. Although still young, his hair was receding. He had a pale face and metal glasses perched on a girlishly turned-up nose. As Felix watched the man moved away into the shadows.

Felix was as sure as he could be of anything that what he had seen was the living Gavin Piercey.

Chapter Twelve

'A Mr Felix Morsom is ringing you from a call-box and wishes you to accept the charge.'

'What?'

'Will you accept the charge?'

'Yes?' Septimus Roache, his hair standing on end and his eyes swollen with sleep, had straightened up in his bed, wearing the sort of striped flannel pyjamas which were obligatory in the school dormitory where he had once been happy. His Yes? was a question meaning I'm here and bloody well explain yourself, can't you?, not I'll pay for the call. However, the result of it was a click and an urgent and excited voice.

'Mr Roache, I'm sorry to call you so early.'

'It's bloody near two o'clock in the morning.'

'Felix Morsom here. You remember giving me lunch at your club?'

'Look, if you just want a friendly chat, piss off. Write me a thank you letter.'

'You remember I was in a spot of trouble?'

'Spawned a bastard? Nothing much to boast about. Most authors could do better.'

'No. This is rather more serious. It seems I'm wanted on a charge of murder.'

There was a pause. Septimus switched on his bedside light and put on a thick-framed pair of reading glasses. Now he could see better, he felt he could hear. 'That *is* most interesting,' was what he said.

'I think I've got a defence.'

'Everyone, however unattractive,' Septimus assured him, 'has got a defence of some sort. If not, they can be given one.'

'The man I'm meant to have killed was found beaten to death in his van in Bayswater.'

'Which man?'

'Gavin Piercey.'

'I think I read something . . .'

'Well, I just saw him get on to a bus.'

Septimus was silent, struck dumb once again by the inability of clients to dream up defences which have anything more than a snowball's chance in Hades.

'You saw,' he said, 'the deceased man, whom you may be suspected of doing in, getting out of a bus?'

'On to a bus.'

'When?'

'This morning. Five minutes ago.'

'An early riser. Up with the lark. How did he die?'

'His head was beaten in with some blunt instrument. Apparently there were also wounds to the face.'

'This character you saw getting on to a bus, this ghost, this revenant, this resurrection specialist, did you see his face?'

'For a moment I did.'

'Horribly injured?'

'Not at all. He looked, well, perfectly normal.'

'So you have woken me at this ungodly hour for the pleasure of telling me you've seen a miracle?'

'I could have sworn it was Gavin . . .' Felix sounded less certain.

'I suppose' – Septimus's voice was icy – 'there's some sort of biblical authority for what you're suggesting? Where was this?'

'On the Embankment.'

'*Hardly* the road to Emmaus.'

'But if it was Gavin, I mean, surely I'd have a defence?' Felix had, at best, a sketchy knowledge of the law.

'It's been a miracle to get some people off.' Septimus never thought it necessary to talk about law to clients. 'But I've never had to rely on a miracle as a defence. You'd better come into the office. I'm always there by nine thirty.'

'I can't do that.'

'Why not?'

'I might be caught.'

'That's bound to happen sooner or later.'

'Not till I've got the evidence.'

'What's the evidence?'

'Gavin Piercey.'

'Where are you now?'

'I told you. On the Embankment. There are some people here getting fed.'

'At the Savoy?'

'No. Near the Savoy. I'll call you later.'

Felix was gone. Septimus put down the phone, then lifted it, dialled another number and left a short message. Then he looked at the sleeping face of a boy only known to him as Yorkie Bar, whom he had attracted by the simple expedient of waving a fifty-pound note through the car window outside the Golden Pavement amusement arcade on his way home from the club. Septimus thought that he had never seen such innocence as there was in the face of the sleeping Yorkie, a look as pure as that of the child Septimus when he first shivered in his striped flannel pyjamas in the icy dormitory at the school from which he had never completely recovered.

'Gavin!' Felix had called out to his persecutor, a man who was certainly dead, as though to an old friend, the person who, most in the world, he would have wanted to meet in the small hours of a morning on Victoria Station. And then a porter, driving a long chain of swaying, rattling trucks, turned to stare at him and he shrank into the shadows.

Felix had the idea that the figure, the spectre, the double or even, perhaps (and this was his single hope), the living Gavin, had left the station. He found himself running, something he hardly ever did, but it had been a night of physical exercise. He was panting, gasping, muttering 'Gavin' and occasionally shouting it. In the entrance hall he passed a little posse of cleaners who looked after him as though he were mad, a sleepless Englishman driven crazy by loneliness and fear.

Gavin, or the ghost of Gavin, had not, Felix was sure, been wearing his inevitable blue business suit. His legs were encased in grey, shapeless material, perhaps the bottom of a tracksuit, and he wore a maroon anorak which, when he turned, had a dangling hood like a monk's. Felix ran out of Victoria Street with no idea whether to start up towards the park or down towards the river. Either way seemed equally hopeful or hopeless. Then he remembered that Gavin had told him at an author event which now seemed to have taken place long ago and in another life that he knew what it was to doss down in doorways. One of the sayings of Felix's father, words of warning or advice which he heard echoing from his childhood, was that more people could be found sleeping on the Embankment because they didn't lead out trumps. In his childhood, before he knew much of London, he had a picture of a high sandbank in front of a dark sea, with crowds of ragged and penniless card-players sleeping on it. He knew that the Embankment was where people bedded down for the night so he turned towards it.

He was still running past sleeping blocks of flats and offices, past a dark Chinese restaurant and a lit shop window in which brightly coloured fish swam lazily and pointlessly under a notice, Tasteful Tropicals. Halfway down Victoria Street a man lurched out of the darkness and collided with Felix who apologized profusely. The man shouted, 'Idiot! You know how many cells you had in your brain the day you were born? Three hundred thousand, would you believe it?' Felix was looking across the road. He could be sure he saw, far down on the other side of the street, in the cold glare of another light, a figure in a maroon anorak which was not running but strutting very rapidly, with its elbows tucked into its sides as though in a walking race. When he tried to move away he found the expert on brain cells attached to his arm. 'And how many have you got left today? How many, my friend? Let me tell you. Precisely three!' As the man started to laugh, Felix shook him off and ran across the road but somewhere down a side-street or in a doorway the maroon anorak was hiding from him.

At the end of Victoria Street, before he caught sight of the stone fretwork of the Abbey, Felix saw letters on a glass door: PARENTAL RIGHTS AND OBLIGATIONS DEPARTMENT. High above it there still seemed to be lights in several windows. Were they at work all night, ruthlessly pursuing careless, delinquent and disappearing fathers? He had no time to worry about them. Soon, he was sure, somewhere by the Sphinx and Cleopatra's Needle, on a bench or a wall, or under a black lamp-post with an iron dolphin twisted about it, he would see Gavin for a third time and be out of danger. He went on, sometimes running, sometimes walking, filled with the single-minded enthusiasm he felt when he hit on a watertight plot, a workable story and had only to summon up his strength and keep going to achieve some sort of success. The idea would become reality as it did when he passed Cleopatra's Needle and found, near Waterloo Bridge, what he now knew would be there.

He saw a parked Volvo Estate with its back open. A red-haired man wearing a dark suit and a dog-collar was pouring something steaming from an urn. Two women were helping him hand out food and drink to a collection of shadowy, ghostlike figures. Felix saw only one colour among them: a man in a maroon anorak was warming his hands on a mug.

They couldn't have been more than twenty-five yards apart when the man in the anorak, the possibly dead man, the murdered man, turned and they looked at each other silently, because now they were so near Felix was silenced. He heard the muted roar of a bus which had stopped on the other side of the road and, as the lights changed, it now started to lumber off. The maroon anorak flickered towards it and the man jumped on to the bus and was carried away, leaving Felix standing.

He didn't feel helpless, however. He was determined. He walked across to the corner of Savoy Gardens, shut himself carefully into a telephone kiosk and made a transfer charge call to the legal adviser who had promised to put out the red carpet for him if he was ever in trouble on a charge of murder.

Although Septimus had poured a certain amount of cold water on his defence Felix was not discouraged. Gavin, if it could be Gavin, was moving around London at night, going down to the Embankment for a snack, sleeping in doorways. He would find him again, track him as he had from Victoria Station. Meanwhile Felix was unexpectedly hungry.

'Homeless?' The smiling, carrot-haired vicar approached Felix with a steaming mug and a sandwich.

'Well, in a manner of speaking.' He didn't know how best to explain the situation.

'Because this is EMH. Sorry, Embankment Meals for the Homeless.'

'Well, yes I am. Quite homeless.'

'Looking at your clothes —' the vicar was anxious — 'they hardly look slept in.'

'Stolen.' Felix found an immediate explanation for his cashmere sweater.

'Well, of course I understand. My name is Brian.' The vicar handed him the homeless meal. 'What's yours?'

'Gavin.' Felix had an absurd idea that the vicar would say, No. You're not Gavin. Gavin was here ten minutes ago and took a bus to the hostel at Centre Point — or pass on some such valuable information but he only nodded understandingly. 'Greetings, Gavin. I recognize that you have as much right to our love and concern as those with four walls and a mortgage. We're up from Dorking every night, me and my sturdy volunteers. You only have to see us and ask.'

Felix stood among the shadows. Now he could see them more clearly. There was a short fat man who wore a bobble hat, a raincoat and woollen gloves and an unusually tall witchlike woman with a cloud of dark hair who was holding a sandwich very close to her face and sniffing at it with deep suspicion. Behind them, frowning ominously, there was a huge ox of a young man, his fist clenched round a mug, his jaws working with what seemed quite unnecessary vigour. Felix took a gulp of some hot, dark, anonymous fluid and looked up from it, puzzled.

'It's like a blind tasting, isn't it?' The man in the bobble hat spoke in a high, precise voice. 'Impossible to tell if it's tea or coffee.'

'It's soup!' The vicar looked young and smiled industriously. The gawky woman said, 'I don't touch it. I hear you put softeners in it, to damp down our urges.' Felix thought she was probably mad. 'You shouldn't spread such rumours, Peggy,' the vicar told her, 'when you know they're not true.'

'What's in this sandwich, then?' Peggy's question was an accusation.

'It's a sort of veggie spread, which I personally find quite delicious.'

'I reckon I'll wait for the prawn and mayo.' Peggy threw her sandwich over her shoulder, in the way people throw spilled salt to scare away the devil. 'I'll wait till they bring round the chuck-outs from Marks & Spencer, thank you very much. I've not long finished the funny curry those Hari Krishnas bring round and it's lying heavy on my stomach.'

Felix looked across the road. An anonymous car had stopped by the kiosk where he had made his transfer charge call. He saw the bald head of the plain-clothes officer emerge, tortoiselike, from the passenger seat, then the driver appeared, casually dressed. They opened the door of the telephone box and stood looking into it for a long time, as though to make sure it was empty. When they crossed the road to speak to the vicar and the shadows, Felix had left as quickly and as silently as possible.

He felt safe behind the shrubs in Savoy Gardens. He stood and saw, through the bushes, the bald policeman showing the vicar a newspaper – the *Meteor*, he felt sure – and the photograph illustrating Lucasta's article. Then, to his surprise, the Furies got back into their car and drove away. The vicar and his helpers were packing up the Volvo. Felix longed for sleep and felt detached, as though none of the unthinkable things that might happen to him would matter any more.

Outside the river entrance of the Savoy a late party in black ties and long dresses were shouting at each other and laughing. Felix stepped out of the headlights of the car which crawled to pick them up. There was a gust of wind and he felt rain in his face. He took shelter under the arches behind Shell Mex House and found himself in what looked like a long dormitory. On the line of stone seats, the sleeping-bags and cardboard-box bedheads were laid out. It was a dry place, full of middle-aged people, mainly men, who had arranged their few possessions as carefully as sailors or monks. Many of them had transistors going at full blast and they were reading paperbacks or the *Evening Standard*, with a puff of cigarette smoke, like a camp-fire, marking each position. Felix saw an empty marble slab with nothing on it but an empty cardboard box and sat, leaning his back against the wall. Then he wondered where else he might have been that night. His house was surely being watched, as was Miriam's. He had absolutely no desire to meet Brenda Bodkin's boyfriend. He ruled out Huw Hotchkiss as a host. There were a few women he had slept with in Coldsands and London, but they were married now and some had children, and he doubted if they'd have welcomed a murder suspect late at night in their family circle. Tubal-Smith of Llama Books had him to dinner occasionally in his Hampstead house but how would he react to a call from a potential criminal? Fergus Campion, his Llama editor, was a serious young man with a turned-down mouth, thin hair pulled back in a pony-tail, and a disconcerting smell of antiseptic. He disapproved of so many things from motor cars and the consumption of animal fats to smoking and calling God 'He', that Felix doubted if the house he shared with a partner in Tufnell Park would provide sanctuary for an author on the run from a murder rap. It was far better to stay where he was.

He thought of what the novelist Trigorin said in *The Seagull*: 'We will talk about my splendid, bright life. Well, where shall we begin? I am haunted night and day by one persistent thought. I ought to be writing. I ought to be writing. I ought . . . What is splendid and bright in that, I ask you? Oh, it is an absurd life!' Night and day, also, the same thoughts, the obsession and the guilt, had haunted Felix. Since pursuing Gavin, and being pursued by his own Furies, he hadn't felt the need to write anything. Under an archway, among those who do their best to forget, his heavy eyelids drooped and his world became blank.

Chapter Thirteen

'This is more or less an informal chat, Miriam. Just to go through the statement you have made and matters arising. You have cooperated hereto, I say that in all honesty, and let's hope this will continue.' In spite of the informality, Detective Sergeant Wathen had not removed his raincoat and had refused what was left of the bottle of sake, when, earlier that evening, he had visited the flat at World's End.

The living-room was unnaturally tidy. Miriam was wearing a black T-shirt and dark glasses. She seemed to be in mourning. She sat on a hard chair by the lamp. Ian was at the table doing his homework and sighing heavily when anyone spoke. Detective Sergeant Wathen was perched on the front of an armchair with broken springs and a seat with leaking stuffing. His Detective Constable, who chose not to recline on a purple beanbag and preferred to stand, was holding his notebook at the ready.

'I rather gathered from your statement that the deceased, whose body you identified, had been with you in an intimate relationship?'

'Had been. Yes.'

'You'd had a sexual connection, hadn't you, Miriam?'

'Had, in the past.' Miriam found the bald officer's use of her Christian name not in the least comforting.

'When you went to visit the deceased at the Carisbrooke Terrace address . . . ?'

'Round Bayswater, yes.'

'Round Bayswater, indeed. Was this a visit, Miriam, made for the purpose of sexual connection?'

'Not specially.'

'By that, I take it to mean sex was a possibility?'

'I suppose everything's possible in this world. I was extremely fond of Gavin.' With her eyes hidden behind her black glasses, it was impossible to judge Miriam's sincerity.

'Everything's possible in this world, you said. And I take it that would include sexual connection?'

'I suppose so. Yes.'

'Mum' – Ian was exasperated – 'I *am* trying to do my homework.'

'Perhaps, in view of the lateness of the hour and the turn this interview is taking, the young lad should now withdraw?'

'All right. Why don't you go to your room, darling?'

'Because I hate my room.'

'I think you'd best run along . . .' Detective Sergeant Wathen spoke in a terrifying fatherlike way to Ian and added, as a final insult, 'Sonny.' Ian rose slowly, packed his pencil-case even more slowly, gave the officer a look of withering contempt and departed.

'Did that little lad' – Wathen turned to Miriam after the slamming of Ian's door had died away – 'show much grief when he heard of Gavin Piercey's death?'

'I don't think so. Ian doesn't show much emotion.'

'No emotion on hearing of the death,' the Detective Sergeant repeated. 'I'd like a note taken of that, Leonard.' Detective Constable Newbury started, as though awaking from a dream. His taste ran to suntanned blondes with enormous tits. He couldn't see why anyone would want to have sexual connection with Miriam Bowker. He wrote down 'No emotion'.

'Like father, like son.' Wathen shook his head as though to say, Sad but true.

'What do you mean?'

'I mean that, to quote your previous statement given in the presence of myself and Detective Constable Newbury, you are now satisfied that Felix Morsom is the father of the young lad Ian?'

'Well, what about it?'

'Bad breeding! That's what's about it, Miriam. In my view, it's in the blood.'

'What do you mean, bad breeding? Felix is an intelligent man. A well-known man. He writes books.'

'Please. Don't distress yourself unduly, Miriam. I'm not suggesting he doesn't write books. However, I am suggesting that your Felix, whom we have not yet had the pleasure of meeting, is perfectly capable of a particularly brutal homicide. All I'm saying to you, Miriam, is watch out as far as the young lad's concerned. It's in the blood!'

'Are you trying to tell me' – Miriam pulled off the shades from her eyes, which were glistening with fury – 'my little Ian's capable of beating someone to death with a spanner?'

'To be frank with you, Miriam, we've had children do considerably worse than that around the Paddington area, haven't we, Leonard?'

'Oh, yes. *Far* worse.' The Detective Constable wanted, above all things, to sit down but didn't know whether it would look right to collapse in Ian's chair and nor did he wish to sit too close to Miriam.

'I don't believe he'd do that for a moment!' Miriam was

contemptuous. 'And, what's more, I don't believe Felix would either.'

'Then perhaps it would come as a surprise to you to know' – Detective Sergeant Wathen was calmly triumphant – 'that your precious Felix uttered death threats about the deceased Piercey in the presence of witnesses!'

'I don't believe that either.'

'Entirely up to you.' The Detective Sergeant seemed no longer interested in persuading her and put on his most formal expression. 'I propose to ask you a number of supplementary questions to elucidate matters already referred to and I will ask Detective Constable Newbury to make a contemporaneous note. I take it' – he returned to what seemed to be his favourite topic of conversation – 'that you have had sexual connection with the man Morsom, whom I shall refer to as Felix for the remainder of this question and answer?'

'Well, seeing as Ian is in that room doing his prep' – Miriam's tone was icy – 'I rather think so.'

'And when did such a connection last occur? Give me the date approximately.'

'About eleven years ago. On the beach at a place called Coldsands.'

'On the sands?' Detective Constable Newbury asked, as though amazed.

'On an inflatable mattress, if you want the full details.'

'The full details' – the Detective Sergeant's voice was now drained of all expression – 'will not be necessary. And when did you last see Felix?'

Detective Constable Newbury wrote: 'After a short pause Miriam Bowker said, "When I went to Coldsands a few weeks ago to introduce him to his son Ian." Detective Sergeant

Wathen said, "Have you not seen him since then?" And the witness answered, "No."'

'Felix was last heard of on the Thames Embankment area making a phone call to his defence lawyer. There, you see, Miriam, I'm laying my cards out on the table. Face upwards. He's not far from here. Not far, you might say, down the river. If you see him or if he makes any attempt to get in touch . . .'

'Yes. Then what?' Miriam was still angry.

'Then you will contact us at Paddington Green immediately. My DC will leave a telephone number which I will ask you to keep by you at all times. That right, Leonard?'

'And if I don't?' Miriam challenged him.

Detective Sergeant Wathen sucked air through his teeth and shook his head again. 'If you don't' – he looked sad – 'we may have to change our view of your own involvement, Miriam.' He stood up, turned and dusted down the back of his raincoat with his hand, as though to get rid of any spillage from the armchair. 'And, if you take my advice, you'll see that young lad is not out roaming the streets after five. This is not an official warning, as yet.'

After the police officers had gone, Miriam let Ian out of retreat. 'If that bald-headed bastard ever comes in here again, don't you say a word to him!'

In the car Detective Constable Newbury said, 'I wonder how she knew it was a spanner?'

'That, Leonard' – the superior officer gave the ghost of a smile to indicate, quite falsely, that it was something he had noticed himself – 'is a question you may well ask.'

Chapter Fourteen

'You! Whoever you are, shitface! You get your arse out of there. That's Flo's place. I'm keeping it safe. Saving it for Flo. You fuck off out of it!'

Felix seemed hardly to have slept at all. A moment of blessed unconcern and then Peggy, the middle-aged woman, was pulling at his arm and cursing him horribly.

'There wasn't anyone here.'

'Course there wasn't. Flo's in hospital, isn't she? She won't tolerate that. Not indoors. Not stuck in a ward with tubes all pushed in her. She won't stay. The Queen of England couldn't make her stay. She'll want the fresh air. That's what she is used to, so you piss off. You creeping monkey. You slithering snake, you. Piss off out of it.'

'Of course.' Felix rubbed his eyes, shook himself and stood up. 'Of course, I'll move. I wouldn't want to take anyone's place.'

He had often tried politeness as a way of manipulating publishers, editors, even students. Never before had it had such a devastating effect. The witch-woman looked stunned. She ran her fingers through her hair so that it stood up in an even more Medusalike manner. Then she said, 'Where are you from, anyway?'

'Hospital.' Felix, at a loss, returned to his trade of creating fiction.

'Hospital? You didn't see no sign of Flo there, did you?'

'Oh, yes.' Felix was now at his ease. 'I saw Flo. She said she wouldn't be out. Not for a couple of days at least.'

'She wouldn't want to be in there. Not for a couple of days even. She always said she couldn't breathe in those places.' The Medusa's eyes narrowed. 'How did you know it was Flo, anyway?'

'Flo? Everyone knows Flo, don't they?'

'I suppose they do. What else did Flo tell you?'

'She said I could have her place. At least till she got back.'

'Flo said that?'

'You know Flo.' Felix found the dialogue flowing easily. 'She'd give you her last fifty p. She'd do anything for a friend.'

'Flo's got more than fifty p!' The woman laughed. 'Where've you been sleeping? Up Lincoln's Inn Fields? Or the Kingsway?'

Felix opted for the Kingsway.

'Dole office doorway?'

'That's it. Of course I always wanted the chance of coming down here.'

'Down here's better.'

'Of course it is.'

'Cleaner.'

'That's what I think.'

'Better class of person. More middle-aged and responsible.'

'They're all young up the Kingsway,' Felix agreed.

'Well, if you're staying, I'll get you Flo's sleeping-bag to lie on. You don't want to lie on the cold stone.'

Felix was nervous of Flo's sleeping-bag, which, he imagined, would be a soggy item, saturated in urine and worse. But when it came, it looked as clean as when Flo had first spread it on the cold stone. He lay down on it gratefully. 'You're very kind.'

'Any friend of Flo's,' she told him. 'Nothing else you want?'

'One thing you can tell me. You never heard anything of a man called Gavin Piercey?'

Peggy shook her head. 'Sleeps round here, does he?'

'Possibly. Bloke with a maroon anorak. Sort of . . .' – Felix struggled for words to describe Gavin – '. . . pale and serious-looking.'

'Gavin? Never heard of him.'

'And those two men that stopped in a car?'

'Never seen them before. Coppers from out of the area. Don't you worry your head about them.'

'They showed that vicar a photograph in the paper.'

'Showed Brian? His sandwiches is awful. God knows why he brings them.'

'Did he recognize anyone?'

'He didn't say. He knows we want nothing said to the police. Not about any of us.'

'Did the others see the photograph? Did you?'

'I didn't bother with it.' Peggy squatted on her haunches beside him. She had a strong individual smell of musk and mildew, the smell of damp churches, which he found he could cope with perfectly well. 'Some may have had a glance at it. But we don't tell the coppers anything. Even when the taxmen beats us up.'

'The taxmen?' Felix had a sudden, surprising vision of dark-suited Inland Revenue officials assaulting street-sleepers.

'What lays claim to half your begging money and kicks it out of you. Not our age group. Surely you have taxmen up there?'

'Oh, yes,' Felix remembered, 'we've got plenty of them up the Kingsway.'

★

He dreamed that he was a boy again at Coldsands, sitting in the shallow water at the edge of the sea, feeling the dark, gritty sand being sucked away from under him as the waves retreated, and then they returned, high-crested and yellow-foaming, to cover his goose-pimpled body in a salt shower. He woke up to find Peggy yanking the sleeping-bag from under him and with hoses sluicing down the arcade as the sleepers picked up their belongings and skipped away from the advancing flood.

'They're not attacking us,' the man in the bobble hat, his possessions neatly rolled, tied with string and lodged under his arm, reassured Felix. 'They don't mean us any harm, you know. No harm at all. We just have to go when they start cleaning up. We'll all be back here this evening. You coming for a bite of breakfast?'

'Where to?'

'Weaver Street. Best breakfast in London.'

'I haven't got any money.'

'It's the order of St Agatha. They don't expect money. And, even if you had it, it's better to keep quiet about it. Take your stuff. Can't leave it here, you know.'

'I'm afraid I haven't got any stuff either.'

'What happened? Did the taxmen rob you?'

'Yes,' Felix answered without difficulty, 'that's what happened.'

The rain had stopped and there was sunshine above early morning mist so, as they crossed Waterloo Bridge, Somerset House and St Paul's seemed to be floating over the water. The bobble-hatted man, who had introduced himself as Esmond, walked with a staccato trot and Felix found it hard to keep up with him. Striding ahead of them on the bridge, silent and unaccompanied, carrying only the smallest, tightest bundle of belongings, was the ox-like young man he had seen by Brian's sandwich van.

'There goes Dumbarton,' Esmond told him.

'Is that his name?'

'Probably just his address. Boy was in the army and when his time was over, you know, he couldn't cope. Used to doing everything at the word of command. Having it all laid on for him. Couldn't manage life on his own. What did you say your name was?'

'I said it was Gavin.'

'Unusual sort of name.'

'Not really. There must be thousands of Gavins.'

'Yes, I suppose there must be.'

Esmond had been right about the breakfast. There was bacon and egg on a fried slice, bread and marmalade and mugs of sweet tea which tasted nothing like soup. They ate at long tables in the crypt of an old Catholic church with the ageless nuns in white habits sailing between the rows of hungry dossers.

'How long have you been on the streets?'

'Not too long,' Felix confessed. 'How about you?'

'Coming up for five years.' Esmond was using his bread to mop up what was left of his egg, polishing the plate. He said, quite without boasting, 'You won't believe this. I was manager of a supermarket in Bexley Heath.'

'Made redundant? I know. They were slimming down the operation?'

'No. I was married to a lovely girl. Sandra. Quite lovely. With a birthmark which I didn't mind at all, although she'd been teased at school about it. And our Barbara. Four years old. Well, of course, I'd have done anything for that Barbara. Died for her quite happily. Only it was her that had to die.' Esmond spoke quickly in the way he walked and quite cheerfully. Felix saw a yellow trickle of egg at the corner of his mouth and tried not to notice it.

'Four years old. On her way home from nursery school with her mother. Drunk driver did for both of them on a pedestrian crossing in Henshaw Avenue. Chap who did it got six months. I got life. Or at least I thought I did.'

'But you got over it?'

'Took me four years. I went to Italian classes in the evening. Trying to forget my wife and daughter. Classes at the Adult Institute. That's where I met her. Lucrezia. Italian girl. Father was an ex prisoner of war and she worked in the National Assistance. She managed to convince me it was love at first sight. I found myself spending hours when I hardly remembered Sandra and young Barbara.'

A nun glided towards them with a huge tin teapot and refilled their mugs. Felix didn't feel that this was a story which was going to end happily, although Esmond was smiling as cheerfully as ever. 'Six months,' he said. 'That's how long it lasted. My Italian marriage. Then she went off with one of our suppliers. A traveller in toiletries. Well! That's it, I said. That does it. That just about puts the tin lid on it. I've had enough. I'm just not prepared to take any more. Know what I did?'

Felix didn't know.

'I had a detached residence, mortgage nearly paid for. I had a Toyota and a job with a decent salary and I couldn't stand the sight of them any more. Not my home. Not my car. Not those crowds of people pushing wire wheelbarrows round my shop loaded up with stuff they never really wanted in the first place. So I locked up the house and posted the keys in through the letter-box. I spent the money I had on a train to Charing

Cross, a little bit of camping equipment and a bloody good dinner at Rules. Then I looked for a nice quiet doorway to sleep in. That was five years ago.'

'And are you happy?' Felix couldn't believe it.

'You think about surviving. That's all you think about. No bills. No rates. No wives. No children. Just how to keep warm and where to walk during the day. The days do seem long sometimes. How about you?'

'What?'

'Are you planning on going back to it?'

'I don't know. I really don't know what's going to happen.'

Silence fell between them. To Felix's relief, Esmond took out a clean handkerchief and wiped the corners of his mouth. Then he lifted his mug of tea and looked at Felix over it.

'I saw a photograph of you last night,' he said. 'Members of the constabulary came and showed us a photograph of you in the paper.'

Felix felt he had gone through a door and stepped on nothing, space and a fall with no end, to nowhere.

'They said they were looking for you and you'd been over in the telephone box.'

What could Felix say?

'Your name's not Gavin, is it? Your name's Felix. Felix Morsom. You're a writer.'

If he kept quiet, Felix thought, it would soon be over. He drank tea and tried to look uninterested.

'I read one of yours. Paperback. We had it in the rack at the checkout. *The End of the Pier.*'

'Did you like it?' Felix wondered why he should care.

'Very interesting. Could have done with a bit more sex and story in my humble opinion. They want a good bonk every three pages, to go with the groceries. You're not a supermarket author, quite honestly, are you, Felix?'

'Please. Don't call me that.'

'But that's your name, isn't it? You're not Gavin, are you?'

Peggy and Dumbarton were eating far away at the other end of the long table. No one round them seemed to be listening. Felix looked at Esmond and decided to trust him.

'No. Gavin's someone I knew. He was murdered.'

'A bad business?' Esmond looked seriously concerned.

'Bad for me. They think I did it.'

'They?'

'The police.'

'You don't have the stamp of a murderer. Not to me.'

'Thank you. I haven't murdered anyone. As a matter of fact, Gavin Piercey's not even dead. I saw him when Brian the vicar was handing out sandwiches. You remember him, don't you? Pale. With a turned-up nose. And a maroon anorak?'

'As a matter of fact I *don't* remember. I was busy trying to identify the refreshment the Rev. Brian had on offer.'

'Perhaps the others will?' Felix looked down the table. 'At least they'll remember the anorak.'

'I think you'll find their memories are miserably short, particularly when the police have shown an interest. I even find I've forgotten your name. Was it Gavin, did you say?'

Felix leant forward and tried to say as quietly as possible, 'Will you help me find him?'

'Why?'

'Well, if he's alive I can't have killed him, can I?'

Esmond thought about it. 'A bit of a tall order. London's a big place. Needle in a haystack job.'

'But he's with . . . well . . . people like you. He was eating on the street. It looks as though he wants to keep hidden. At least from me. He seems to want to disappear.'

'Perhaps that's what you ought to do.'

'What?'

'Disappear. Forget everything. I have. I never believed it was possible to forget Sandra and our Barbara. But can you imagine? That's the first time I've thought about them since Christmas. Christmas Day, I thought about them but never since. Lucrezia and Sandra and even my Barbara. They're going away now. I can't even remember exactly what they looked like.'

But Felix didn't want to forget. He wanted to find Gavin.

Chapter Fifteen

Brenda Bodkin heard the news in her Fulham Road flat. It came from Radio London when she was having breakfast with Paul, her Australian boyfriend. She wore an old camel-hair dressing-gown, left behind by a previous lover, and was eating muesli. A pink towel covered her damp hair like a turban. 'The police are anxious to trace the missing novelist Felix Morsom. They think he may be able to help them in the inquiries into the death of a publisher's representative, Gavin Piercey, who was found dead in his van parked in Carisbrooke Terrace, Bayswater. Anyone who has seen Mr Morsom or knows where he is to be found is asked to get in touch with Paddington Green police station. And now here is Miss Tina Turner with *What's Love Got to Do with It*.'

'*Felix* wanted by the police? I can't believe it!'

'I'd think they're the only people who do want him.'

'I wanted to make him a bit more newsworthy but not *that* notorious.'

'Stop worrying about him, Pavlova.' (This was Paul's pet name for his recently acquired girlfriend. It was a reference to the pudding not the dancer.) 'I mean, he's not that great is he? He's not Balzac or Martin Amis or any of those?' Although he had over-the-ears hair and the blond moustache of a professional footballer, Paul was, in fact, Professor of English at a Queensland university and was over on a sabbatical. The novel he was trying to sell to Llama Books was about a sensitive boy growing up in the remote Riverina district of New South Wales.

'He was very talented. And he was extremely fond of me.'

'What do you mean *was*? He's still alive and kicking.'

'And I was fond of him too.' Brenda drank orange juice. 'In a way he found me very attractive and I found him clever.'

'You didn't do it, did you?' Paul lived through an unusual moment of insecurity.

'No. As a matter of fact we'd already done it, if you want to know the truth.'

'Done it where? On one of those tarty book tours of yours?'

'No. We did it in our heads.'

'Bloody funny place to do it, Pav.' Sometimes he shortened her nickname in this affectionate way.

'Not funny at all if you've got a literary imagination.'

'And are you saying I haven't?' The author of *The Budding Groves of Wagga Wagga* took offence.

'I'm sure you have but not for doing it in your head. I should have kept in touch with Felix. I thought it was odd he hadn't called me for days.'

'He called you here.'

'When?'

'Couple of days ago.'

'You didn't tell me?'

'You were out at some late-night book launch.'

'The new Sandra Tantamount. We've taken her over.'

'Well, he rang up and asked for you. I didn't think it was that important.'

'Did he say where he was?'

'Not a squeak on the subject. I asked him if he found you a good fuck.'

'Because you thought he had?'

'Because I knew he hadn't.'

'That wasn't exactly kind!' But Brenda, in the act of lighting her first cigarette of the day, was suppressing laughter.

'Kind? *He's* not exactly kind. Looks like he's wanted for murder.'

'That's ridiculous. It can't be true.'

'You didn't know he'd got a kid tucked away somewhere? It seems this scribbler is full of surprises.'

'And I thought his life was uneventful!'

'Ought we to tell the police?' Paul, the Australian, wondered.

'What?'

'About the call?'

'No need. It can't help them find him. Poor old Felix.' She stood up and her dressing-gown fell open, revealing the still damp body of pale Pavlova.

Paul said, 'I think we ought to do it.'

'Tell the police?'

'No. *It*. But not in the head.'

'Where on earth?' But she was jabbing out her cigarette in a saucer.

'The floor's nearest.'

In the end they settled for the bed and Brenda was half an hour late for work. Sandra Tantamount had called early and left a message that on book tours she wanted a suite at each hotel with caviar, Dom Perignon, Badedas and Prozac in the fridge. She never wanted to go to a literary lunch again where more than one person, that is, herself, was talking and she hoped that Llama Books would refuse to publish any book which Felix Morsom might write to make money out of crime.

★

It had been a long and fruitless search. They called in at King's Cross and Euston Station. Esmond advanced some of his begging money to obtain entrance to the Superloo, where middle-aged men entertain boys from the North on their first visit to London. They visited Victoria and Centre Point. They walked down to the Cut in Waterloo and on to the gardens round the Imperial War Museum, to Battersea Park and back, down the whole length of the Embankment and up to the Kingsway and Lincoln's Inn Fields. They asked the regulars they met in each place if they had seen someone called Gavin who had a turned-up nose and wore a maroon anorak. When asked for his name, Felix no longer said he was a Gavin in search of Gavin, but called himself Anton in tribute to his hero.

Under St Martin-in-the-Fields Esmond had his feet attended to, after a short wait, by the regular chiropodist, whilst Felix washed his shirt and underpants in the launderette which spun perpetually under Wren's calm and untroubled church. Then he took a shower and discovered how to work a spin-drier, surprised to find that he had not, as yet, met any smell, including his own, he found unbearable.

In a greasy-spoon café off Holborn, Esmond bought them both a cup of tea and a slice of toast. Felix, embarrassed by his lack of money, asked his host's advice.

'You either beg or you go without,' Esmond told him. 'In your position I wouldn't go near the National Assistance, and I wouldn't think you had much of a talent for stealing.'

'I don't know how to set about begging.'

'You've done it before, haven't you? In your work or in love. Everyone begs for something. You must be used to it.'

Felix thought about his propositions to Brenda. Were they

begging? At any rate, they had been conspicuously unsuccessful.

'Do it when the shows come out. The opera's best. People
feel guilty about going to the opera and all that money they've
paid. Bit near Bow Street nick for you, however. Try the
theatres in the Strand. They've got the new musical *Anna
Darling*. I believe it's loosely based on Anna Karenina.
Wouldn't go near it myself but it's not a bad play to beg
outside.'

In the evening when they were talking to an ageing Irishman
who was preparing his bed and box for an early night in Great
Turnstile Street, they heard drums and chanting and saw the yel-
low-robed Hari Krishnas advancing remorselessly towards them.
'For God's sake!' Esmond gripped Felix's arm. 'Don't risk the
curry.' So they retreated to the back door of Rules where two
big steak and kidney pies were being prepared for the homeless.
They each got a generous portion when Esmond told the chef
that he was a patron of the place and had enjoyed his last supper
there before he opted out of so-called civilized society.

The boy said, 'You can sit here if you like. I'm not afraid of
competition. Anyway, I think we'll attract a different class of
customer.'

He was good-looking, hollow-cheeked, deep-eyed, with
long thin arms like a Blue Period Picasso. He sat cross-legged
with a blanket over his knees, doodling on the cover of a
paperback called *The Economics of Poverty*. His position was
between two theatres in the Strand. Felix sat in his clean
clothes in the shadows of a shop doorway. There was not
much passing trade and he and the boy talked across the space
between them for company. 'What sort of customer do you
hope to attract then?' Felix asked.

'Men, perhaps. Mostly men who'll want to take me down a dark street.'

'Will you go?'

'Only if they put their money out first. Spent the night with an old bloke who showed me a fifty pound note, then kicked me out without a penny.'

'Don't you mind doing it with them?'

'I won't say I like it. You feel like a cut off the joint sometimes. That's why they call it the meat rack.'

'What's the meat rack?'

'Round Eros's statue. Where the boys go who ain't learnt their way about. You're new about here?'

'Quite new.'

'I thought I hadn't seen you. What's your name then?'

'Anton.'

'What sort of name's that?'

'A Russian name.'

'You Russian then?'

'Not at all.'

'Oh, right!' the boy said as though he understood perfectly. 'I get called Yorkie Bar on account I'm from the North. You can call me that if you like.'

'Well, thanks. I just wondered' – Felix was taking the last chance of the day – 'if you happened to see a bloke called Gavin round here? Perhaps sleeping rough. Pale sort of person in a maroon anorak?'

'Why do you want him?'

'Well, as a matter of fact, people are saying he's dead. But I know he's not, you see.'

'How do you know?'

'I saw him last night. Down on the Embankment. After it had said in the paper he was dead.'

'Why was it in the paper? Is he famous or something?'

'Not famous. Just that . . . Well, I'm supposed to have killed him.'

'Then I don't know anything about him,' Yorkie Bar said firmly. 'I don't know anything at all.'

Waiting for the theatre crowds to come out they chatted sporadically. Felix asked the questions. How long had Yorkie Bar been on the streets? Why did he start? What were his plans for the future? The answers were two years. Because his foster parents hated him, only wanted him for the money, and his probation officer wanted to trade a good report for sex. He supposed he'd go on as he was. It wasn't a bad life so long as hairy old men didn't take you home and cheat you. When Felix told him he was finding it pretty comfortable under the arches behind Shell Mex House, he said, 'I wouldn't use it. There is none of my age group down there.'

So the time passed quietly until the theatres emptied. A group of girls out on an office party dropped a shower of pound coins on to Yorkie's blanket. An anxious-looking man in spectacles, who reminded Felix of himself, passed by hurriedly, his face carefully averted, and then stopped, wrestled with his conscience, lost, and gave Felix three pounds twenty p, all in small change. He put the money in his pocket and, feeling the weight of it against his leg, felt ridiculously secure again. A Rolls pulled up and was parked by a chauffeur who was playing loud country and western with the window open. He looked across the pavement at Felix and Yorkie with amused contempt.

And then the pavement was full of legs, feet and chattering voices. Felix found his arm irresistibly lifting, his hand held out like a cap or a begging-bowl. From time to time he heard himself say, 'Can you spare a bit of change?'

Yorkie only grinned modestly, cast down his eyes and his blanket was heavy with contributions. A group of young men in blazers stretched tight across muscly shoulders came out of *Anna Darling*, found an empty Coca-Cola tin in the gutter and ran off dribbling and kicking it across the street, their girlfriends laughing as they followed. A man with a red face and suspiciously dark hair came out with a girl who looked not much older than Yorkie Bar. He was complaining loudly, 'Whoever heard of a darkie playing Vronsky? Should've asked for our money back!' As he pushed his way towards the Rolls the girl, lagging behind, opened her handbag and sent a five pound note fluttering down towards Felix. It gave him the same feeling of unexpected joy as when he got a good notice for a book.

Felix was calling across to the girl, who was being helped by the chauffeur into the back of the now silent Rolls, 'Thank you, lady. Good luck! God bless you' – words which he thought appropriate to such an occasion – when he saw something which made him retreat again into the shadows, lowering his head as he stuffed the note into his pocket. Brenda Bodkin had cried at the end of *Anna Darling* and Paul, who had only agreed to go because 'someone wanted to do a musical of *Budding Groves*', clearly despised her for it. Now she paused, looking at Yorkie Bar. 'Don't dream of giving them anything,' Paul told her. 'Drug money. That's all it is! Every penny'll go on crack.' Brenda allowed him to pull her to the edge of the pavement where he was shouting for a taxi. But she was shocked to have seen one of her best-known authors, certainly the one who loved her most, begging in the shadows of a doorway. She also knew he was wanted by the police. For the moment she kept quiet about it.

★

By the end of the evening the score stood at Yorkie Bar twenty-nine pounds, Felix eleven pounds forty p. Felix felt his alcohol content had sunk to a dangerous low and realized he hadn't had a drink for two days. With his new-found wealth he invited Yorkie to join him in a pub. There were moments, and this was one of them, when he felt that his new way of life was, in itself, a hiding-place, and he had no need to keep his face in the shadows. Yorkie led him down a dark street between the Strand and the Embankment and into a pub called the Garden of Eden in which he was, apparently, well known. Felix bought them lagers and stood surveying a scene which was, living quietly in Coldsands, unusual to him.

The pub was an old one, with frosted patterns on big mirrors and threadbare plush, which had been invaded and taken over by a new world. Humming neon lights exposed the cracked ceiling and peeling plaster, the bar throbbed with heavy metal and bleated with flashing Space Invaders. The clientele seemed to go in for bright yellow hair, cut short, pierced noses and ears, leather trousers, caps which might have been worn by storm troopers, tight shorts and patent leather boots. They yelled greetings or abuse at each other and quarrelled in corners. As Felix stood drinking with Yorkie, he saw a young man leaning on the bar, apparently alone, looking at him with particular interest. His hair was cut into short bristles at the side and flat as a table on the top of his head. He wore a black T-shirt with BASIL written on it in green phosphorescent script, white jeans and purple boots. His face was decorated with designer stubble and a single earring. What was unusual about him, in those surroundings, was that he wasn't looking at Yorkie with desire but at Felix with what was clearly suspicion. Felix's fragile sense of security was shattered as he gulped what was left of his lager and, forgetting to say goodbye to Yorkie, moved quickly to a door marked Gents.

As he went, his watcher moved to join Yorkie Bar. There followed a brief conversation during which Basil asked after Yorkie's health, said he had seen him begging earlier (but didn't intend to report it) and who was the newcomer to the area? Yorkie gave him what details he could of Anton, including the fact that he seemed very keen on finding some guy called Gavin who wore a maroon anorak. He remembered that particularly because Anton had told him that it was put in the papers that this Gavin had been knocked off by someone, perhaps him.

'Sounds as though he's a bit daft!' was Basil's comment.

'That's what I thought,' Yorkie Bar agreed. 'I mean, what's the sense in going around looking for blokes that are dead?' Basil was particularly interested in this information and bought Yorkie another lager, after which he stood watching the door of the Gents, waiting for Felix to emerge.

Felix didn't emerge. When he got through the door he had found himself in a passage with a staircase leading down to the porcelain from which came cries of anger and delight. A door from the passageway led into the public bar, a bleak, unpopular area of the Garden of Eden, in which only a few late-night cleaners, about to go on duty, were drinking Guinness. Felix walked by them and out of the pub door, leaving Basil wondering if he hadn't passed out or shot up in a cubicle.

Felix walked into Villiers Street and down towards the river. As he arrived on the Embankment at Hungerford Bridge, he saw an extraordinary procession moving inexorably towards him. In the lead strode Peggy, her hair standing out like a nest of serpents. She marched, as though she were a guard with a red flag before an antique train, in front of what was undoubtedly a moving hospital bed, its iron frame shaking and groaning as its castors hit the road or mounted unsteadily on to the pavement. In it, a very old woman, with long white hair, was sitting bolt upright and shouting. The moving bed was being pushed by the giant Dumbarton, beside whom Esmond in his bobble hat trotted enthusiastically. Awaiting their approach Felix knew what had happened. They had sprung Flo from hospital.

As the impressive cortège approached him, Peggy screamed, pointing, 'That's him, Flo! Him what told lies about knowing you. So he could sleep in your quarters!' Felix stood amazed at the sudden wave of hatred from the wild-eyed woman who had spread out Flo's sleeping-bag for him. But Flo, like some ancient queen arrived by chariot, pronounced a final judgement, shouting, 'Get away with you! We don't know you! You're not welcome any more round Shell Mex!'

'Nothing I can do about it.' Esmond was beside him and apologetic. 'You could try top of the steps across Blackfriars Bridge. Used to be quite decent. Haven't been there lately.'

'That's right. You go down under the bridge. We don't want you round us! On we go, Dumbarton. And if he don't move, run him over!' The bed lurched forward and Felix moved out of the path of the approaching juggernaut.

When Flo and her bed had been settled in her favourite spot at the end of the arches, and Peggy and Esmond were enjoying a smoke before getting their heads down, Basil arrived. He was greeted by Peggy as a friend who'd always done his best to protect the respectable and elderly people sleeping in Shell Mex, and only issued a summons for begging after countless warnings – or when his wife told him he'd never make it as a sergeant if he didn't get the layabouts off the streets.

'I hear you had a newcomer sleeping here, Peggy? Middle-aged and going thin on top, that's how he was described to me.'

'We had an intruder. Put it that way.'

'Does the name Anton mean anything to you?'

'Nothing at all. It means absolutely nothing,' Esmond assured him.

'Does the name Gavin Piercey mean anything to you?'

'Sorry, can't help,' Esmond said.

'You say this man was an intruder?'

'He wanted to sleep in Flo's place,' Peggy told him.

'Only when she was away.' Esmond was trying to be reasonable. 'Anyway, you helped him sleep there.'

'He thought he could lie his way in.' Peggy's eyes were blazing and a thin column of smoke emerged from each nostril. 'Flo wasn't having it. Flo told me he was a liar.'

'Not your sort was he, Peggy?' Basil was understanding.

'You can say that again! Did you mention something about Gavin?' Peggy was making an effort to remember.

'Gavin Piercey. Bloke who got himself murdered.'

'Gavin. Yes. Now I come to think about it, I feel sure he mentioned him. Murdered, did you say? Anyway, he was still looking for him.'

'You know where he is now?'

'Blackfriars Bridge steps. Esmond sent him there to sleep.'

'That right, Esmond?' Basil turned to the retired super-market manager but Esmond had gone off, as fast as he could trot, in the direction of Blackfriars. Basil took the mobile phone out of the back pocket of his jeans and dialled a number. When he had finished his conversation with Detective

Sergeant Wathen he put away his phone and looked into the shadows under the distant arches. 'Fuck me!' he said, 'if that's not a hospital bed you've got there.'

'Donated to us by the Sisters of St Agatha,' Peggy told him. 'We are *very* saintly girls!' Constable Basil didn't believe a word of it but he had more important things on his mind.

Esmond had set out to give a warning. Although he hadn't greatly admired *The End of the Pier*, he felt that Felix had been unfairly treated by Flo and Peggy, who had broken the firm rule of the colony of sleepers at Shell Mex, which was not to give out any information, even to such friendly and sympathetic members of the police as Constable Basil Bulstrode of the Homeless Squad.

Esmond had seen the mobile in Basil's back pocket and knew that he could be swiftly in touch with more powerful and less humane members of the force. Moreover, he had taken to Felix, he felt they hit it off, and he had enjoyed spending an otherwise fruitless day showing him round the street-sleepers in London, and thought he had made a friend with whom the next few years of anonymity could be pleasantly spent. So he was trotting along towards Blackfriars, fully intending to find Felix and tell him to get as far away, and as quickly, as possible.

Then he saw a cheerful crowd of young men with their laughing girlfriends coming down the steps to the Temple Station. He remembered that he had treated Felix on a few occasions during that day and had earned nothing. A crowd who'd enjoyed a happy evening ought to be good for a quid or two. He took a quick detour, stood at the bottom of the steps, held out his hand and said, 'Can you spare a bit of change?' The whole transaction would be over in a minute.

It was, in fact, over very quickly. Esmond heard someone shout, 'Give him change, shall we? Let's all give him change!' He was surrounded, overwhelmed, by a sea of faces, most of them laughing. He heard a girl's voice and felt a heavy weight, which seemed to fall from a great height on to his chest and forced him to his knees. Feet were kicking him, trampling him. He was lying on the ground, stretched out as though he were going to sleep, and then he felt a shuddering pain inside his head and he was falling into darkness. He heard someone shout, 'Good night, Charlie!' and then silence.

His attackers had had a great night out. Starting with dinner and plenty of drinks at the Strand Palace, then *Anna Darling*, the musical, with a lot of whisky in the interval, finishing off with drinks in the Crow's Nest before they went for their train. Meeting Esmond was just a bit of fun and everyone ought to join in keeping beggars off the streets. They were in a high mood as they got into the tube and ignored one of the girls who insisted on sitting alone at the far end of the carriage and cried softly to herself.

Chapter Sixteen

The first thing Felix heard as he started up the steps near Blackfriars Bridge was a dog barking. It was a sharp, angry bark, which seemed to be the product of a dog infuriated by life and eager to bite by the throat, and shake to death, any passing stranger. And then, as he climbed the stairs, he got a great waft of the smell he dreaded, which had made him shamefully sure that he could never have followed Chekhov into the cholera wards and the penal colony. It was the sharp, acrid smell of urine, over which hung the sweet, clinging odour of shit, mixed on this occasion in a cocktail which included stale sweat and mouldering carpets. He was about to see those street-sleepers whose lives were far removed from those of the middle-aged patrons of Shell Mex House, and whom even Constable Basil couldn't tolerate because, as he used to say, of 'their habit of defecating over the side of their staircase, regardless of the safety and comfort of passers by'.

Felix remembered the books in his grandmother's house: carefully preserved, hardly read copies of Dickens and Victor Hugo. When turning the pages he had passed quickly over the hard engravings of poverty, lean wolf-like faces, some crowned with tall, battered hats, peering out of the dark recesses of a London or Parisian slum – gaunt men, toothless crones and pallid, starved children. When he found himself in such a scene at the top of the steps, he wanted to turn the page quickly to the illustration of a groaning dinner table or a candlelit ball where men with drooping whiskers and bare-shouldered women waltzed eternally. The top of Blackfriars steps had changed utterly since Esmond had last visited it and the colony of dog-lovers and dog-stealers had moved in.

The group was momentarily lit by a flaming cardboard box and, as Felix approached it, he saw that there wasn't one baying dog but a whole pack of varying shapes and sizes, some bounding to the limit of the string that held them, others lying as though dead and one spaniel curled on the stomach of a sleeping man to keep him warm. As he moved towards the group, Felix saw that the faces were white and masculine, except for one girl who seemed very young, a skinny teenager, who stood in the middle of the dogs and young men, not like a captive but as some sort of ruler. She added her voice to the chorus of the dogs and shouted a stream of words which were lost on Felix as he turned and tried to walk slowly back down the steps, afraid that his panic decision not to spend the night with the dogs would rouse the group to anger. As he got back to the level of the street he heard the girl laughing. But when he walked away she and the dogs fell silent.

The baying and the barking started up soon after when Detective Sergeant Wathen and Detective Constable Newbury arrived. They didn't find who they were looking for but resolved to tell the Homeless Squad to get the place hosed down and the whole lot moved on in the morning. Detective Constable Newbury decided he could do nothing whatever about the stolen dogs.

Felix walked westwards along the South Bank, glad to be alone, with no one to talk to or depend on except himself. Some time, he knew, he would have to return to the world and explain. He would soon run out of hiding-places and he couldn't find a home among forgotten people. All he needed was to come back with what he was convinced was the truth: that the man he was suspected, for whatever improbable reason, of killing was alive and eating free sandwiches intended for the homeless.

He tried to imagine what Gavin would do if he were still alive but wanted, perhaps as another stage in his persecution of the author he pretended to admire, to remain hidden. Where would he go? Who could be trusted with his secret?

He felt in his pocket for his money and found he still had some change. He also pulled out a piece of paper which seemed to come as an answer to his questions for on it Huw Hotchkiss had written Miriam's address and number. It was getting on for midnight and he made for the telephone boxes in Waterloo Station.

The telephone rang and no one answered. At first he thought she was asleep, curled up in the pile of rugs, blankets and old clothes, white and naked as he remembered her, with the television bleating, and the smell of joss sticks and Chinese take-away. He thought he'd outwit the Furies again, climb the dark stone stairs, knock on the door and tell her about the inexplicable sightings of Gavin. Then, as there was still no sound of her voice, he became convinced she'd gone out and left Ian alone in the bleak bedroom, sleeping, his glasses neatly folded on the floor, locked in his private and impenetrable world. But then it became worse. The ringing seemed to him to echo in a completely empty flat. They had both gone, sold up, cleared out the junk or poured it in armfuls into the back of some friend's pick-up truck – and the odd couple he had regarded as an intolerable intrusion into his life would never reappear. As he listened to the hopeless ringing he felt unreasonably betrayed. And then he heard a coin tapping the glass of the kiosk and turned to see the pale, hollow-cheeked Yorkie Bar gazing at him like a fish in an aquarium. Felix, seeing him mouth the name Anton, put down the unsuccessful telephone and pulled open the door on Yorkie who said, 'I seen him.'

'Who?'

'The bloke you were after.'

'Not Gavin?'

'Yes. Gavin.'

'Where? Where did you see him?'

'After I came out of the Garden of Eden, after you ran away from that Basil.'

'I didn't like the way he was looking at me.'

'I don't like the way most of them look at me round the Garden.'

'But Gavin. Where did you see Gavin?'

'I went back up the Strand and there he was in the doorway of the camera shop.'

'How could you know . . . ?'

'Purple anorak with a kind of hood like you told me. Gingerish hair. I just thought it was a might be, so I said it out, "Gavin," I said. You see I knew you were looking for him. So I wanted to help you out.'

'What did he say?'

'Well, he turned round and said "Yes?" before he'd thought about it. I don't think this Gavin wanted it to be known he's kicking about.'

'I don't think so either.'

'So I said I had a friend Anton which I don't think's his

real name. If you don't mind, I said that. I said he thinks you are dead like it's given out.'

'What did he say?'

'He said, Describe Anton.'

'"Going thin on top," I said. "Thin face, glasses, looks a bit nervous, speaks plummy, like he's reading the news." Anyway he seemed to know who you were.'

'That's surprising.' Felix couldn't recognize himself.

'Anyway. He wants to meet you. Says he's got something to tell you.'

'Where?'

'I wrote it down. He lent me his Biro.' Yorkie opened his *Economics of Poverty* and found a scribble. 'Six o'clock. National Gallery steps.'

'Six?'

'In the morning. I think that's what he meant. Anyway he was keen to have a meet. Funny that,' Yorkie Bar grinned, 'a meet with somebody dead.'

'If you see him again . . .'

'I don't expect so.'

'Tell him I'll be there.'

'You can tell him. When you see him.'

'Thank you. Thanks, Yorkie. I ought to give you something.' Felix felt in his pocket for the few remaining coins but Yorkie Bar was saying, 'No need for that. I did quite well tonight. Exceptionally well. Must go now. Got a bit of a meet myself.' And the boy was gone into the recesses of the station where the bars were shut and the trains had almost all stopped running.

Someone had left the *Evening Standard* on the shelf over the directories and he found himself looking down at his own face. The paper told him he was a missing author, once nominated for the Booker Prize, whom the police wanted to interview in connection with the Bayswater murder. No problem, he thought. The Bayswater murder would soon be proved no murder at all. He and the living Gavin Piercey would meet on the steps of the National Gallery at exactly six the next morning.

He walked down to the river, stood for a while looking at the water and at the floodlit buildings opposite where Flo was no doubt sleeping peacefully in her stolen hospital bed, grateful for the fresh air in her lungs. He was cold and walked up and down until he was tired. There were more possibilities than he could count. Gavin had been hit but managed to recover. He had some reason to hide and wanted Felix to help him. More probably he wanted to implicate Felix again in some way and the missing author, the wanted ex-Booker nominee, had better be careful. Well, he was being careful. He had proceeded strictly in accordance with the law. Gavin would be seen by reliable witnesses and the mystery would be solved. When he had tired himself out, he lay down on one of the benches outside the National Film Theatre and fell asleep.

He was awake with the first grey hint of daylight. There were only a few early workers waiting for buses in Whitehall and, as he crossed Trafalgar Square, the startled pigeons fluttered into the air. The National Gallery steps were empty and Felix sat down to wait on a little patch of grass where the statue of George Washington stands. He leant his back against a wall on which a long streamer advertised Goya and the Depiction of the Nightmare. Beside him, on the ground, an elderly man was asleep clutching, as though it were a much-loved partner, a placard which read A SMILE COSTS NOTHING. GIVE GENEROUSLY. At three minutes to six Felix woke the sleeper up, gave him a pound coin and told him that something was going to happen on the steps which he wanted to be seen by a witness. He discovered that the old man's name was Mr Deakin and he promised him another pound when the meeting was over.

He needn't have worried. As the clock on St Martin-in-the-Fields struck six, and as Felix went up the steps to meet someone who wasn't there, Detective Sergeant Wathen and Detective Constable Newbury got out of their car, walked up behind him and arrested him for the murder of Gavin Piercey. Detective Sergeant Wathen then gave Felix the new, complicated caution which warned him of the dangers of silence in words which neither the Detective Sergeant nor Felix were able to understand. Felix protested, pleaded, shouted and resorted to charm after this warning but nothing would persuade the officers to wait for Gavin. Indeed, the idea seemed to the Detective Sergeant decidedly comic. 'You are speaking of the deceased now, Mr Morsom.' Wathen gave a thin smile. 'And no one could be more deceased than the late Gavin Piercey, which is why we are taking you in, sir.' Before he was removed from the steps Felix managed to throw another coin in the direction of Mr Deakin and shout, 'Wait for a man in a maroon anorak!' Deakin trousered the money and, when he was alone again, went back to sleep.

In the car Detective Sergeant Wathen said, 'What've you got against kids then, Felix?'

When Felix said he had nothing whatever against them, Wathen asked, 'Have you considered, for one moment, how it will affect the life of young Ian having a killer for a father?'

At Paddington Green Wathen said, 'We're going to introduce you to the custodial suite.' After further formalities, and after his fingerprints had been taken, Felix heard the cell door bang behind him.

Chapter Seventeen

'You're not having my baby's blood!'

Miriam stood with her legs apart, her chin up high; a lioness protecting her cub. WPC Brisket looked distinctly shaken. She had come to the flat at the World's End armed with an order signed by Mr Percival, a stipendiary magistrate, and a paramedic called Nigel stood holding what looked like a bright blue lunch-box which contained a hypodermic syringe, among other more or less alarming equipment. 'I've made up my mind,' Miriam added on a higher, shriller note. 'You're not getting a drop of blood out of my Ian!'

'Come on, Miriam.' The policewoman's use of a Christian name was meant to be reassuring but Miriam Bowker winced and backed away as though horribly insulted. 'Nigel's not going to hurt your boy. Just a drop of blood. It happens every day in hospitals.'

'It may happen every day in hospitals but it's not going to happen under my roof. And I know why you want it.'

'Why?'

'You want to give it to those police that came here. I know just what they think.'

'I'm not sure I'm quite with you, Miriam.'

The WPC was a dark-haired, kindly girl with large breasts and a motherly expression. She was prepared to wait as long as it took.

'What do they think?'

'They think Ian's got bad blood. They think it's inherited. Because they think Ian's father's a murderer.'

'Is he a murderer then, Miriam?'

'You're trying to trap me now, aren't you?'

The maternal smile remained fixed, although the accusation was true. WPC Brisket had recognized the name in the letter from PROD as someone on whom the police force were relying for help.

'Are you telling me that Ian's dad is a murderer, Miriam?' she repeated.

'I don't know.'

'What *are* you telling me then, Miriam?'

'I don't know about Ian's dad.'

'Are you telling me you don't know who his dad is?'

'Of course I know my own child's father!'

'A good many don't, Miriam. It's a funny old world we're living in nowadays.'

'I don't see what's funny about it.' Miriam was panting for a cigarette but felt nervous about lighting up. She was unsure if to do so had now become an arrestable offence.

'It seems you weren't always so sure. Not judging by the correspondence we've had with the Parental Rights and Obligations. You once said the father was someone else entirely.'

'I was covering up for him. But I know who it was. And I know why you want Ian's blood. You want to prove there's something wrong with him, don't you? The killer instinct. You want to prove it's in the blood so you can prove your case. Well, I'm not having it, see. I'm not having my Ian exhibit A handed round the jury. Not whatever Felix did.'

'What do you think Felix did, Miriam?'

'I don't know. I don't know what he did recently. I only know what he did on the beach, what he did to bring Ian into this world. My child you want the blood out of.'

'Miriam' – the WPC sighed and her voice became more gentle and exhausted, like a mother's when her child won't stop kicking the cat – 'why do you think I came here?'

'I don't know. You ask those other detectives. See if I didn't cooperate with them. I even . . . Well, I cooperated fully.'

'I'm here because you wrote to PROD about Felix Morsom being the father of your child.'

'All right, I did that.'

'And he denied it. So, in cases where the paternity is in dispute, PROD asks the parties for a blood test.'

'I didn't know that.'

'PROD wrote to you on no less than four occasions asking you to agree for a test on Ian.'

'*Did* they?' Miriam was incredulous.

'Didn't you get the letters?'

'Possibly. I don't open them. Not if they are brown envelopes with OHMS written on them.'

'So they had to get a court order. That you permit your son to take a blood test. You know what a court order is, don't you, Miriam?'

'I suppose so.'

'You have to obey it or you get locked up.'

'Lock me up then! Go on! Kick me out of here! Beat me up! Drag me down the stairs! Chuck me in the bloody paddy-wagon!' Miriam held out her wrists as though for the handcuffs. At which point the door of Ian's bedroom opened and he put in an appearance.

'It's awfully hard to get any work done,' he said, 'with all this noise going on. Can't you keep quiet, Mum?'

'Ask *them*! Ask them to keep quiet!'

'All we want of you is a drop or two of blood for a test.'
WPC Brisket cheered up considerably at the sight of Ian.
'Nigel will see it doesn't hurt a bit.'

'All right.' Ian started to roll up his sleeve. 'I don't see why
not. It's better than doing homework. Do stop fussing, Mum.'

Defeated by her child, Miriam decided to forget about the
future and lit a cigarette. Nigel, the paramedic, plunged the
needle into the boy's white matchstick arm and drew out
blood. Although Ian didn't blink, Nigel, who hated giving
injections, felt horribly faint. The room lurched and he was
glad to get out into the fresh air before he collapsed.

Simon Tubal-Smith, head of Llama Books Worldwide, lay
on a square white sofa in his office with his shoes off and a
smile of simple beatification on his face. He had yellowish
skin and soft brown eyes and spoke very rapidly, as though
he were trying to sell a carpet before you noticed that it was
full of holes and covered in mysterious stains. He had come
to publishing because of his huge success in the pet food
company which had given him his first job. He rewarded it
by stripping it down, selling off the wholly owned pet shop
chain, firing a lot of people and declaring a huge profit. Deeply
impressed, Catesby Communications PLC, which had bought
Llama Books for the sake of prestige, head-hunted him. For
the first time in his life he put on a bow-tie, because he thought
that was what publishers wore, and sacked seventy-five Llama
employees, including four of London's best editors. Brenda
Bodkin, a survivor of the massacre, was one of the few people
who could enter Tubal-Smith's office without fear. She now
sat at his desk (Tubal-Smith would have considered it humiliat-
ing ever to use that piece of furniture) and she thought how

thin and long his arms and legs were. Given all that, his distended stomach came as a surprise. It was as though a skinny woman, past the appropriate age for childbirth, had become heavily pregnant.

'Guess who was on the plane from New York?' he said and rolled the name round his tongue as though it were a fine old wine. 'Only Sammy de la Touche.'

'Who on earth's Sammy de la Touche?'

'Only the most notorious of all fashion designers!' Tubal-Smith began to feel insecure. Had he not been travelling with a real celebrity?

Of course Brenda, dressed in her baggy, checked trousers, trainers and a T-shirt which read SYDNEY-SIDERS DO IT IN THE SOUTHERN HEMISPHERE, knew all about Samantha de la Touche, but she wasn't going to allow Tubal-Smith the pleasure of his name-dropping.

'Did you speak to her?' she asked, sure that he hadn't.

'She wasn't next to me,' Tubal-Smith admitted. 'And she was asleep most of the time, wearing one of those masks they give you as a present. But I passed her quite often on my way to the john.' He always came back from New York speaking in American. 'And I thought of telling people that I'd spent the night with Sammy de la Touche.'

They really ought to give you a knighthood, Brenda thought, so you could drop your own name occasionally.

'And who else do you think was on the plane?'

'Well, I suppose there was you . . .'

'Only Jim Clothard. The software king. One of the world's great communicators.'

'You mean someone like Dickens or Shakespeare? Or Tolstoy perhaps?'

She saw, with some satisfaction, that she had now gone too

far. Tubal-Smith levered himself off the sofa and started to pace the office in his stockinged feet. 'Brenda,' he said, 'I don't know if it's slipped the attention of the publicity department but one of our authors has just been arrested on suspicion of murder.'

'It'll mean a fantastic interest in his book! It really started to move after Lucasta's article. Now it's bound to make the bestsellers'.'

'Not' – he turned on her triumphantly – 'if we don't get it into the shops! I called into the Fulham Road Millstream's on the way in and there wasn't a single Morsom on the shelves. Moreover, I want you to know, they told me they hadn't seen our rep for weeks.'

'That's not strictly my business.'

'Then *make* it your business, Brenda.' Tubal-Smith's voice sank to a low whisper which used to terrify the board at Noah's Ark Pet Foods. 'No good getting all this stuff into the papers if we can't get the books in the shops.'

'We've had a rep off recently. I believe he's sick.'

'Don't believe anything, Brenda. Find out! We've got no immediate plans for slimming down the publicity department. Yet.'

To this rather feeble threat, Brenda played her trump card. 'Let me know when you've decided,' she told him. 'I've been offered considerably more money by Four Corners, so feel free.'

Tubal-Smith looked a little like the Thane of Cawdor who, about to sit down to a dinner party, notices that his place has been taken by Banquo's ghost. He had read on the aeroplane the rumours that Catesby's was considering selling Llama Books off to Four Corners, which would end in his being personally slimmed down. Brenda passed him on her way to the door and he smelled the faint odour of fruit not yet ripe.

'And don't worry about Felix either,' she said. 'He didn't do it.'

'How do you know?'

'He never does. *Not* doing things is his speciality.'

'I wonder,' he said, trying to sound friendly, 'if the plane had crashed, would the headline have been WELL-KNOWN PUBLISHER IN AEROPLANE DISASTER or QUEEN OF FASHION KILLED?'

'I should think that would have been absolutely no contest.'

'Thank you, Brenda.' Tubal-Smith was sure he'd been paid a compliment. 'Thank you very much. You know I'm having dinner with the Gantries? He's just running up the new Oxford lottery college. Just wait till I tell them I know the star of the newest murder.'

Felix Morsom, Brenda realized, had become a name to be dropped.

She had in her mind the indelible and disturbing picture of one of her favourite authors, Booker nominee and occasional bestseller, sitting in the shadows outside *Anna Darling*, lifting a beseeching hand for small change. She had told nobody, not Tubal-Smith, not even Paul, and certainly not the police, about what she saw. She couldn't guess how he had come there but she felt guilty. Perhaps, if she had been more accommodating, he might not have had to go to such horrifying lengths in search of excitement. Although she had, she now remembered with regret, urged him to add more colour to his life, she had never meant to drive him to the lurid role of a suspected murderer begging in the street. She resolved to help Felix although she had not the remotest idea how to start.

★

Brenda sat in her office, a glass-walled pen in the corner of the publicity department, where girls were sticking review copies into Jiffy bags and phoning nervous authors to ask if they were prepared to 'do the Denny Densher'.

And, as she thought about Felix, Brenda Bodkin was surprised to discover how much she missed him. There was no one else to whom she could give pleasure so easily. Pleasing Paul entailed close attention, flattery and considerable effort. But she could bring sudden happiness to Felix, she knew, simply by ringing up, or holding his hand in the car, or smiling at him in public as though there were secrets between them. She felt that he was kind, considerate and thought of her when she wasn't there. She wanted to comfort him, to cheer him up, to put her arms round him unexpectedly.

Then she looked in her book for the number on which she always called Terry, the rep, and found him in his car, or in a bookshop, or some bar where he was enjoying a short rest, a pint of Murphy's stout and a packet of bacon-and-egg-flavoured crisps. What she got was a bright female voice repeating, 'The cellphone you are calling has been disconnected.'

There was another number in her book, written in some years before. The pencil had faded and she remembered that Terry had asked her not to use it. When she rang she got a woman whom she seemed to have interrupted in the middle of a nervous breakdown. She said she hadn't seen Terry for a month and had no idea where he'd got to. He was meant to take the kids out at the end of last week and didn't show up. If that was his job speaking they might like to know that the Parental Obligations were after Terry again for back maintenance. Ten thousand pounds. And what did his job intend to do about it? Then a child could be heard screaming and the woman shouted, 'Shut up, you little sod!' Brenda replaced the telephone gently, unwilling to intrude on private grief.

Chapter Eighteen

Banged up in the police cell Felix, clenching his fist and digging his nails into his palms, sat on a bench as far as possible from the entrance, determined not to move. He knew that if he did so he would throw himself at the door in the ridiculous hope that it would open and, when it didn't, scream in panic. In his childhood, taking his father's advice and making use of the facilities in the Princess Beatrice Hotel, Coldsands-on-Sea, he had managed to lock himself in the Gents and sentenced himself to just under half an hour's imprisonment. When his screams at last alerted a dozing attendant and a carpenter was sent for, the hall porter, a bulbous man with a slight cast in one eye, said to the nine-year-old boy, 'Let that be a lesson to you, sonny. Never lock a lavatory door again as long as you live.'

It was advice Felix had always remembered. Wherever possible he avoided lifts, held his breath in revolving doors, and the lavatories he occupied always had Vacant written on them. He had once, long ago, seen a play in Coldsands Rep in which a young man, falsely imprisoned, concluded Act One by feeling slowly and methodically round the walls of his cell. He didn't do that, nor did he pace out his prison's measurements as Dantès did in the Château d'If. He sat very still, closed his eyes, and pretended he was sitting on a beach near Coldsands pier, or staring from his window at the grey, uneventful sea. This worked so well that the pretence seemed reality and when the cell door was unlocked to admit a visitor, he felt that he had slipped back into a bad dream. A whiff of eau de cologne covering stale cigar smoke and the tang of an unchanged shirt announced the arrival of Septimus Roache, legal adviser to authors in distress.

'What are *you* doing here?' The sleepy, half-awake Felix had the instant and understandable impression that the lawyer himself was in trouble.

'Because you had the good sense and decency to send for me. You couldn't have done better.'

'*I* sent for you?'

'They asked you if you wanted a solicitor. They've got to do that. So naturally you mentioned my name. Well, you owed me a favour. I did rather resent being woken up in the small hours to be told you were having breakfast at the Savoy.'

'You're going to defend me?'

'I told you I would.' Septimus smiled, exposing a row of nicotine-stained teeth, and Felix felt a growing sensation of unease. 'If you got yourself into a decent sort of scrape, something with a bit more meat to it than a boring little bastardy, we'd roll out the red carpet for you. I'll get you a sparky young QC. Chipless Warrington's had quite a run of luck in murder lately.' A shadow of a doubt fell over the contented solicitor. 'You do earn more than ten thousand a year, I hope?'

'Quite a bit more.'

'And you've got a house? Unencumbered?'

'Well, yes.'

'Thank God' – Septimus closed his eyes as though in prayer – 'you don't qualify for legal aid! Legal aid's out of bounds as far as I'm concerned. My partners won't allow me to touch it. All right then? Stage one. The police are going to ask you questions.'

'I'll do my best to answer them.'

'Oh, my God!' Septimus rolled his eyes towards heaven. 'You authors are all the same. Clean characters! Never been in trouble before, I suppose?'

'Only parking fines.'

'Parking fines!' Septimus seemed to be about to spit. 'So one has to start by teaching you the alphabet. You have to learn from the very beginning. You will not do your best to answer them. You will answer nothing. You will listen to me saying, "We are not prepared to answer that question until we have been formally charged and have had an opportunity to make further inquiries. For the moment we reserve our defence." We're not going to load Chipless, QC with a lot of incriminating answers he'll have to say were beaten out of you. As the officer in charge of the case looks like the winner of a gorgeous granny contest, that might cause even Chipless a little difficulty.'

'But I want to tell them . . .' Although the whole conversation seemed unreal, and he still felt half asleep, Felix knew he had something of great importance to communicate. 'I want to tell them that Gavin Piercey's still alive.'

'Not that rubbish you talked when you rang me up in the middle of the night? Not that old resurrection defence story?'

'I'm sure I saw him. Three times.'

'Like I said. On the road to Emmaus.'

'The first was Victoria Station . . .'

'What'd you been drinking?'

'Quite a bit of beer, half a bottle of sake and a double brandy.'

'Add a few rum and cokes if anyone else asks you to explain these hallucinations, which let's hope they won't.'

'But I told them. I told the Furies.'

'*Who* did you say?'

'The Furies.'

'That was what I thought you said. The Furies. The Eumenides. The ones we fear to name. For God's sake! I know you authors. You live in a world of myth and make-believe.'

'My Furies are two police officers. One tall and bald, the other short and casually dressed. I told them when they arrested me.'

'Do I have to be with you every minute, night and day, holding your hand?' Septimus stood, his legs apart, his thumbs stuck in the pockets of his waistcoat, and looked sadly at his client. 'What did you want to tell them a thing like that for?'

'Because it's true.'

'That's no sort of excuse for opening your mouth about anything. Not if you're a defendant. Well, there's two ways we can go on this one. We can agree you said it and plead insanity. I know a couple of friendly quacks who'd be kind enough to find, at the very least, diminished responsibility. The trouble is, do you want to spend the rest of your life in a funny farm for mad assassins, awaiting Her Majesty's Pleasure, or do you not?'

'I don't.'

'Then you were still a bit pissed, old boy. And thought you'd seen a ghost.'

'A ghost?' Spirits, dreams, phantoms? Septimus had twice mentioned the road to Emmaus and Felix thought of the improbability of Gavin as a Christlike figure, magically immortal. He hadn't seen him call for boiled fish and honeycomb; he hadn't known him by the breaking of the bread. He had only thought he'd seen him warming his hands on a cup but that was at night, from a distance, when Felix was tired and full of sake. He had been haunted by Gavin for a long time. Was he still haunted? His belief began to drain away as, at an earlier age, had his acceptance of miracles and his faith in God. 'I suppose,' he said, 'I might have imagined it.'

'That's good!' Septimus smiled in an encouraging fashion. 'We're coming along nicely.'

'But if Gavin isn't alive' – Felix knew he ought to be worried about something – 'what's my defence going to be?'

'Don't worry your head.' Septimus was looking so cheerfully avuncular that he might almost have said 'pretty little head'. 'We'll deal with that in conference with Chipless. After all it's his business to provide defences. Now I expect the gorgeous granny will be about ready for us. That is, if someone's shown her how to work the tape-recorder!'

'I have just returned from a visit to my landlord, the solitary neighbour that I shall be troubled with.' The recording machine, its little red light glowing, spoke these words in Detective Chief Inspector Cowling's soft and educated voice. The Detective Inspector herself was wearing a beige suit, tan shoes, a cream shirt discreetly open at the neck to display only a few of her row of pearls, and her hair looked as though she had a quick shampoo and set every morning on her way in. She said, 'I expect you know where that comes from?'

'Of course!' Felix felt that this, at least, was a question he'd be allowed to answer. 'It's the opening sentence of *Wuthering Heights*.'

'What a relief!' – the Detective Inspector's teeth shone to match her necklace – 'to find someone literate at work. And that doesn't only go for the villains.' Detective Constable

Newbury, seated with his notebook at a small table in a corner of the interview room, looked pained. 'I shouldn't have said that about DC Newbury,' the Detective Inspector hastened to add. 'He's a tremendous admirer of *Watership Down*.'

'They're all rabbits,' Leonard Newbury told them. 'You wouldn't believe it!'

'I put that test sentence in the machine especially for you.' The Detective Inspector's smile was almost flirtatious. 'So much more interesting than 'one, two, three, testing'. When I hoped we'd meet again, I didn't imagine it'd be exactly in these circumstances. I'd wanted to ask you about something they told us in our creative writing course.'

'What was that?' It was Septimus Roache who asked the question sharply, suspecting bias.

'Only the post-modernist view that the creator is of no interest in a study of the text. I mean, when it comes to an alleged crime, we can't help being interested in its creator can we?'

'I suppose not,' Felix had to admit.

'Oh, by the way, I've finished *Molehill*.'

'You've finished what?'

'Remember we were talking about my novel *Here on This Molehill*? I've submitted it to Llama Books. Thanks for the recommendation.' And before Septimus could refuse to take the conversation further she pressed the button on the tape-recorder, restored the red light and said, loud and clear, 'Interview with Felix Morsom, conducted by DCI Cowling in the presence of his solicitor and DC Newbury. 11.05 hours on Friday, 13th September. Mr Morsom, you are a highly respected writer of contemporary fiction, earning a comfortable living, are you not?'

Felix was about to agree with becoming modesty when

Septimus came growling in with 'We are not prepared to answer that question until we have been formally charged and we have had an opportunity to make further inquiries.' And that was the answer to every question during the next three quarters of an hour, during which Detective Chief Inspector Cowling remained smilingly polite and Detective Constable Newbury fell into a light doze.

Chapter Nineteen

Brenda walked down the long straight road between parked cars towards the main gate. She was not alone. Asian and Caribbean children, lanky blonde English girlfriends with Princess Di hairdos and little jewels in their noses, panting black mothers, their voices high with complaint, ageless women in saris, gliding along under the shadow of the wall, here an imam and there a rabbi – these were with her on the walk to the visitors' entrance. Brenda Bodkin hadn't had occasion to visit such a place before.

That morning, as she sat in her office, a person with soft brown eyes and a small moustache, who had a reputation as a Don Giovanni in the accounts department, had brought her a list of so-called expenses. Terry Whitlock, the rep, wanted them sent to an address in Chandos Street. He'd asked if they could be justified as the signature on the letter didn't bear much relation to Terry's. Brenda made a note of the address but had no further time to deal with the matter. She was on her way to prison.

Once inside the visitors' section, she was searched and had a metal detector passed over her body. Then she was allowed into a long room, one end of which had been fitted out like a day nursery, with a slide and a climbing frame, tables with sheets of paper, coloured chalks, picture books and jigsaws, where the children of the convicted, or those on remand, could entertain themselves, twittering like birds in an aviary, whilst their parents exchanged news, had suppressed quarrels or just sat having long since run out of sympathy, encouragement or regret.

Brenda had been given a number and found her way to a similarly numbered table, a process which reminded her of a hundred literary lunches. Felix was brought towards her by a fat, ginger-haired officer whose great bunch of keys jangled as he walked. 'Remember,' this screw said, 'visiting regulations. Quarter an hour minimum, three quarters maximum. Visit stops if you get abusive.' She was left alone with her author.

'It's good of you to come.'

'You asked me. I got a letter.'

'I know. You didn't mind?'

'Of course not.'

'I couldn't really think of anyone else.'

'Well, thank you, Felix, thank you very much.'

'I didn't mean that. Thank you for coming anyway.'

At the next table a very young couple, pale with stringy hair, wearing identical T-shirts and jeans, were holding both hands across the table, saying nothing. Brenda felt that she too had run out of conversation and there were still fourteen and a half minutes, minimum, to go.

'I've been out with Sandra Tantamount,' she told him.

'Was that good fun?'

'Marvellous! In Edinburgh she tried to get the manager sacked because there were no white lilies in her bedroom. In Dublin she wanted me to shoot vitamins into her bum with a hypodermic syringe before she'd go on the Gay Burns show. In Manchester she threw a pair of shoes at me and said, "Get these mended, girl!" And in Cardiff she wanted me to organize a male voice choir to carry her on their shoulders to a signing session. It wasn't good fun, exactly.'

Felix, who hadn't had many compliments lately, fished for one now. 'Was it more fun with me?'

'Yes, Felix.' She was being patient with him. 'It was more fun with you.'

'Not half as much fun as it'll be when we go abroad.'

'If I were you I shouldn't think about that.' She was being deadly sensible.

'Why not?'

'I suppose because you're not going to be in a position to travel. Not for some time.'

'Do you think I did it?' For the first time Felix sounded depressed.

'No, I'm sure you didn't.'

'I wish *I* was.'

'What on earth do you mean?'

'After all that's happened, I'm not really sure about anything.'

'Who's defending you?' She came down to practical matters.

'A pretty ghastly solicitor called Septimus Roache who has hair growing everywhere and smells peculiar and a rather unbearable young QC called Chipless Warrington.'

There was a silence while Brenda absorbed this information. Then she said, 'Why Chipless?'

'Because his father was a rubbish collector in Bermondsey and he went to a South London Comprehensive but he's got no sort of a chip on his shoulder. He's very democratic and behaves just as though he went to Eton.'

There was a long pause and she said, 'Cleansing operative.'

'What?'

'That's what they call rubbish collectors nowadays. Have you got faith in him?'

'Who?'

'This Chipless?'

'Not at all. It's difficult to have faith in anything much in here. Only the Moslems seem to manage it. Perhaps I should ask to see the Imam. Oh, there was a time when I began to believe in miracles.'

'When was that?'

'When I thought I saw Gavin rise from the dead. I saw him three times, you know.'

'Felix' – Brenda was now at her most severe – 'I'm not going to bother with you if you're going dotty on me.'

'I thought you'd probably say that.'

'I've got quite enough of all that with Sandra Tantamount.'

'I suppose it could have been a mirage. Not that they have many mirages on the Thames Embankment.'

'You've got to pull yourself together and get out of this mess. Someone's got to help you, even if this barrister of yours is several chips short of a take-away.'

'Who?'

'What?'

'Who's going to help me?'

'Well, I will. Within reason,' she promised him un-expectedly.

He asked her for a favour to start with. 'I'm wearing these clothes because there's no one to bring in my other stuff, or to see it gets cleaned occasionally.'

For the first time she noticed that he was in a blue striped shirt and a pair of trousers that looked as though they had been cut from a grey army blanket. She then agreed to go to Coldsands, find his cleaning lady and bring up clothes to

London, including a best suit for his day in court. He looked at her with as much gratitude as she might have deserved if she'd organized his instant acquittal.

'Whatever you say' – he told her – 'I shall think about our going abroad together. In the end.'

'I suppose there's no harm in thinking about it. If you need to.'

'I can't help it. Oh, if you come again . . .'

'I shall come again,' she promised. 'I'm not leaving you to Chipless.'

'. . . Chekhov's *The Complete Plays*. On the shelf over my desk.'

'I'll bring it,' she said, 'together with the y-fronts.'

'No.'

'What?'

'Boxer shorts. It's true. You never found out.'

'Quarter of an hour,' the screw with the jangling keys came up and told them. 'Do you want another fifteen?'

'No,' Brenda said firmly, 'that's quite enough to be going on with.'

The proceedings at the Magistrates' Court had been extremely brief. Septimus sent down a clerk and Chipless's junior. This was a young barrister called Quentin Thurgood who had been to Eton and was decidedly chippy about it, forever fearing that the best briefs in the really highly paid cases went to ruthless women barristers of Ugandan descent or to the products of North Country comprehensives. He would carry on for hours about snobbery at the Bar and deep-rooted prejudices against white, upper-class males, but he had very little to say on the subject of bail. 'I'll ask for bail if you like,' he told Felix in the cells, 'but it'll be bloody useless.' He did and it was. Felix was remanded in custody. For the short trip from the court to the bus, a security man was good enough to lend Felix a blanket to put over his head. Recent events had promoted him to the status of famous author, liable to be photographed at any and every opportunity.

Getting into prison was an endless process of form-filling by large men with very white shirts and jangling keys. Felix was taken behind a screen, stripped naked, showered, pushed and prodded in various ways, and examined by an exhausted young doctor who seemed to have emerged from medical school with his confidence shattered. Through most of this process Felix did as though he was at the dentist or having his hair cut; he kept his eyes shut and tried to recite to himself the poem *Ulysses* by Alfred Lord Tennyson which he had learnd at school. He had just reached

> Yet all experience is an arch wherethro'
> Gleams that untravell'd world, whose margin fades
> For ever and for ever . . .

when a voice shouted in his ear, 'You got anyone near and dear to bring you in clean clothes and keep them washed and tidy?'

'What? Oh well, not really.'

'Right then.' And the voice called to another distant screw, 'Prison clothing!'

So Felix had put on the regulation underclothes, then the shirt and the trousers which were so stiff and scratchy that they might have been left to stand up by themselves. When his few possessions had been locked up and signed for (only to emerge at the time of his release), when his money (one pound twenty-four p) had been carefully counted in his presence and removed, he was led through endless doors which had to be ceremoniously unlocked, past a yard where a few prisoners were playing basketball and into a building of high balconies with iron railings and nets stretched between them to catch those prone to suicide. He was surprised by the sullen quietness of the place, broken only by the click of balls on the ground-floor ping-pong and snooker tables, the murmur of voices on the prisoners' telephones and the eternal clanking of keys when the warders – a few of whom were women with elaborate hairdos – made the slightest movement. The yellow paint on the stone walls was an attempt at cheerfulness, like the laughter of lawyers in the corridors of the Magistrates' Court.

'You share a cell here till we can assess your conduct,' the thin screw with glasses told him. 'If you keep your nose clean, you may get enhanced to A block.'

Most of the prisoners were out of their cells and the door of Felix's future home was open. The cell seemed to be filled with two huge objects: a lavatory with a seat and cistern to replace the old-style chamber-pot, and a man lying in the shadows of the top bunk who was doing absolutely nothing. The screw departed and Felix, edging his way into the cell, sat down on a small chair at a smaller table near the door. A Scottish voice spoke from above his head saying, 'So, you've turned up again.'

He had only heard the man speak rarely but peering upwards he recognized Dumbarton. 'I thought from the way you carried on in the street you'd soon be in trouble.' The tall young Scotsman was far more loquacious in prison than he was under the arches of Shell Mex House.

'Dumbarton! What're *you* here for?' Felix didn't know whether to count himself lucky in his cell mate.

There was a long silence, then Dumbarton said, 'They got Esmond.'

'You mean the police got him?'

'No. Party-goers got him. Pubbers got him. Evening-outs got him. They kicked his head in. He's dead.'

Gentle Esmond, who posted his keys back through his front door and rejected the world, dead? Who else? Who now? Felix said, 'He was kind to me. I'm sorry.'

'Ah. But I paid them back for it.'

'Did you?'

'I killed one.'

'One of them that did it?'

'I couldn't tell that. All I know is he was a pubber. And he had drink taken. And he was coming down the steps where Esmond was done. So I knocked him down and kicked his head in for Esmond's sake.'

'You killed him?'

'Thoroughly.'

'But he might not have been one of them that did for Esmond.'

'Maybe not. But that was no concern of mine. Or of Esmond's either.'

There was another long silence and then Dumbarton said, 'What did you do?'

'I'm on remand. Accused of a murder I didn't do.'

'Like all the rest of them in here!' Dumbarton spoke with undisguised contempt. 'I'm the only one in here for a murder I did do. You'll not use that toilet in here. Not ever!' He'd been talking in a quiet, deliberately controlled Glasgow accent and his final command was yelled out like a parade ground order.

'Why? Doesn't it work?' Felix found the courage to ask.

'Of course it works! It'll take the place over if you let it. We've not got a cell with a toilet in it. We've got a toilet with a few inches of cell round it. I've got to eat my dinner in here. I've got to think my thoughts. If you want to go, you go when you're out of the cell. Just remember that!'

'All right. But what's it like in here?' Felix, already feeling queasy, was anxious to change the subject.

'It's good. Very good. They tell you what to do. Like the army. No worries if they tell you what to do. I never got on well down the Embankment. It was all up to you where you went for breakfast. It's better here or in the army. Give me a bit of quiet now, and don't dare use the toilet.'

That night Felix lay entombed on the bottom bunk, conscious of the inconvenient stirrings in his stomach and listening to the heavy breathing of the young giant who, it seemed, killed at random.

Weeks later, he was told he had a visitor. He combed his hair carefully in the little square of a mirror and, doing his best to look cheerful, went off to his date with Brenda Bodkin.

She stood looking at his desk, empty and waiting for him, and was struck by his sense of order. Hers was always piled high with books, shoes, ashtrays, half-drunk mugs of tea and coffee, opened packets of biscuits, letters, photographs and ideas for point of sale publicity. On Felix's desk the long, ruled sheets of paper were lined up in a neat block, the clock and the metal duck stood like sentries on each side of the photograph of Chekhov, lolling on a verandah in the sunshine with his dog – a smiling writer with tired eyes on his way to death. She pulled down the fat paperback collection of plays and put it in the bag in which she collected shirts and trousers, socks and boxer shorts, and the suit for Felix's day in court.

She had called on Mrs Ives in Mermaid Crescent, the cleaning lady, who had handed over the key in response to Felix's note with a trembling hand and a look which meant Good luck, Miss. Rather you than me! Mrs Ives hadn't been in to clean since the arrest. What, Brenda wondered, did she expect to find? Dead bodies, severed limbs, floorboards torn up for the concealment of butchered victims? She said she'd make sure everything was in order and that she'd see Mrs Ives got paid for regular visits and for keeping his place as no doubt Mr Morsom would have wanted it kept. She got to the flat and blinked at the lightness of it, the low autumn sunlight bouncing off white walls and the tidiness everywhere. She went into the bedroom and, opening a cupboard, found the stack of clean shirts, kept in order by a man who was interested in laundry.

She zipped up the bag full of Felix's possessions and looked round his writing-room as though to say goodbye to it. The window in front of the desk was filled with his view of the sea: a greenish colour with a gold burnish where the sunlight struck it. She looked at the shelves, the neat row of box-files and notebooks, and the press-cutting albums in which Felix pasted his good notices. (He could smell out the bad ones almost without reading them and destroyed them rapidly.) There was a shelf for tapes and compact discs, under which stood the black box which was the centre of his Orpheus sound system. On top of the box lay a tape, unmarked but perhaps recently played. What was it? Some favourite piece of music? The tune he'd take to the desert island if he were only allowed one? She was in no hurry and so far the flat hadn't divulged any secrets about an author who had managed to land himself in such sensational trouble. She slotted in the tape and pressed a few buttons. A red light glowed, the Orpheus hissed and Gavin spoke.

'They told me to get in the motor. I would describe their manner as peremptory. They were hostile. You might say unpleasant . . .' Brenda was listening so intently that the cigarette between her lips was unlit, the lighter with its flame was flickering in her hand, as Gavin continued, '. . . The police cell was by no means spacious and a great deal of room in it was taken up by a man wearing a crumpled blue suit and a number of heavy rings. On one of them I noticed was a sphinx's head which might have come into use as a knuckleduster. I do not exaggerate when I say that he smelled like a bar parlour on the morning after. I noticed in particular that his hands were not clean and his fingernails were what my mother used to call "in mourning for the cat's mother". By this time I was in considerable distress and I asked if he objected to my making use of the very inadequate toilet facilities provided. His words to me, spoken in a slurred voice, were, "Be my guest, sunshine." It was while I was relieving myself that my cell mate approached, pulled down my clothing and bent me over the toilet. The next thing I was aware of was a sharp pain in my rear passage and a feeling of resentment.'

Brenda lit her cigarette and listened until the voice said, 'I shall watch your future career with interest.' Then nothing could be heard except another faint hiss. She remembered the *Sentinel* literary lunch and the drink in the bar where she had noticed the heavy, silvery ring with the plump face of a sphinx. It was on the hand of Terry, the missing rep, and no doubt it would come in useful as a knuckleduster.

★

Lying in the bunk under Dumbarton, who had now sunk back into silence, Felix read *Uncle Vanya*. He was disturbed by the depths of despair and the cruel depiction of life by an author whom he had come to regard, he now realized quite mistakenly, as gentle. He closed the book, turning away from such remorseless creations and, when let out of his cell, joined the other prisoners in watching Australian soap operas on the big television set at the end of the gallery. He sat enthralled by their undemanding plots. The next time he visited the library he took out *Grand Slam* by Sandra Tantamount.

Chapter Twenty

'I don't know, Mr Roache, if the client appreciates . . .' Chipless Warrington, QC was tall and sturdy, the descendant of a long line of dustmen who had carried overflowing bins of rubbish. His yellowish hair toned with the colour of his skin and flowed gently over the top of his ears and down to his collar so that he looked more like a trendy banker or a person in advertising than an Old Bailey hack. He had a prominent, fleshy nose, a generously rounded chin and the sharp, white teeth of a carnivore. He spoke in the upper-class drawl in use when Lord Curzon, whom he somewhat resembled, was Viceroy of India – and he managed to avoid speaking to Felix or looking at him directly. '. . . I mean, I don't know if the client fully understands that if we establish provocation we might reduce it to manslaughter?'

'I think you can take it,' Septimus Roache assured him, 'that the client understands absolutely nothing whatever about the law.'

'If the client were to tell us – and I do say *if* – that he went round to see Piercey to stop him giving the tabloids the story about his bastard child, and if – and, once again, I must stress this *if* – the client should tell us that, when he saw him in his van, Piercey was abusive and then started to blackmail him, demanding, shall we say, twenty or twenty-five grand as his price of silence, and even if – and again I lay stress upon the *if* – we should be instructed by the client that Piercey upped the ante and asked for, well, let us suppose thirty grand, or that he'd tell the papers quite untruthfully, of course, that the client raped the infant's mother or gave her a transmittable sexual disease, *if*, as I have quite clearly said, those are the instructions from the client, well, then, bingo, Piercey becomes a blackmailer and juries don't at all mind blackmailers being bonked on the head with spanners.'

'What would be the tariff?' Septimus wondered. 'If we reduce it to manslaughter?'

'Five years. Maybe four, given a fair wind and a soppy judge. I understand the client is of good character.'

'He was nominated for the Booker Prize.'

'Are you suggesting that's a criminal offence?'

They laughed, Chipless and his junior, Quentin Thurgood, and Septimus Roache. They were grouped round a table in the glass-walled prison interview room. Felix, looking at them, thought they were as remote and patently artificial as the characters in Australian soap operas.

'I just don't see it,' Chipless's junior said when they had stopped laughing. 'I just don't see manslaughter.'

'All the same, perhaps we could get them to accept a plea to it.' Chipless was still jovial. 'Who's prosecuting?'

'Marmaduke Pusey,' Septimus told him.

'Dear old Marmalade! There was a girl in his chambers pestering him and I took her off his hands. Marmalade owes me a favour.' But Quentin Thurgood still didn't see it at all. 'Provocation,' his junior told Chipless, 'has to be instant, on the spur of the moment. You know the law.' Chipless conceded, 'One relies on one's junior for that.'

'You can't plead provocation if you'd been planning it for a long time' – Quentin turned the pages of a bundle of prosecution statements – 'like the client in the instant case.'

'Remind me, Quentin. Refresh my memory. Merely refresh it.' Chipless was doing his best to sound like someone who'd read his brief.

'"You can drop dead, Gavin. Drop dead!" The client was heard to say that to a man answering descriptions given of Gavin Piercey outside a bookshop in Covent Garden. That is the statement of Sir Ernest Thessaley.'

'I was talking to the officer in charge,' Septimus told him. 'Apparently Ernest rang the police to give them that little nugget.'

'Really? Why would he want to do that?' Chipless was shocked.

'He doesn't like other authors,' Septimus told them, as though that explained it all.

Hearing the evidence of Sir Ernest Thessaley, to his great relief, Felix felt as angry as when he was approached by Gavin in Covent Garden. He intruded on the private consultation, saying loudly, 'I'd better make it quite clear that I never saw Piercey in his van. He never tried to blackmail me and, once and for all, will you get it into your heads that I never hit him with a spanner!'

The lawyers turned to look at him as though a strange apparition had just wandered into the room. Then, as the apparition said no more, they returned to their intimate conversation. 'I notice,' Quentin Thurgood said, 'that the client denies striking the man Piercey on the head with a heavy weapon.'

'We shall be in deep shit' – Chipless had no doubt about it – 'if we attempt to deny the attack. It will create an extremely bad impression.'

'Always best,' Septimus agreed, 'to accept as much of the

prosecution evidence as possible. Confess and avoid always looks better than barefaced denial.'

'Barefaced denial,' Chipless agreed, 'never sits well with the jury.'

'I don't care who it sits with,' Felix intruded once more. 'I never hit Gavin.'

'The client wishes to go for denial.' Septimus was saddened.

'The client would do far better to leave things to his legal team,' Chipless agreed, 'and not go wandering off on a line of his own.'

'A particularly hopeless line,' Quentin, the junior, was delighted to point out, 'because of the fingerprint evidence.'

'Ah! The fingerprint evidence. Just remind me.' Chipless settled back in his chair, preparing to enjoy it, while Quentin made another search through the depositions.

'The client's fingerprints' – Quentin found the place – 'found on the door-handle and side window of Piercey's van.'

'I tried the handle,' Felix told them.

'Trying door-handles, dear me!' Chipless was greatly amused. 'Not trying to pinch cars, are you, when things are a bit slow in the writing trade?'

'I called at Gavin's flat. I wanted to see him. Urgently.'

'You will recall that the client was seen going in and coming out of the flat,' Quentin reminded his leader, who said, 'Of *course* I recall,' as convincingly as possible. 'No doubt to utter more threats. We shall have to deal with the message on the answering machine.'

'"I'll be compelled to take steps to silence you",' Quentin read out the bit in the evidence he'd highlighted in pink.

'I meant legal steps, of course,' Felix assured him.

'If the client meant legal steps,' Septimus murmured, his

attention directed at the ceiling, 'one wonders why he didn't say so.'

'And then wasn't there a final note left in the flat?' Chipless remembered.

'"Don't think you can get away with this. I'll be back."' Quentin had that highlighted also.

'And of course' – Chipless was still smiling – 'the client came back.'

'No, I didn't! I didn't see any point. I got a train back to Coldsands and went home.'

'Did he see anyone who might remember him on the train?'

'I don't think so. There was no one I knew.'

'Or meet anyone in the street?'

'The town was fairly empty.'

'Does it come to this' – Chipless was looking, seriously now, at his instructing solicitor – 'that we can't call any witness to support an alibi?'

'Naturally we've made inquiries,' Septimus told him.

'Naturally you have as a first-class defence solicitor. And drawn, I suppose, a blank?'

'A complete blank!'

'So we're left with the fingerprints on the door of the van?'

'There must have been all sorts of fingerprints,' Felix protested.

'But the client's prints were the ones the police have put in evidence.' Quentin sounded quietly satisfied. 'And then we have the fact that the client sought to avoid arrest.'

'By seeking refuge,' Septimus agreed, 'among the poor and dispossessed.'

'And the murder weapon was never found?' Chipless's questions were quiet now but, he clearly thought, probing.

'I didn't dispose of it. Anyway, if I'd've attacked Gavin like that, I'd've been covered in blood . . .'

'You went home. Plenty of time for a bath,' Quentin suggested.

'My clothes?'

'You live by the sea, don't you? Mightn't you have dropped them in?'

'But on the train . . .'

'A quick wash-up in the Victoria Station Gents?'

'Anyway, I told you' – Felix was looking at Septimus – 'after all this was meant to happen I saw Gavin Piercey alive. At least . . .' And as he spoke he felt his certainty draining away, 'At least I think I saw him.'

'I offered the client insanity,' Septimus Roache told Chipless. 'I offered him Broadmoor but he didn't seem too keen.'

'I *must* have seen him!' Felix found a sudden confidence in his defence. 'I was in a telephone box on Waterloo Station. Yorkie Bar – that's a boy who slept in the street – Yorkie tapped on the glass. He said he'd seen Gavin, who wanted to meet me by the National Gallery in the morning. That's why I went there. Because Yorkie Bar told me that.'

There was a long silence during which the three lawyers now looked at him steadily. Then Chipless began to speak, quietly, in the way he always began his most effective cross-examination of a hostile witness. 'Didn't you think it rather odd that when you went to the National Gallery, police officers were there to arrest you?'

'Not particularly. I assumed they'd been following me.'

'Knowing where you were on the Embankment?'

'I suppose so.'

'But not arresting you until you got to Trafalgar Square? Can you think of a reason for that?'

'Well, not really.' Felix knew he was sounding lame.

'Well, let me help you.' Chipless was all smiles. 'Let me suggest a reason. Someone had tipped them off. Someone made sure you'd be at the National Gallery at precisely six o'clock in order to be arrested.'

'Someone?'

'Someone who spoke to you when you were telephoning at Waterloo.'

'Yorkie Bar?'

'I think you ought to know we've been served with some additional evidence by the prosecution. I will ask my learned junior to read you the relevant passage. Give it to him, Quentin.' And Chipless, lolling back in his chair, gave his junior the statement, a gesture a retired bullfighter, who has entertained the audience by a series of dazzling passes with the cape, might make to some underling to whom he has handed over the sword.

'Statement of William Mansfield, otherwise known as Yorkie Bar, aged sixteen, of no fixed address.'

'He had an address,' Felix told him. 'The pavement. Between the theatres in the Strand . . .'

'Never mind about that. Blah, blah, blah . . .' Quentin read on. 'Oh yes, here it is. "Anton". It seems you gave him a false name. "Anton had told me that he was supposed to have killed this bloke Gavin, but Gavin was still alive!"'

'You see! He bears me out.'

'Not quite so fast!' Chipless warned him. 'My learned junior will continue.'

'"As a result of what Anton told me, I had a conversation with PC Basil Bulstrode of the Homeless Squad. After this conversation, I went in search of Anton and when I found him I told him that I had seen Gavin Piercey who wanted to meet Anton next morning on the National Gallery steps. This was quite untrue but designed to get Anton to a place where he would be arrested."

'"Although homeless I am reading books on economics to better myself and am always willing to cooperate with the police, who are doing a grand job looking after those of us compelled to sleep rough round the area."'

It was at that moment that Felix knew total defeat. A huge conspiracy, embracing Miriam, Gavin, Sir Ernest Thessaley and his lawyers, had been mounted against him and, now it was joined by Yorkie Bar, he knew he could no longer fight it.

'So you see,' his QC ended the cross-examination, 'it is much better for you to take our advice and go for manslaughter by reason of provocation. You have a wise and experienced solicitor who would agree. Wouldn't you, Septimus?' And the wise and experienced Septimus agreed.

'Why should I get five years for something I didn't do?' Felix protested half-heartedly, a final spasm before helplessness set in.

'Because' – Chipless now sounded gently reasonable – 'it's better than doing life for something you didn't do.'

As they left the prison Septimus Roache reminded himself to be out of court, engaged on an important case in Chelmsford, on the day that William Mansfield, otherwise known as Yorkie Bar, gave his evidence.

Chapter Twenty-one

'I just can't wait for my kids to take up crime! I mean, I'm longing for them to do a bit of mugging so they can be locked up for their own good. And mine. Or at least be taken into care.' Brenda looked at Terry's wife and wondered if she was joking. For the sake of her peace of mind, she decided that she was. 'Are they such little criminals then, your children?'

'No. That's the whole trouble! They're law-abiding. They take after me. I'm completely honest. I can't pluck up the courage to pinch a pair of fancy tights from Tesco's. So they never get into trouble. They'll be home straight after school to get under my feet and drive me round the twist. Oh shit!' Terry's wife cried out in genuine distress as the never switched-off West London radio announced that it was two o'clock and time for the news. 'Only half an hour and it'll be time to fetch Sheena from nursery. Bloody soft these nurseries nowadays. They won't even keep them in after school for misbehaving. Can you really spare a fag? Thank you. I'd be ever so grateful.'

Brenda had found the address by telephoning and promised to bring the money claimed by Terry as expenses, cash reluctantly released to her by Don Giovanni in Accounts. This had assured her of a warm welcome by a woman who, although well into her thirties, looked at first sight like a young and fairly attractive boy. She had straight, straw-coloured hair, high cheekbones and lines at the corners of her eyes which might have been printed there by laughter or grief. She wore an old tweed jacket, designed for a small man but which was too big for her so she had turned back the sleeves, and jeans. Her voice was husky and she chainsmoked as many as she could get of Brenda's cigarettes. She had short, blunt fingers with bitten nails. Having been christened, and she said it was worse luck, Antonia, she preferred to be addressed as Tony.

Tony and Terry had lived together before his disappearance in a semi-detached on an Acton estate called Woodlanders. The next-door neighbours had gone, Tony said, berserk with their front garden. It was a blinding mass of dahlias, late roses, geraniums, hollyhocks and Michaelmas daisies. A crazy-paving path led over a handkerchief of lawn to a gleaming front door, beside which stood a white plaster lion couchant. Tony and Terry's front garden looked like a patch of the Somme brought back as a memento of the 1914 war. A gaunt swing and a seesaw stood on the bare and muddy earth. Indoors, toys that must have once been expensive were broken and abandoned. Little piles of washing – clean knickers, vests and T-shirts – lined the staircase. Inside the front door there were assorted children's shoes, and small sweaters and anoraks which had fallen off the banisters. In the kitchen plastic buckets full of dirty clothes stood in front of a washing-machine which throbbed constantly. Brenda and Tony sat at the kitchen table smoking and drinking the cooled bottle of Kalinga Creek Chardonnay Brenda had bought at the offy down the road to loosen Mrs Whitlock's tongue.

'So you've no idea where Terry's got to?' Being among the uninitiated so far as children were concerned, Brenda had decided not to waste time discussing the names, ages, personal habits and talents for destruction of the Whitlocks' brood. She came straight to the point after handing over the money and a celebratory glass of Chardonnay.

'Hiding, I expect. He did that before. When PROD were after him.'

'And they're after him again?'

'Oh, yes. I had to go for income support because of the kids and they made me set PROD on Terry. Pity, because we do get on sometimes. In spite of all the problems, Terry and I do get on.'

'You mean the problems with money?'

'No. I mean the problems with sex.'

'What problems?'

'Basically, the fact that Terry's gay.'

'But' – Brenda looked at the whirling, vibrating machine – 'all this washing . . .'

'Well, I know. You see, the only person Terry feels in the least bit bi with is, well, me. I suppose I look like a boy.'

'He must have thought you looked *very* like a boy!' Brenda refilled their glasses.

'Hardly any tits and a small bum,' Tony admitted. 'Well, I suppose he did. It seems hardly fair, does it? PROD chasing him so much when he's gay basically. I mean if he'd only stuck to that he'd never have got into trouble.'

'Were you fond of Terry? I mean *are* you?'

'Well, you'd be surprised. You wouldn't guess it but he can be very loving, very gentle. I do love him. I suppose that's why I got so mad when he bolted without telling me.'

'Don't you get jealous?' Brenda was genuinely interested.

'What? You mean other blokes?'

'Well, yes.'

'Not really. They're no sort of challenge to me. Know what I mean? I'm different. The one thing he couldn't get anywhere else. Mind if I pinch another fag? No, I never got jealous of his boyfriends. They came and went, after all. They couldn't provide what I gave him.'

'You mean children?'

'I'm not so sure he thought that was an absolute plus. Nice mouthful, this wine. Good of you to bring it.'

'Compliments of Llama Books.'

'No, the only time I got jealous of Terry is when he started mucking around with this girl.'

'Who?'

'I don't remember her name. She used to ring up here and he'd told her I wouldn't mind if she were a bloke, so she put on a ridiculous, deep bass voice and said, "Would you mind telling Terry that Fred called?" I nearly tore his head off when I found out about that.'

'When Terry disappeared last time because PROD were after him . . .'

'The time he got locked up for non payment, you mean?'

'Yes, that's when I mean.' Brenda registered the fact that Terry, the rep, had been sent to prison, filed it away for further reference and asked, 'Did you know how they caught him?'

'I had an idea. I think he slept in his car sometimes. Some-times round his sister's. I never told PROD that, though. I didn't want to get him into real trouble. It was one of the other drivers that shopped him.'

'One of the drivers at Llama?'

'No, not in Terry's job. But you know the book reps round London. They have evenings. Get togethers. Piss-ups, I suppose you'd call them.'

'I know.' Brenda shuddered at the memory of one such social occasion. Terry had pressed her to come, promising wine, cheese and good music. She had ended up in a cellar somewhere near Ludgate Circus with slopping pints, doner kebabs and a karioke.

'Well, Terry got pissed I suppose and told one of the other reps where he was staying to keep away from PROD, and this rep gave him away. I think he was a bloke in trouble over child support himself and wanted to butter up the authorities. And he wasn't a rep for any proper firm either. Some sort of vanity publishers or a dirty book merchant.'

There was a silence and then Brenda decided to try it. 'Not Epsilon Books by any chance?'

'Yes . . . Yes, I think that's what Terry said.'

'And you wouldn't remember the bloke's name? Did Terry tell you that?'

'Funny you should ask that. I saw it in the paper the other day, bloke that got murdered.'

'Not Gavin Piercey?'

'That's right! Wherever he is, I bet Terry was glad when he read it in the paper. I bet he gave three small cheers when he read that!'

On her way back to Llama Books, Brenda stopped her Golf in Chandos Street outside a tobacconist and newsagent squashed between an office block and the Last Chance Saloon. Inside, a Mrs Singh, a gentle woman with a caste mark and a cardigan, was warming her hands at a small electric fire behind the counter and viewing, with mild disapproval, those members of the Sheridan Club who had come in after a late lunch to search, on her top shelf, for the magazines which were suited to their particular interest.

In the shop window Brenda saw cards advertising rooms to let, cleaning ladies wanted and strictly supervised ballroom dancing lessons offered. She went into the shop and, after a certain amount of money had changed hands, Mrs Singh confirmed that her shop had been nominated as an address for letters by a Mr Terry Whitlock. After a further exchange of money she agreed to ring Llama Books, or Brenda's home, if this Mr Whitlock, whom she was no longer able to describe accurately, called in for his post.

The car park was at the back of Llama Books' office block, a covered, concrete area guarded by Donald, a small Scotsman who used a curious crouching run to seek out and clamp any unauthorized shopper or careless author who parked in the spaces provided for the higher reaches of management and, of course, for the reps. Brenda, after a good deal of political manipulation, threats to leave and buttering up of Tubal-Smith, had got her slot and when she drove into it she stopped at the glass-walled booth from which Donald kept watch over his domain. She asked after Terry's Vauxhall Astra and was told that it had been taken out a couple of weeks ago. It was the habit of the reps to sign the cars in and out and a book was available on a shelf in the booth.

Brenda, who could charm Donald out of his usual mood of beady hostility, helped him find Terry's scrawled name by a date well after Gavin's murder. Donald hadn't seen Terry go. He was, wasn't he, entitled to a lunch break, during which the booth was open so that reps could get at the book.

Donald seemed to remember that the car had been there for quite a while. He remembered Terry saying, at the end of one day, that he was going to a meeting of RPU (officially the Representatives of Publishers' Union, but unofficially, and more accurately, the Reps Piss-up) in the old Jane Shaw pub round Ludgate Circus. Terry was determined to get drunk, anxious to avoid arrest and so had decided to leave his car in its parking space. Donald was a little surprised by the time it had stayed there, but assumed Terry was either drunk for a good many days or had been working in Central London.

When she got into her office Brenda rang Tony to tell her that her husband had taken out his car and was no doubt with it somewhere, alive and well. She didn't say, and it wasn't yet time to say, that there was a strong possibility that Tony's sexually uncertain husband had committed murder and was in flight from the police.

Chapter Twenty-two

'Any history of mental disease in your family?'

'My father was a bank manager who took up golf. Oh, and my mother became interested in the novel late in life.'

'You put that down to mental disease?'

'I can think of no other explanation.'

'Can think of no other explanation,' the doctor repeated quietly as he made a note. 'How's your health otherwise? Waterworks?'

'Does it?' Felix looked confused. The doctor explained his question with weary patience. 'I mean are you passing water easily?'

'All too easily.'

'Bowels moving regularly?'

'I try to suppress them.'

'Tries to suppress bowel movements . . .' The doctor made another note. 'Have you a rational explanation for that?'

'I was sharing a cell with rather a large murderer. He didn't want me to use the lavatory.' The doctor looked searchingly at Felix, as though he had some fascinating but hitherto undiscovered complaint. This doctor had what Felix thought of, and would have described, as a silly hairdo. His dark wavy hair, in some attempt to recover lost youth, was brushed forwards and towards his eyes, so that he seemed to have a villainously low forehead. He had a square face and large, white hands. He wore, again in the search for youth, a floppy, unstructured suit made of some lightweight material. Felix was beginning to tire of his company. He said, 'I've been enhanced since then. I'm now in a cell on my own but I'm still nervous about going to the lavatory.'

'Still nervous of the toilet' the doctor wrote down. 'Other effects of prison life on your mental state, are there?'

'I do think' – the doctor had hit on a subject which interested Felix – 'your surroundings influence your mind. My mind's a chameleon. I live by that sad sea, the English Channel. A lot of wind and white paint flaking off boarding-houses. Rain on the pier. So I write about lonely people.'

'I have to confess' – the doctor seemed to take some pleasure in the confession – 'that I haven't read any of your books.'

'Here on remand' – Felix was explaining it to himself – 'I seem to have absorbed the prison culture.'

'You mean you're learning how to steal cars?'

'Not that exactly. I've come to enjoy Australian soap operas and the novels of Sandra Tantamount.'

'I doubt if the court would accept that as evidence of an abnormality of mind arising from a condition of arrested or retarded development.'

'Would they not? You surprise me.'

'Let me explain.' The doctor leant forward earnestly and Felix got a strong whiff of aftershave (Pour les Jeunes Hommes by Carcinette). 'Murderers often obliterate the act from their mind. The brain, bit of a clever dick in many ways, tidies it away, pushes it under the sofa, so you genuinely forget you've ever killed anyone.'

'I know I've never killed anyone.'

'There, you see! The brain's done a magnificent tidying-up

job in your case. But the subconscious works overtime, as you well know. So it makes you see something that, well, just isn't there.'

'What isn't there?'

'Gavin Piercey.'

'I saw him. After he was supposed to be dead.'

'The man you killed?'

'I didn't kill him and I saw him three times.'

'How comforting' – the doctor leant back now, all smiles – 'for you to see the man you killed still alive and walking about London! How reassuring. That's one thing you can say for the old subconscious. It always tells you what you want to know.'

Felix looked at the doctor and said, 'Who sent you?'

'What do you mean?'

'You're not the prison doctor. Not in that suit. Did Roache send you?'

There was silence. The doctor put his notes and fountain pen carefully away in a leather briefcase. Then he said, 'Septimus and I go way back. We've worked together on hundreds of cases. We've got an excellent track record.'

'And Roache wants you to say I'm insane?'

'Oh not insane. Not the full monte, I wouldn't say that. Diminished responsibility by reason of an abnormality of mind under Section 2 of the Homicide Act 1957. Septimus just wants to use that as a backstop in case provocation becomes unstuck.'

'I wasn't provoked and I'm not loopy.' Felix rose to terminate the interview. 'I just didn't do it. I'm going to read all the evidence now and work out my own defence. I'm sorry but I don't think I need you or Section 2 of the Homicide Act.'

'You're making a big mistake,' the doctor told him. 'Looking at you I can see that you're clearly diminished.'

Septimus Roache had sent Felix the big bundle of prosecution statements after their last conference. He'd put off reading them as he'd wanted to finish *Pot Red* (sex and shenanigans in world-class snooker) by Sandra Tantamount. He went back to his cell and read them now. With the documents came a slim volume of photographs in bright colour. Felix took off his glasses in order not to see too clearly the disfigured body slumped in the van or, stretched naked and defenceless, in the mortuary. But he looked carefully at the interiors of Gavin's flat, presumably taken to establish the dead man's identity. The bedroom was as he remembered it, the cupboard door open and, on its coat hanger, he could see the sleeve and shoulder of a blue suit.

'All these events. One thing after another. Things happening. Well, to someone like me. Someone to whom things hardly happen at all. It seemed, well, totally unreal. Like a dream. Something I'd never dare put in a book because no one would believe it. But then I lay down on my bunk with that bundle of statements and I read them all through, like a novel, and I thought, well, that's true. That must be it. That really happened. I suppose it's because it was written down.'

Brenda said, 'So Gavin shopped Terry, the rep, to PROD.'

Felix and Brenda were in the visitors' room. At the next table a big black man with grizzled hair was telling his blonde girl visitor, who looked very young, a joke to cheer her up. His shoulders were shaking with laughter whilst she was in tears. Brenda said, 'Don't you see what that means?'

'Not exactly.'

'PROD were after Gavin for some money. He thought if

he told them where they could find Terry, they'd be grateful. Perhaps give him a discount, time to pay or something. God knows how they work.'

'One thing I noticed, reading through those things . . .'

'So Terry went after Gavin to protest,' Brenda carried on with her solution. 'There was a quarrel. Terry hit Gavin with a spanner. Probably he didn't mean to kill him at first but he got into a panic.'

'. . . It was something about the clothes found on the dead body.'

'Anyway, Terry killed him! Then he went into hiding. Just like he did before. Went missing. Didn't tell his wife. She said he used to sleep in his car. They must find out what's happened to the car.'

'It said the dead man was wearing a blue suit.'

'The police have only got to look for the car. Put out a message. All over the country. The car must be somewhere.'

'And there was a blue suit in the cupboard. In Gavin's flat.'

'Will you tell them to search for Terry? Put out his description. You can tell your police inspector that. She's a woman. You can probably get her to do what you want.'

'You're a woman and I can't get you to do what I want.'

'Oh, please! What do you expect me to do? Lie down under the table? I'd be arrested and you'd get about three years.'

Felix dismissed the vision of Brenda under the table firmly from his mind and said, 'Do you think Gavin had two blue suits? I imagine he only had one. One business suit.'

'Does it matter?'

'Perhaps not. All the same I'd like to know the answer.'

'Why?'

'Because they said he died in a blue suit. But when I saw Gavin . . .'

'After he was dead?'

'That's what they say! He wasn't wearing a blue suit at all, although there was one in his cupboard. He was wearing a maroon anorak and grey baggy trousers . . .'

'So he'd died in a blue suit, gone upstairs, changed into leisurewear for comfort and decided to go for a walk along the Thames Embankment?'

'Of course not!'

'You've got to give up this story, Felix. There's no future in Gavin's mysterious resurrection.'

'A future for Gavin, possibly.'

'Just tell Ms Police Inspector. She's got to find Terry. Promise me?' She wrote down the number of the car and gave it to Felix.

'All right, I promise. But Mirry would know how many blue suits Gavin had. And about the anorak.'

'Mirry?'

'Miriam Bowker. I should have asked her when I had the chance.'

'The mother of your child?'

'So she says. But I'm sure there's a lot more she could tell us.'

'All right. Where do I find her?'

'Thank you, Brenda. Thank you very much,' Felix said and told her about the flat at the World's End.

She wrote down the address in her Filofax. 'Think nothing of it. Anything to keep your mind off sex.'

'You're saying you saw a miracle?'

'I'm not saying that. Not exactly.'

'Good! Very good! I don't think we'll be seeing miracles. Not nowadays.'

'You mean God can't do them?'

'Can't? Why do you say can't? There's nothing God *can't* do. Miracles are just things he doesn't care for any more. He's given them up.'

'I see. Like smoking?'

'I know of nothing,' the Reverend Lionel Doone, prison chaplain, told Felix, 'either in the Scriptures or subsequent theology, to suggest that God was ever a smoker.' He had come stooping into the cell, an exceptionally tall man with a puzzled expression. Now he loomed over Felix, who sat on his bunk enjoying, as he always had, discussions about the God he couldn't bring himself to believe in. He said, 'What about water into wine, the feeding of the five thousand, restoring sight to the blind? Wasn't that all a bit miraculous? Anyway, how did you know that I thought I saw Gavin Piercey after his murder?'

'Your lawyers gave me the brief history.'

'The raising of Lazarus. Isn't that a case in point? Anyway, my solicitors want me to be insane.'

'They don't want that. Their hope is that you're a person of diminished responsibility.'

'Do you think Lazarus was of diminished responsibility?'

'Lazarus was a long time ago.'

'Does that make any difference? Under the great arch of eternity?'

The Reverend Lionel seemed a little shocked by Felix's ecclesiastical manner of speech. He said, 'There's no doubt God could go on creating miracles. When our faith was young it needed, perhaps, a bang on the drum, a trumpet call to attract attention. Nowadays, I believe, he finds that sort of thing, well, how can I put it?'

'Cheap publicity?'

'Exactly!'

'Nowadays he prefers a programme without commercials . . .'

'Let us say he doesn't seek out faith by mere . . .'

'Conjuring tricks?'

'You put it *very* well.' Far above Felix's head the chaplain nodded. 'Of course, that's your business, isn't it?'

'You're quite sure, are you, that God wouldn't just try a small miracle if he happened to find a man dead in a van in Bayswater?'

'I'm convinced that he would think such a thing hideously vulgar. What would be the point of it?'

'Perhaps just to keep his hand in?'

'No!' The chaplain was without doubt on the subject. 'His hand has never been out.'

'So no more miracles?'

'I'm sure he thinks that sort of thing quite out of date.'

Silence fell between the prisoner and the prison chaplain. Then Felix said, 'I just wondered . . .'

'What?'

'Well. Exactly what clothes Lazarus was wearing. When he was raised from the dead.'

'Oh, I can tell you that,' said the chaplain. 'He was wearing grave clothes. He'd been four days dead.'

Chapter Twenty-three

When he was ten years old Felix found the book he enjoyed most in the glass-fronted bookcase in his parents' sitting-room, sharing the space with a couple of china shepherdesses, a Staffordshire spaniel and a mysterious piece of stone which his father always told him had fallen from a meteorite one stormy night over Coldsands, but which had, apart from a certain glint noticeable in some lights, a distinctly earthbound appearance. There were three neat rows of books and between *The Life of Field Marshal Montgomery* and *The World's Best Golfing Stories* he found *The Adventures of Sherlock Holmes*. As he lay on his bunk he thought about 'The Engineer's Thumb'. What was it all about? A man who unwound a handkerchief and showed a horrid red, spongy surface where the thumb should have been. How had he been so damaged? Something to do with fuller's earth, whatever that might be. Felix had no idea. But what he remembered was the unfortunate engineer being shut in a cell-sized room, and seeing, after a slight hiss, that 'the black ceiling was coming down upon me, slowly, jerkily, but, as no one knew better than myself, with a force which must within a minute grind me to a shapeless pulp'. As he looked upwards Felix imagined the sound of distant levers and the ceiling falling to crush him. The fears which had forced his fingernails into the palms of his hands on the first day of his imprisonment came creeping back.

That day seemed decades ago, years, he thought. Great stretches of helpless, tedious and useless time extended the gap. He was doing time and it demanded his full attention.

There had only been one diversion since Brenda's visit. He had asked to make a further statement to the police and, when he was taken to the interview room, he told Detective Sergeant Wathen, who had arrived with his Detective Constable, all that Brenda had discovered about Terry, the rep, and the number of his car. Wathen promised to bring the matter to the attention of his Detective Chief Inspector but clearly thought little of Brenda's ideas or her suggested line of inquiry. 'I very much doubt,' he said, 'if I shall be able to persuade Her Majesty to spend more police time and money on further inquiries. We're satisfied we've got the right answer on this one.'

'Oh yes?' Felix asked. 'And what's the answer then?'

'You.'

Felix was taken back to his cell, where, after more seemingly endless days had passed, he took to lying on his bunk and thinking about 'The Engineer's Thumb'.

The bundle of prosecution statements lay on his table. He no longer read them. He no longer read anything. Even his last Sandra Tantamount was unfinished. He had been excited by something he remembered at the time of Brenda's last visit – apart from the colour of her hair, her thin wrists and pale fingers, the slight pucker of her lips as she examined his case with a shrewdness apparently beyond the reach of Septimus Roache or Chipless, QC. What was the thought which had struck him and seemed so important at the time? He tried to recapture it but it was sucked down into the swamp of lethargy into which he was slowly sinking.

For the thousandth time he gazed round his cell and, for

the thousandth time, he found nothing much to look at. There was one change, however. Over the wash-basin and the in-cell lavatory a photograph of a solemn child, wearing spectacles and a school blazer, was Blu-tacked to the wall.

When the cell doors opened, the screw told Felix he had a visitor. For a moment he wondered if it was Brenda back, or was he being taken out for trial? Such hopes faded when he faced the lofty clergyman who had come to lend him a book called *Faith without Miracles*.

'After all,' his visitor told him, 'we don't need to see a woman sawn in half to know that the conjuror exists.' Then he noticed the photograph on the wall and went to examine it with approval. 'I'm glad to see you're a family man,' he said.

Felix thought it would take too long to explain who Mirry was, and that she had sent him a note saying 'Sorry you got yourself into such a pickle. I thought you'd like to see Ian's latest school photo. I know who he reminds me of.' Felix couldn't explain why he had promoted Ian to a place on his wall. Now he got off his bunk and went over to the table. He was waking up and remembered something that might be just as important as the blue suit.

'This is yours, isn't it?' the chaplain asked, still looking at the boy's face.

'Oh, yes.' Felix didn't bother to ask if he meant the photograph or the child. He was searching through a list of exhibits but in a little while he forgot what he was looking for.

'He looks –' The chaplain was searching for a word and finally settled for 'dependable'. Then he left Felix to get on as best he could without the miraculous.

★

'I've got a pimple. A really disgusting spot! It's appeared on the side of my nose and it's a sign of the stress I've been put to during this book tour. I've been pressurized and it's given me a pimple!' Sandra Tantamount's usually imperious voice had acquired a querulous note, a threatening sign that all might end in tears. Brenda heard it on her mobile phone as she crawled along with the traffic in the outer reaches of the Fulham Road. 'You've got an interview at four thirty,' she told Sandra.

'Then I must rest. I must rest in peaceful and sympathetic surroundings. I know me. It's only complete relaxation that cures my spots. Get me a suite at the Galaxy Hotel. Mention my name and they'll give you the best. What's the time now?'

'Ten thirty. But I don't know if they've got a suite.'

'I told you, girl. Mention my name. Complete rest or the interview's off.'

'But, Sandra, does it really matter about the spot?'

'Does it matter? Of course it matters! What do you mean, does it matter?' In Sandra Tantamount's voice grief had given way to astonished anger.

'I mean it is a *radio* interview. I think they want to talk to you about your shopping habits.'

'Get the suite!' Brenda held the screaming mobile away from her ear. 'Or the jig's off!'

Somewhere near the Fulham football ground Brenda rang the receptionist at the Galaxy, who, being a dedicated admirer of García Márquez, knew nothing of Sandra Tantamount but was ready to reserve the suite for Llama Books. Then she dropped her phone into her handbag and lit a cigarette. She was on her way to her first meeting of the day in a block of flats near the World's End.

★

Brenda had tried ringing the flat for days but wasn't satisfied by a phone that didn't answer. She went to the address Felix had given her and found the lift gaping open and motionless. She climbed the stairs, past the scrawled threats to Pakis and Nig-nogs, and found a door with the screwed-on number hanging loose. She rang, knocked, and was rewarded by the sound of movement, a door closing, a light, perhaps, switched off. She put her mouth to the letter-flap and shouted, 'I've got to talk to you. I'm a friend of Felix's!' Miriam opened the door almost at once and let her in. When Brenda had seen her at the Bath Millstream's, she had thought of Mirry as a kind of joke. If she had noticed Felix taking her up, she'd have told him to put her down at once. Now she thought she could understand that he might, ten years ago, have fancied the pale-faced, darkly dressed woman who had risen, quite neatly, from the garish and crumpled confusion of her room.

Brenda introduced herself with unusual formality. She was a representative of Felix Morsom's publishers she said, and naturally they wanted to help their author in distress if they could. There were some questions they felt only Miriam Bowker could answer but Mirry, talking rapidly, was anxious to be off. 'I'm sorry. It's not convenient. I'm going out to lunch. I've got a date, actually. Someone's invited me.'

'You see, you seem to be the only person who knew them both.'

'Both?'

'Both Felix and the dead man Gavin Piercey.'

'I'm off to Puccini's in the King's Road. A friend of mine invited me. You know Puccini's, do you? It's awfully nice there . . .'

Mirry was making for the door but Brenda stood firmly

blocking her path. 'You see, we can't find anyone else who really knew Gavin.'

'My friend always chooses the risotto with mushrooms there. I don't know if you've ever had the risotto with mushrooms. It's really delicious.'

'You knew Gavin?'

'Not all that well actually . . .'

'Well enough to say he was the father of your child?'

'Ian's at school,' Mirry said as though it were a final answer to the question. 'He keeps on with his schooling through it all. He's doing well. That's his report I've got pinned up there. It says "Works well but does not participate in group discussions."'

'Then you changed your mind and decided Felix was his father.'

Mirry looked at Brenda and came to a conclusion. 'Are you Felix's girlfriend?' Asking the question seemed to give her momentary confidence.

'Not his girlfriend. His friend.'

'Oh.' Mirry was back in confusion. 'I'm sorry.'

'Nothing for you to be sorry about. Why did you fix on Felix for Ian's father?'

'We worked it out and went into all the details. It had to be Felix.'

'By we, you mean you and Gavin?'

'Are you trying to trap me?' Mirry did her best to sound outraged but only seemed shrill and frightened.

'Why should I want to do that?'

'I don't know. Coming here. Worse than the policemen. Asking questions.'

'Did they ask if you knew Terry?'

'No. No, they didn't!' The two women stood looking at

each other, both suspicious and silent. 'Who's Terry, anyway?'

'You must know.'

'Why must I? I don't know any Terrys. Terry's not the sort of name my friends would have.' Brenda said nothing and, as though afraid of the silence, Mirry added, 'The bloke meeting me round Puccini's is called Magnus.'

'Terry Whitlock. He's a rep like Gavin was.'

'Gavin knew lots of reps. He was on the Committee. They trusted him to arrange the meetings of the Book Reps Association or whatever.'

'Did Gavin go to a meeting the night he died? Was he at some sort of a piss-up at the Jane Shaw in Ludgate Circus?'

'I'm not sure. I'm not sure where he went.'

'But you said he'd asked you to meet him late that night. You said that's why you went round to his place.'

'Did I? Did I say that?'

'That's what you told the police.'

'I can't be sure what I told them.' Mirry was looking round the room, retreating into vagueness and uncertainty.

'That's when you found Gavin dead.'

'Dead,' Mirry repeated, as though hearing the word for the first time.

'So you could identify the body. It must've been terrible for you.'

'Yes. It was terrible . . .' Mirry said it like a frightened child, repeating a lesson she hadn't learned properly. 'Now, I really can't keep Magnus waiting. He's ever so impatient. Being in management, he's used to punctuality. He likes people,' she said, unaware of any ambiguity in the phrase, 'to be dead on time.'

'But you say you never heard him speak of Terry?' Brenda was searching in her shoulder-bag. After she found a cigarette and stuck it in her mouth, she continued to burrow for her lighter.

'Terry? No. Never that I remember.'

'Terry and Gavin had been arrested. They were in a cell together.'

'He never told me about that. Gavin never spoke about it at all.'

'He only put the whole story on tape.'

'Tape? I don't know anything about a tape.'

Brenda, who knew she was getting nowhere, saw a big box of kitchen matches among a litter of scarves, tissues, candles, mugs of cooling tea and cold coffee, Tampax boxes and a half-eaten doughnut on a paper bag. She moved to strike a match, lit her cigarette and blew out smoke. 'Only one other thing. Felix wanted an answer to this question.'

'What?'

'Did Gavin own two blue suits? And a maroon anorak?'

She looked at Mirry's face, which had betrayed nervousness, uncertainty, vagueness and some resentment. Now what she saw was pure terror. The path to the door was clear and Mirry, in a few steps, was out and it banged shut. Brenda was left staring after her. She had seen Mirry's hand on the door knob and, for the first time, had noticed what was on her third finger – a heavy, silvery ring with the face of a sleeping sphinx on it, something that might be brought into use as a knuckleduster.

Chapter Twenty-four

Left alone in the chaos of the World's End flat, Brenda smoked her cigarette and stood awhile in thought. Then she took a look at Ian's report and discovered that he was good at English, desultory in his attempts at Science and Mathematics, and seemed to have a deep-seated dislike of physical exercise. That, she thought, figured. Over the sink she saw a photograph pinned to the wall. It was a booksigning, she thought probably in a Millstream's shop. The author signing was undoubtedly Felix. The proud signee was, wasn't he?, someone like the Gothic companion she had noticed in the company of Miriam, colourfully clad in Bath. Feeling that it might come in useful, she detached the picture from the wall and put it in her handbag. She had become a woman with a mission; the mission being to spring Felix from gaol by discovering the truth about Gavin Piercey's death.

She now wondered, particularly when in the company of the Aussie Paul, if she loved Felix or, more particularly, if she were in love with him. She couldn't mention his name to Paul without bringing on a burst of contempt, mainly, it seemed, caused by the fact that Felix had never slept with her and yet their relationship, however described, born in signing sessions and literary lunches, had survived imprisonment and a grave criminal charge. To Paul, Felix was a wimp for not having seduced Brenda. If he had ever been permitted to try, Paul was sure, Felix would have shown himself hopeless in bed with as much knowledge of the niceties of oral sex as a Benedictine monk. Probably considerably less, the way monks carried on these days, particularly in Brisbane. And yet Brenda doubted Paul would have put up with prison with the stoicism, almost the gallantry, which Felix had shown on her visits.

She had picked Paul up at a publisher's cocktail party, where she behaved as ruthlessly as Don Giovanni in Accounts, who roved among the temps and made his selection, and now, like the moustached lover on the second floor, she was preparing to ditch her conquest. The business of getting Felix out of prison was going to demand her full attention. It was that task and not the progress of her author's pimple, which filled her mind as she stood by the sofa on which Sandra Tantamount lay stretched in the darkened sitting-room of her Galaxy suite and said, 'We've got a hired car to take you to West London Radio. It's waiting by the side entrance.'

'It's not *only* the spot,' Sandra Tantamount said, very near to tears. 'It's the sex.'

'Perhaps you need a new husband? A lover? Something of that sort?' Brenda managed to sound as detached as a nurse suggesting a different brand of laxative.

'Not for *me*, girl!' Sandra Tantamount coldly rejected such palliatives. 'For my golf novel I need some entirely new ideas. I can't do the melon bit again.'

'The melon was good,' Brenda reassured her. 'Was that in *Grand Slam*?'

'No, *In off the Red*. What's the matter, girl? Don't you *read* my books?'

'Of course I read them! Terrifically good yarns. Unput-downable. Compulsive page-turners.' Brenda, who had read none of the Tantamount oeuvre, remembered the quotes from the *Croydon Advertiser*.

'Well, then, you'll know it's not for me. Henry never troubles me in that sort of way. It's for the work!' Brenda remembered Sandra's husband, Henry, a silent older man who wore tweeds and seemed emotionally concerned with the growing of vegetables. Seated next to Henry at a launch dinner, Brenda had learned much she had now forgotten about the cultivation of prize-winning runner beans ('similar length is what they're looking for') and cucumbers ('difficult little buggers to get straight'). She said, 'What do you mean "for the work"?'

'All those bonking sportsmen of various kinds and their managers and mistresses. Isn't that what Llama's going to make its money on? Well, where's it coming from now?'

'I rather imagined it came from life.'

'Really, girl! What do you think I am? It was Hilary McCrindle who used to tell me about sex.'

'She was a woman of some experience?'

'In the Sixties, yes. She had a number of friends in the BBC. And some on the Coal Board.'

'Well, I suppose that accounts for it.'

'Of course she settled down and married the vicar.'

'Which vicar?'

'Our vicar.' Brenda was silent, turning all this information over in her mind. Sandra said, 'I mean the vicar where Henry and I live. Near Haslemere.'

'Oh, I see. *That* vicar.'

'But Hilary took it into her head to die on me. So where do I get my material? Tell me that, will you, girl?'

'I think . . .' Brenda looked at her watch. They were going to be late for West London Radio. Then she smiled and said, 'I might be able to come up with someone.'

'Someone?'

TWENTY-FOUR

'Who could possibly help with some research.'

'Really?' Sandra sat up on the sofa, awake and interested. 'Who?'

'I'll let you know tomorrow. In the meantime . . .'

'What?'

'The radio. It's live.'

'Has the spot gone?' Sandra was still anxious. 'I daren't look in the mirror myself. Come on, girl. You've got to tell me!'

'Totally cured!' Brenda said. She was delighted to still see the pimple, plain as a pikestaff and flourishing.

'What did I tell you? The relaxation did it. Now then, girl. Get moving or we'll be late for "Teatime Rap".'

It was first thing – about dawn – Brenda thought – in the park. An early frost powdered the grass; the leaves had turned and were falling. A party of soldiers rode chattering under the trees and the traffic was a distant and muted roar. A white-haired couple, a man and his wife in bathing-suits, walked, shivering, towards the icy water of the Serpentine as though they were parties to a suicide pact. Brenda, in a thick sweater and shorts, was running to keep up with her Australian lover, a pursuit she was beginning to think unnecessary.

'I was talking about you,' she panted, 'to one of my authors. I was telling her about your prose style.'

'Lucid and yet poetic. That's what I try for.' Paul slowed up a little, anxious to discuss a favourite subject. 'Whatever you may think about *Wagga Wagga*, it's beautifully written.'

'*Just* what I told her.' When she and Paul first got together she'd driven him to the park with enthusiasm for their morning jog, delighting in what the early sunshine did for the golden hairs on his legs, laughing as she struggled to keep up. Now, all she wanted was to sit down with a cup of coffee, a cigarette and the *Meteor*. However, she struggled on gamely.

'What this author needs is a sort of master class.'

'A what?'

'A class with a master, such as yourself. She has problems with repetition, her chapter endings can be terribly weak and she has absolutely no idea what to do with the semi-colon. Quite honestly, Paul, she needs help.'

'She? Who is this she?'

'Sandra Tantamount.'

'Isn't she a huge bestseller?'

'Mega.'

'And you say she needs help?'

'Quite honestly she's got into a bit of a rut. And with your teaching experience . . .'

'Is it writer's block?'

'I suppose you could call it that.'

'I'd like to meet her.'

'She'd love to meet you. She's in the Galaxy Hotel.'

Paul whistled as he ran. 'Sounds fine by me. Is she there with some geezer? I mean a husband or something?'

'Oh, no. She's quite alone.' Brenda thought of adding, alone with a pimple, but decided not to mention it. Instead she told Paul she had run quite far enough and she'd meet him back at the car. As she trailed her trainers through the brittle, frosted leaves she thought about the problem which concerned her most. How on earth had Gavin's friend Miriam acquired a ring from Terry, the rep, whom she'd never met?

When he was a boy at school Felix had never minded the work, he had just found playtime terribly hard going. Now he was growing used to his cell and he looked forward to the hour of watching television. What he dreaded was exercise. He stood in the corner of a cold yard, which was wired in like a fruit-cage with weeds growing in the cracked concrete, and tried to keep out of the way of a flying ball. Looking up to a clear blue sky he saw the white cottonwool trail of a jet off to ... Where he wondered? Istanbul? Rome? Athens?

Would he ever see such places again? Or only when he was old, aching, stiff-jointed, and remembered not as a writer but as a murderer? Morsom, the Bayswater killer. If his name was on the back of another book, it would be in the series of Notable British Trials.

A cluster of young prisoners ran past him, shouting. Over their heads he saw Dumbarton towering, his arms stretched up to the sky, his fingers tipping a ball into a torn net. The young lads were cheering but Dumbarton didn't smile. Felix couldn't remember ever having seen him smiling. Dumbarton, the ex-soldier, who marched down the Embankment to Temple Station and killed someone, some innocent man, running down the steps to get back to his wife, his girlfriend, perhaps his children. Someone had to die, anyone would do, to avenge Esmond's death. Had Dumbarton been at large the night Gavin died, Felix wondered, and wandering round Bayswater? Had he taken it into his head, for some obscure reason, to batter a stranger to death in a van? Was London, perhaps, full of Dumbartons, gloomily intent on random murder?

It was then that a flying ball from the game hit him in the face. His glasses fell, turning the clear world into a soft, impressionist blur. He stooped to pick them up and found one lens shattered. But in that act of stooping, he remembered the great, the important thing, the single fact he had to check in the bundle of depositions. His hopes soared high as the vanishing aeroplane.

That morning Ian Bowker had woken early, as he always did, to be on time for school and saw a piece of paper fastened with a safety pin to his blanket. He put on his glasses and found that it was a note from his mother, scrawled in purple Biro in a hand which he complained was more illegible than he, in fact, found it.

> My darling Ian (he read)
>   Mummy has to go away on business. I hope and pray it won't be long. I know you can get to school and manage on your own. Don't answer the door to anyone, particularly the police, or if they want to take more of your blood. I have left money under the telephone so you should be all right for suppers etc. I daren't say where my present address might be in case anyone else's eyes should pry. I love you and here's to when we shall be reunited. Keep your chin up.
> *Mum*

The kisses filled the rest of the page – a line of crosses and one mouthful of smudged lipstick. Ian got up, washed, dressed and collected the money from under the telephone. He hadn't got time then but he thought, as he looked round what he considered a complete tip, that if his mum was away in the evening he'd have a really good tidy-up and throw away a load of rubbish.

He had been fast asleep in the middle of the night before when a Vauxhall Astra had driven up to the entrance of the flats. Mirry, who had been looking out for it, kissed her sleeping son and pinned the note to his blanket. Then she staggered down the stairs with a suitcase bulging with clothes and cosmetics, got into the car and was driven away to a destination she was afraid to divulge even to Ian whom she was leaving to fend for himself.

Chapter Twenty-five

'The Tantamount tour going well, is it?'

Tubal–Smith lay on his couch with his shoes off, one of his toes showing palely through a hole in his sock.

'It's a huge success. I'm not with her all the time now. She prefers to travel with a friend.'

'Really? What sort of a friend?'

'Oh, a brilliant young novelist. He's from the southern hemisphere to be exact. I think she's well into a new story.'

'About sport again?'

'Oh, I think it's about that too!' Brenda told him.

'I'll tell you why I wanted to see you. Fergus Campion. Bright young editor, isn't he, Fergus?'

'Of course. He's Felix's editor.'

'Well, that's the fortunate part of it. He's just had a novel in from a woman called Elizabeth Cowling. And would you believe it?'

'Would I believe what?'

'This Ms Cowling's a copper. A Detective Chief Inspector, nothing less. And can you guess . . . ?'

'Yes,' Brenda told him.

'She's the same copper that arrested Felix Morsom.'

'I think he told me.'

'Well, that's a bit of plum publicity dropped into our laps!

Don't you see it, Brenda? How often do we get one Llama author arresting another?'

'Not very often, I suppose.'

'I suppose never! Can you imagine what Lucasta Frisby would do with a story like that?'

'Yes.' Brenda was seriously concerned. 'I'm afraid I can.'

'What I want you to do' – Tubal-Smith heaved himself and his stomach off the couch on to his slender legs and began to pace, excitedly shoeless, about the room – 'is have a look at the book. Fergus says it's called something to do with molehills. All about people called things like Tarquin and Arabella who spend their time discussing philosophy in a ruined chapel. But that's not the point. The point is that it's by a copper who fingered the collar of Felix Morsom! If you think it's a good idea, have the woman in. Talk to her.'

'I think,' Brenda told him, 'I'd like to do that.'

At the door she said, 'Millstream's shop in the Fulham Road is absolutely bursting with our books. I hope you noticed.'

'I've noticed.' Tubal-Smith beamed. 'You've done very well, Brenda.'

'Not me. It's the reps. The reps have done really well.'

'Have they indeed?' Tubal-Smith was puzzled. 'I thought you said one of them had vanished. Off the face of the earth.'

'Terry Whitlock? No. I've been in touch with him. Terry Whitlock's one of the best. In fact I thought you might have an idea.'

'What about?'

'A sort of prize. For Rep of the Year. Stimulate competition and give them all a bit of encouragement. Isn't that what you have in mind?'

Tubal-Smith asked himself the question and came up with the answer. 'Yes,' he told her, 'I believe it is.'

'That's great! We can always rely on you to come up with new ideas.' Brenda smiled and left the presence.

Ian was on his way home from school. It was the end of the week and he'd nearly spent all the money Mirry had left under the telephone. In addition to food, he'd had to buy furniture polish, Fairy Liquid and something which turned the water in the lavatory bowl blue. The flat was clean, tidy and smelled gently of disinfectant. Each night he had cooked himself toast and spaghetti rings and, after he'd finished his homework, he allowed himself an hour of television before bed. Far from being lonely, he'd enjoyed the happiest days of his life. He was delighted to be without his mother's weeping and demands for affection. He could also do without the strange voice she'd put on when answering the telephone and the occasional rumpus of her making love.

All the same, he was running out of money. He could, perhaps, earn a little by going downstairs to Mrs Pugsley and offering to do her shopping, but her flat smelled like the World's End public Gents and Mrs Pugsley, who had a nose which set off downwards to meet her upturned chin and a black tangle of wiry hair, had gone completely off her trolley and had taken to bellowing through his letter-box, 'Your mum's gone off and abandoned you, hasn't she? You're an abandoned child! Someone ought to tell the Council.' On such occasions he had turned the volume on the television up to its full extent and refrained from answering the door.

He walked now, in the early dusk, between the dark cliffs of the buildings, down alleys where the smell of Mrs Pugsley's quarters was echoed and re-echoed, aware of the dangers. He'd been twice set on by gangs of mixed sexes who had pushed him over, kicked him, opened his school-bag and scattered his geography projects in the wind. Dozens of times he had been offered drugs by school-age dealers to whom refusal was a personal affront. He had been groped and once held pinned to a wall by wandering paedophiles unable to find lonely children other than the solemn boy who stared at them through his glasses with a calm disapproval which finally put them off. So now he always walked through the shadows to his home having removed the compasses from his Geometry set, with the point out and sticking forward as a weapon of defence.

As he walked, he heard footsteps behind him and suspected one of his usual dangers. He quickened his step; the step behind him quickened. Not daring to look round, he started to run; there was running behind him. A hand gripped his shoulder; he turned quickly and lunged with his drawn compass which penetrated a blue skirt and black tights, entering the fleshy thigh of WPC Brisket. She had come with Judy Primrose, a social worker, to investigate Ian as a child totally lacking parental or other control. Later, he was taken into care as a danger to the public, with a record of unlawful wounding and assault on the police. He had spilled some of the WPC's blood in exchange for the blood she had once come to get from him.

'We've got the kid!' Detective Sergeant Wathen was able to report with great satisfaction. 'We've got the kid put away safely. The Council applied for a supervision order.'

His Detective Chief Inspector said nothing. She was studying a piece of forensic, which had only just arrived, in the case of *R*. v. *Morsom*. The labs, she thought, must be entirely staffed with partially mobile geriatrics. It took for ever to get a drop of blood sorted.

'The mother's scarpered. What we need is a law for locking up irresponsible mums.'

One thing was, Elizabeth Cowling thought, that when they'd crept round to do their job, the result had the virtue of certainty. The DNA test was an almost sure thing in a world which could only guess at the reason for its creation.

'I warned her,' Wathen said, not for the first time. 'I gave her a clear warning: "That nipper of yours has bad blood in him. There is the blood of a killer," I said, "in that nipper's veins. He should have been under a supervision order from birth, him being the fruit of a murderer's loins."' Detective Sergeant Wathen rolled his tongue round the last phrase with particular pleasure.

'You're wrong!' his superior officer said, also enjoying the exchange. Detective Sergeant Wathen was getting more than ever up her nose, and she felt a freer spirit since she had heard welcome news about *Here on This Molehill.* 'You're completely wrong. Ian Bowker's not the child of a murderer.'

'Giving the little blue-eyed lad the benefit of the doubt, are you? Bleeding little innocent, is he?' Wathen did a poor imitation of a soft-hearted do-gooder. 'My honest opinion is the only thing to do with lads like that is crack down on them. Crack down on them hard!'

'I'm afraid there isn't any doubt to give him the benefit of. I've got the DNA.'

'Science! That never proves anything.' Wathen said it, but he was already losing confidence. He felt as though Science was stealing up on him with some sort of blunt instrument.

'We've got Ian's blood and that of the deceased Gavin Piercey. Felix Morsom gave us some of his when we took prints. Anyway, the answer is Ian isn't the child of either of them.'

'Not Piercey?'

'No.'

'Or Morsom?'

'Certainly not Felix Morsom.'

'Well, we don't know who his father is, do we?' Detective Sergeant Wathen began to cheer up.

'No, we don't.'

'So it might be another murderer?'

'It's not very likely.'

'Or some violent criminal spawned him?' The Detective Sergeant was hopeful again. 'In which case we did right to crack down on the lad and bang him up.'

'Don't exaggerate, Cecil!' The Detective Chief Inspector was smiling. 'Not all parents are violent criminals, you know.' Elizabeth Cowling knew that her sergeant was particularly hurt by her calling him Cecil, mainly because it was his name.

'You see, when Tarquin lies to Dermot and makes up a story about Arabella and Neville being lovers, and Dermot accuses Arabella and that then puts the idea in her head, so she does go to bed with Neville – or at least has sex with him in the old Coach House – and that leads, however indirectly, to Nuncle's suicide . . . What I'm trying to say is that it's by way of fiction we find out the truth.' Detective Chief Inspector Cowling leant forward eagerly. She wore a mauve dress with a single row of pearls. Her hair had just been done and she was clutching a gin and tonic, feeling somewhat out of place in the Malibu Club, the glimmering white and gleaming chromium 1930s-style cocktail bar in Soho, where she had been asked to meet the girl from Llama Books. Around her the men wore unstructured suits, gold chains on their wrists, shaven heads or beards or small, drooping moustaches. The white-faced, tousled women wore tights like ballet dancers or minute leather skirts. Many were muttering into mobile phones, some into tape-recorders. The strawberry blonde girl she had come to meet, whom she had feared would turn out a hugely efficient female editor with strong ideas, ready to attack *Here on This Molehill* with a blue pencil and a pair of scissors, had a gentle voice and wore baggy tartan trousers and an old football shirt, designed for a man. She made the Detective Chief Inspector feel middle-aged and overdressed. 'I expect,' she said, 'you'll make all sorts of helpful suggestions during the editing process. After all, this is my first.'

'Oh, I'm not an editor,' Brenda told her.

'You're not?' Then what are we doing here in this extraordinary place?

'I'm publicity. I shall be doing all the promotion for *Molehill*. Signing sessions. Literary lunches. All that sort of thing.'

'Well, yes. Provided my work doesn't get in the way.'

'Work?'

'Crime's soaring, I'm afraid. It's really giving me awfully little time for writing.'

'Of course.' Brenda leant forward and talked to her new author confidentially. Detective Chief Inspector Cowling was taken aback by how beautiful she looked. 'Your job? I think we should keep your job out of it.'

'Oh, I agree. Murder and sudden death. Everyone must be bored of that by now. It's becoming as tedious as the weather. I mean, for a topic of conversation.'

'The head of Llama Books is very keen on the story about you arresting Felix Morsom, another of our authors.'

'He does seem to have killed someone.' Elizabeth Cowling smiled defensively. 'So, really, I had very little choice . . .'

'Oh, I'm sure it was your job. But I don't see that as a particularly good way of selling *Molehill*. I don't think your beautiful novel . . .'

'You've read it, of course?'

'Of course.' Brenda lied swiftly but convincingly. 'I don't think it needs that sort of lurid publicity.'

'I'm sure it does not.' The Detective Chief Inspector was getting nervous. 'I mean, I certainly couldn't talk about the case to the newspapers. Sub judice and all that sort of thing. My superintendent would be absolutely livid.'

'All the same' – Brenda looked doubtful – 'Tubal-Smith might insist on it as a publicity peg. He wants you to talk to Lucasta Frisby on "How I Fingered a Famous Novelist's Collar".'

'Oh, I couldn't possibly do that!' The professional policewoman was profoundly shocked.

Brenda frowned, sank her chin in her hands. 'I've been trying to think of a way out for you.'

'Oh, if you only would! Lucasta Frisby! In the upper reaches of the Met *everybody* reads her.'

'The only possible answer,' Brenda had to admit, 'is for Felix to be acquitted.'

'Why?'

'Well, then it would be a non-story! You just fingered the wrong collar. We'd have to fall back on the book.'

'But is it really likely he'll get off? I mean all the facts seem dead against him.'

'All the facts?' Brenda looked surprised. 'I mean, I know you haven't found Terry Whitlock yet, but surely it's only a matter of time.'

'Terry who?'

'Whitlock. One of the Llama reps. He's obviously the chap

who really killed Piercey. I know Felix told you all about him. His car number and everything.'

'He never said a word. Not about this Whitlock or anyone else.'

'Or he told your sergeant. Surely he reported back?'

'Just you tell me!' The Chief Inspector leant forward intently. 'Tell me all you know! There are some channels of communication which need clearing out. Like drains. So tell me about this Whitlock.' When Brenda had told the story, Elizabeth Cowling resolved to reopen the inquiries at once. She might not reach the truth but, and this was even more important, she would make Detective Sergeant Cecil Wathen look a complete prat.

Felix was in the group of prisoners out of their cells and watching 'Southern Cross', the latest Australian soap. Why had April left home? Was she pregnant by the new manager of the BYO Catch of the Day restaurant? Where had they all gone wrong? These were the subjects the Sydney-side family were anxiously discussing as they gathered in the kitchen where Granma was cooking a chook. New papers had just arrived from Septimus Roache, containing scientific evidence. Felix glanced at the conclusion and saw that neither he nor Gavin had been identified as Ian's father.

'Of course,' he said aloud. 'That's it! That figures absolutely.'

'Don't tell me!' Dumbarton, gazing at the screen, was rarely moved to speak. 'You'll ruin the bloody story!'

Chapter Twenty-six

'I'm afraid this is very unconventional but we authors are creatures of impulse.'

'Are we?'

'I've come alone. Without even informing your solicitor.'

'I'm not sure he's worth informing.'

'And no Detective Constable to corroborate my version of the following conversation.'

'So I notice.'

'We're just chatting informally,' Detective Chief Inspector Cowling almost gushed, 'as brother and sister of the pen.'

Felix felt his toes curl in embarrassment but he said nothing to stop the policewoman's flow. 'You see, I've had a most interesting and helpful meeting with Llama publicity department. I do feel it's a wonderful start for me to be sharing publishers with so many famous authors, you in particular. She gave me some very valuable advice. I expect you know her? A nice girl called Brenda Bodkin?'

'I know her' – Felix's voice was full of regret – 'up to a point.'

'She's dead against an idea they apparently had at Llama of using, well, the way we bumped into each other – or shall we say over this case of yours – to publicize *Here on This Molehill*.'

'You don't want that?'

'Well, do you?'

'I must say that, at the moment, it would be the least of my worries.'

'Yes, I suppose it would.' She looked thoughtful. 'I expect you get a lot of time to yourself here, don't you?'

'Not bad. We're banged up about fourteen hours a day.'

'So you have a nice lot of time for writing?'

'I can't write. I read crappy novels and watch television.'

'Oh, I'm sorry to hear that.' Elizabeth Cowling couldn't quite conceal the pleasure that an accepted novelist must feel on hearing that another author can't write. 'But what I wanted, after seeing Brenda Bodkin who took me to that interesting club of hers, no doubt the haven of authors . . . I suppose I'll have to join . . . I mean, why I wanted this little informal chat was that it might possibly help us to help you.'

'Are the police always so helpful?'

'Well, not always. And I doubt if my Detective Sergeant would approve but this *is* a special case. Now is there anything you haven't told us?'

'I haven't told you anything.'

'On legal advice. But now, anything that might help us help you?'

'Something you should have reminded me of. Something that struck me as very important. The glasses.'

'I see yours are broken.' One of Felix's eyes was still shrouded by a cracked lens. 'But isn't that rather a matter for the prison authorities?'

'Not my glasses. Gavin's glasses.'

'I don't remember . . .'

'. . . Seeing them on the scene-of-the-crime list? You didn't because they weren't there.'

'He wore glasses?'

'Obviously not just reading glasses. He wore them always. Every time I saw him.'

'They'd've been broken in the attack.'

'But no bits of them were found. No bent frame, shattered lenses, nothing. I mean, the murderer wouldn't have taken them away with him, would he?'

'I suppose not. What do you think that means?' Felix looked round the interview room. On the other side of the glass he could see a screw with his arms crossed, his head sunk on his chest, apparently asleep. Then he told her what he thought it meant.

'It's a bit of a bloody superstition to think that a preposition is a word you must never end a sentence with,' said Brenda's one-time friend Paul, who was wearing only a T-shirt from the Adelaide Literary Festival on which the bald butler-like head of Henry James stared out with a look of fastidious disapproval. 'Now let me ask you this,' Paul continued in his best tutorial mode. 'Would you rather say people worth talking to or people with whom it is worthwhile to talk?'

'I'm not sure.' Sandra Tantamount, quite undressed, was fastened to the hotel bed by her Hermès scarf, Paul's belt and the cords of two Galaxy complimentary bathrobes.

'Well, then, we'd better have a demonstration.'

'About prepositions?'

'Semi-colons. You've never really understood how to use them.'

'All right. But *do* hurry up. We can't be late for the Llama Books party.'

The activity which they then engaged in is fully described in chapter twenty of *Hole in One* (Llama Books £16.99) in which Brad Eagle, the American Ryder Cup hero, encounters Sally Appledorf, a sports page journalist, in a bunker.

Llama Books didn't need to hire restaurants or assembly rooms for parties. The first floor of its offices, converted from an old coach station, was a cavernous space, once the starting point for tours of the South Coast or the Shakespeare country, now fitted with a marble floor, tall stained-glass windows and potted palms. There a hundred and fifty assorted booksellers, critics, writers, publicists and broadcasters could circulate, grab glasses of champagne, fill their mouths with miniature pork pies and avocado dip and, splutter, from food-filled mouths, unfavourable views of the authors who made up the autumn list. Tonight the reps, complete with their partners, had turned up in force to hear the announcement of the Rep of the Year Award (an engraved tankard and a handsome cheque) to be presented at some point in the proceedings by the bestselling Sandra Tantamount.

She arrived only a little late with Paul, her often discontented face wreathed in smiles. She was met, with a little half bow, by Tubal-Smith, as though she were visiting royalty, who took her to meet Lucasta Frisby. 'She's dying to talk to you for a series she has in mind about star women writers and their unknown husbands. It'll be frightfully good for *Hole in One*.' Paul found himself near to Brenda, who was wearing the long, green dress she kept for ceremonial occasions, so she looked mystic and wonderful as some sort of water nymph in a pre-Raphaelite painting.

'Long time no see.'

'You've been busy with Sandra.'

'She wants me to be with her on tour. Her prose is improving all the time.'

'I bet it is. Does she want you to jab things into her bum?'

'For heaven's sake, Brenda! Don't talk disgusting. There's people from television about.'

'I'm sorry. Silly question. Of course she does.'

'Haven't you missed me a little, Brenda?'

'Not much. I rather like being alone. You can stretch out your legs.'

'Well, you always liked that.'

'Honestly, I'm grateful to you, Paul. What with one thing and another, you've been the most wonderful exercise. I leave you a far fitter woman than the one you took up with all those months ago.'

'Brenda, you're joking?' Paul had always been the one who ended things.

'In a way. But you'll be far happier helping Sandra.'

'If we split up' – Paul was clearly worried – 'does it mean Llama Books won't publish *The Budding Groves of Wagga Wagga*?'

'Not at all. I'm sure Miss Tantamount will see you have a simply enormous print run.'

He walked away from her then and she said to herself, Of course I'll miss you, you long, blond post-modernist child of the outback! In some ways I'll miss you very much indeed.

She saw Detective Chief Inspector Cowling in a cocktail dress, with a samosa in one hand and a glass of champagne in the other. Being in the police, she didn't know many people to talk to. Brenda went up to her and asked her not about her book but about some other preparations they had planned for this event. 'It's all done,' Elizabeth assured her. 'But I was so looking forward to this party. Seeing so many writers I admire in the flesh. Now it's becoming a bit of a busman's holiday.'

'I'm sorry you feel like that. There's someone just come in

I've got to talk to. I'll get Tubal-Smith to come over to keep you company.'

'Will you? Tell me, does he really like *Here on This Molehill*?'

'He thinks you're right up there with Virginia Woolf. In fact *he* thinks Virginia'll be sick as a cat when she reads it!' And Brenda was gone. For she had seen, between the drinking, cheering, laughing heads, a straw-haired, boyish woman, with hands deep in the pockets of a dark jacket, come into the room and look round in a way that seemed not hesitant but amused, as though she'd like to stand and enjoy the joke on her own a little longer. She wasn't left alone, however. Brenda was beside her, holding out a glass of champagne and saying, 'Thanks for coming, Tony. I think Terry's in with a real chance.'

'Rep of the Year! You really think he'll show up?'

'He's probably got to hear about it. We published the shortlist in the *Bookseller*. There are only three on it, so he'll know he might well be up for the big one.'

'How big is it exactly?' Tony screwed up her nose, unaccustomed to the bubbles that sped up towards it.

'Five hundred smackers!'

'Terry'd come for that. If he's anywhere above ground.'

'And if he doesn't show, you'll accept it on his behalf?'

'Course I will. Just so long as PROD doesn't get their sticky fingers on it.'

'Spend it before they notice! How are the kids?'

'Ghastly, thanks. They're driving Terry's mum crazy. Serve her right for giving birth to such a ridiculously fertile bisexual. Is it all right if I have one of those sausages?'

'Look, if you do have to accept the prize, there's no need for you to make a speech. Just say thanks, take the money and run.'

'That's just what I had in mind!'

Three quarters of an hour later the sound of the party had risen several decibels. Deals, takeovers, breathtaking advances, mass sackings and possible prizewinners were debated. Seductions had started in various corners. A plump young historian came up to Miss Bodkin and said, 'Brenda, I know I'm not much good in bed but with you I'd really try hard,' imagining this was the approach irresistible. She gave him what she hoped was a withering look and started to talk with unnatural animation to an octogenarian with a whistling hearing-aid. Don Giovanni in Accounts was making a flagrant approach to Elizabeth Cowling on the basis that, to complete his collection, every serious seducer's list should include at least one older woman. But he was interrupted by Tubal-Smith who told him he couldn't wait to tell the Heritage Minister and the lead singer of the Degenerates at dinner that he'd just captured the most newsworthy officer in the entire Metropolitan force. Then he was called to the microphone to introduce 'our newest bestseller acquisition who has researched, in writing her wonderful novels, almost every sporting activity known to the civilized world'.

Sandra Tantamount, flushed and overexcited by the ever-flowing champagne and the afternoon's activities, had raised her voice an octave and her short speech was punctuated by high and girlish giggles. 'Those of us who have had a little success at writing,' she said, 'owe everything to the unsung heroes of the literary world, the reps!' Laughter at this was drowned in cries of 'Got it right, girl!' and 'Good on you!' from all the reps present. 'This prize is therefore far more important than the Booker and the Prix . . .' She was about to say the Prix Goncourt, but after Prix she abandoned the attempt. 'All those reps on the shortlist have done splendid work and now, if I can only open the envelope . . . It seems to have been stuck down with superglue! Yes, I've got it open. And, yes, I'm so glad about this. The winner of Rep of the Year prize will be well known to you all. It is . . . Terry Whitlock!' Sandra looked brightly round the room. 'Is he here? Mr Whitlock, come and collect the prize. Rep of the Year!'

There were shouts of 'Give him the money!', 'Where's Terry?', 'Probably still down the old Jane Shaw' and, even, 'He's done a runner!' But Brenda appeared at the bestseller's side and told her, 'His wife's here to receive the prize.'

'Good news!' Sandra's voice rose high and excited over the chatter. 'Terry, it seems, is busy. Well, he's always busy, isn't he, our Terry? But luckily his wife, the lovely . . .'

'Tony,' Brenda prompted.

'Tony! Did you say Tony?' Sandra was puzzled until Brenda said, 'Yes. It's a woman.'

'Oh, right. Will Terry's wife Tony please come up and collect his prize? Terry's busy, isn't he?' she asked the short-haired woman who had appeared beside her. 'Always busy! Thank you very much.' And she took the envelope with the cheque in it rather as a hungry young zoo leopard might take its daily lump of horseflesh from a keeper. And then she was pushing her way through the crowd, her head down, not looking at anybody, and out of the door. Brenda gave her a short start before she went after her, and Detective Chief Inspector Cowling left Tubal-Smith in the middle of his anecdote about an 'amazingly star-studded lunch at the Galaxy Grill', the only point of which seemed to be the names of the characters concerned. The movements of Terry's wife Tony were from now on to be carefully scrutinized.

*

The Llama car park was a place of faint lights and long shadows. In a dark patch Brenda had got into her Golf, taking care to shut the door quietly, and sat looking forward, her hand on the ignition, peering through the windscreen. She saw, in a pool of light, Tony ferreting in her handbag for the key to her child-infested, beat-up Ford Fiesta which the HP company might just not reclaim if she could get Terry's cheque cashed. It took her a long time and Brenda could guess at the abuse of life and the universe that went on as Tony shook her bag, shook her head and shaped her lips round various obscenities. At last she found a bunch of keys and Brenda started her engine.

At the same time there was a roar from another car which seemed to bound out of the shadows and aim itself directly at Tony. It came like a torpedo at the woman dazed in its headlamps, a standing bewildered target. Brenda could never be sure what made her drive forward, her foot flat on the floor, to cannon into the side of the advancing murder weapon, to turn it, with the horrible sound of crunching metal, out of its course, so that it hit a concrete pillar broadside and stopped. Both Tony and Brenda could then see it for what it was. The relic of the Vauxhall Astra used by Terry, the rep, to conduct his business.

Figures came out of the shadows. Detective Sergeant Wathen pulled open the door of the wreck and leant over to switch off the engine. The driver seemed unhurt. He was pale, however, and the impact had broken his glasses. He was wearing a maroon-coloured anorak and the bottom half of a tracksuit. He was not Terry but, undoubtedly, Gavin Piercey, alive in spite of everything.

Chapter Twenty-seven

Felix sat in the dock of number one court in the Old Bailey and looked with wonder at his trousers. He thought it was only in another existence, another world almost, that he had worn his best suit – dark grey with a discreet back slit – which Brenda had brought to the prison for his day in court. The prominence to which he had been led by a secret staircase from the cells, blinking at unexpected daylight like a mole emerging from the earth, didn't feel like a position for an important actor but a back seat in the audience. The play, which he had long ago decided would be protracted, meaningless and finally boring, seemed to be starting off at a great distance and, having nothing to do with him, was unlikely to hold his attention.

He saw Septimus, chatting with a man from the Crown Prosecution Service at the solicitor's table. He saw Chipless, lounging with his hands in his pockets, his wig pulled down over his forehead like an Edwardian dandy's top hat, laughing at a joke told to him by Marmaduke Pusey, QC. He saw Quentin Thurgood, who was busy reading a brief in another case. And then there was a knock like that which used to precede French plays and an usher yelled, 'Be upstanding!' and Felix rose wearily as a tiny man in scarlet and ermine, a judge seen through the wrong end of a telescope, bustled into court. When they all sat down again, another voice intoned,

'The Queen against Morsom,' and Felix wondered what exactly the Queen had against him.

When the judge said, 'Yes, Mr Pusey,' he turned out to have a deep bass voice, inappropriate to such a small, fussy person, so that it all seemed like a television play with the volume turned up. From then on the trial proceeded in the shortened version. Felix was reminded of those actors who undertake to do the whole of *Hamlet* in five minutes. The text was as follows:

MARMADUKE PUSEY, QC: My Lord, in this case I appear to prosecute with my learned friend Miss Goldacre. The defence is in the able hands of my learned friends Mr Christopher Warrington and Mr Quentin Thurgood. My Lord, your Lordship will not be troubled long with this case. Certain facts have emerged which have led me to advise the Crown not to offer any evidence against the defendant Morsom.

JUDGE: I understand that the deceased victim is, in fact, still alive?

PUSEY: Indeed he is, my Lord. It was an event which the Crown could not possibly have foreseen.

JUDGE: Quite so, Mr Pusey. I understand it was entirely unexpected?

PUSEY: Indeed it was, my Lord.

JUDGE: But being without a fatality is somewhat fatal to your case?

[*Polite, if muted, laughter in court.*]

PUSEY: Your Lordship puts it so much better than I could have done. When it comes to costs, it is our contention that the defendant Morsom brought these proceedings on his own head by constantly threatening the man Piercey with death. The threats are referred to in the depositions.

JUDGE: I have read the depositions. What have you to say on costs, Mr Warrington?

WARRINGTON: My Lord, I agree with every word which has fallen from my learned friend. These proceedings were undoubtedly due to Morsom's conduct. That is not disputed.

JUDGE: Brought it on his own head, did he?

WARRINGTON: He did indeed, my Lord.

JUDGE: Then I'm most grateful to you two gentlemen for not wasting the time of the court. [*He looks towards the dock.*] Are you Felix Morsom? [*As though he didn't know who he might find sitting there.*]

FELIX: Yes. [*For some reason he couldn't bring himself to say 'my Lord'.*]

JUDGE: Then you are free to go. There will be no order for costs against the prosecution.

The privatized dock officers opened a small door and Felix walked out of the sinister playpen. Septimus came strutting up, his fingers in his waistcoat pockets, sniffing through the hair in his nose and smelling, as usual, of eau de cologne and sweat.

'I think your chestnuts have been pulled out of the fire,' he said, 'by the best legal team in the country. Are you coming to say thank you to Chipless?'

'No, thanks.' Felix was looking up at the public gallery, where he saw the bright hair of the person he needed to thank. She smiled, waved and pointed to show that she was coming down to join him.

'He's not allowed to speak to anyone. Sorry. No story! Mr Morsom's reminiscences are the sole copyright of Llama

Books. He's under a contractual obligation. Just let us through, will you? Sorry to disappoint you.' Lights were flashing, lenses and microphones were pushed towards him. There were cries of 'This way for the *Sun*, Felix', 'Quick smile for the *Meteor*', 'Just a couple of words for the BBC'. There was even a faint and distant cry of 'Radio Thames Estuary'. Brenda gripped Felix's arm, steered him away through the traffic, ran with him down the side-streets to where her car (a hired job, the Golf convertible was still very sick indeed) was parked outside the Mother Bunglass pub. She started the engine as the news gatherers, weighed down with cameras, recorders and bags of equipment, came panting round the corner of the alley-way.

'Where are you taking me?' Felix, for not much reason, found himself laughing.

'Where do you want to go?'

'I suppose home. Unless . . .'

'Unless what?'

'. . . you can think of anywhere else?' He was trying not to sound hopeful.

'I'll take you home.'

She used back ways and short cuts for getting out of London. Then she avoided the motorways, but drove fast down dual carriageways and through straggling, endless suburbs and small towns from which the charm had been resolutely removed by urban developers. They were heading for the sea, the flaking white paint and the windswept pier of the place he lived in, had known and wrote about – the world of Felix Morsom.

'I never guessed. I was wrong all the way. Right up to the end. I thought it was Terry who'd killed Gavin. So you think that poor Terry . . . ?'

'Battered to death in a van. Dead with his pockets full of Gavin's papers. Falsely identified as Gavin by the only witness they had time to bother with – Gavin's girlfriend. Buried under the name of the man he hated . . .'

'Not a nice way to go. But when did you guess?'

'Well, it was pretty odd when I saw him on the Embankment. And then everyone told me I was dotty, or it was not God's way, or it was a defence that would do me more harm than good, and I began to doubt, seriously doubt, if it wasn't some kind of dream. And then, when I'd been banged up long enough, I began not to care.'

'But you didn't give up hope?'

'I've never given up hope about one thing.'

'Getting acquitted?'

'No, getting you. I've never given up hope about that.'

'Not much good in hoping for me if you were doing life.'

'Why ever not? I might have got an open prison. You're allowed connubial visits. Wouldn't an open prison count as abroad?'

'Hardly.'

They had stopped at lunchtime in a country pub. At least from the outside it looked like a country pub of the thatched and oak-beamed variety. Inside it had all the modern advantages of Indie music, flashing Space Invaders, plastic tabletops disguised as wood, electrically lit-up logs in the fireplace and kebabs and chips from the microwave. On this diet the landlady, who wore a low frilly top and the sort of checked cotton trousers favoured by clowns, had grown alarmingly stout.

Irritated by the decor Brenda, when they ordered lunch, asked for a Ploughman's Kebab. What she got was a pale, hairy, grey chicken leg in a basket. She nibbled at a chip and said, 'So it's all solved, the mystery.'

'Not altogether. I guessed some of it.'

'When?'

'I thought about the glasses. If there'd been a battered Gavin in the van, there'd've been shattered optical glass. The figure I'd seen on the Embankment was wearing glasses. Definitely.'

'I thought Terry had gone to kill Gavin – or at least beat up the other father who'd shopped him to PROD.'

'I think that's what happened. They met at the reps' knees-up in Ludgate Circus. Terry didn't have a car. So he asked Gavin to give him a lift home.'

'Gavin agreed? He gave a lift to the man he was scared of?'

'Probably too scared to refuse: "Take me to Acton. Just a bit out of your way. On past Bayswater." He was a big man, Terry. A big man with a heavy ring. When the car stopped, Terry told Gavin what he was going to do to him. Drunk, of course. Gavin must have got him pretty quickly, before he started.'

'Got him with what?'

'Something he had in the car – a spanner, a jack handle. I don't know what. And I don't expect he meant to kill him.'

'You always think the best of people.' Brenda looked displeased.

'I'm sorry.'

'You forget. He made an unrecognizable mess of Terry.'

'He had to, if he was going to turn him into a dead Gavin.'

'Is that an excuse?'

'Not an excuse. A reason.'

Brenda shivered. 'He did all that in his van. And no one noticed.'

'Probably no one would've noticed if he did it in the street.

Under a lamp-post. I imagine it happened when they stopped in Acton. Before Terry got out.'

'You mean, outside Terry's house?' Brenda couldn't believe it. 'With his wife and children asleep? That's what you imagine?'

'That must have given Gavin the idea. There was a dead man in his van. All right, the dead man could be him. Gavin would never be caught because he was dead. He liked plots, Gavin did. He liked mysteries. He saw himself loitering in some safe limbo until the police gave up their inquiries and he could return as someone else entirely.'

'So you think he drove the dead Terry back to Bayswater?'

'And left him outside his flat. He had to, if Terry was going to be him. He took everything out of Terry's pockets and put it in his own wallet – driving licence and stuff. Oh and he must have taken off Terry's sphinx ring so he could give it to Miriam some time or other.'

'That was horrible,' Brenda said, as though the rest was all right.

'Then he went upstairs. Lucky for him no one saw him. He changed his clothes and phoned Miriam to tell her to come and identify the body as him. That was one of the cruellest things he did. She must have been half mad to do it. Can I get you another drink?'

He went to the bar and the landlady, when she had finished a lengthy phone call, slowly poured a draught Guinness for him and a glass of white wine for Brenda. When Felix asked her if she'd turn the music off, she asked, 'Why on earth?'

'We can't hear ourselves speak.'

'Our customers prefer the music.' She seemed surprised. 'It's what they came out for. They get quite enough talking at home.'

'All the same, we want to talk.'

'You want to get intimate, you mean?'

'At least some of us do.'

'I'll put it down a notch for you. That's the best I can do. Any more and my husband'll go bananas.'

Felix didn't like to say that he saw no sign of a husband, nor indeed of any other customers. Brenda had to pay for the drinks from Llama expenses. Tomorrow he could cash a cheque like an ordinary person. She said, 'Didn't Gavin take a ridiculous risk, hanging round the Llama party?'

'Of course he's a bit mad and beating Terry's face in made him madder. In a way he must've felt he'd become Terry. He'd got Terry's car as probably the keys were in the dead man's pocket. He'd got Terry's expenses by writing in to Llama. No doubt he knew Terry might win the prize and, if Terry's wife collected it, he'd get it straight off her.'

'By driving his car at her?'

'By then he'd got used to killing.' Felix finished his Guinness.

'Is that what you imagine happened?'

'More or less.'

'It may not be true?'

'Perhaps it wasn't exactly like that.'

'The truth may come out at the trial.'

'If Gavin's got Septimus Roache and Chipless defending him, I should think it's extremely unlikely.'

They sat in silence for a while as the image of the happenings in Gavin's van slowly faded. Then Felix said, 'Tomorrow, when I'm able to pay for things, can I take you out to dinner?'

She didn't answer that. Instead she asked, 'When did you become sure?'

'When I got the DNA report which said the child couldn't

have been Gavin's. Of course it said that because they never tested Gavin's blood.'

She was leaning back in her chair, running her finger round the rim of her glass to make it sing. 'You mean,' she said, 'it is Gavin's child?'

'I don't know,' Felix said. 'The author's not all wise. The author doesn't know everything. I don't know who Ian's father is. I only know it's not me.'

Coming over the Downs the distant sea was only a shade greyer than the sky. The fields were drenched in autumn rain. He said, 'I'm dreading this.'

'Why?'

'My house'll be staked out. They'll be poking cameras and microphones at me.'

'No, they won't.'

'I'm afraid they will. It's quite easy to get my address. Why won't they?'

'I got my secretary to ring around. She told them you were going straight to stay with your publisher in Hampstead.'

'Tubal-Smith?'

'No less.'

'Won't he be furious?'

'Of course not. He loves having his name dropped in the papers.'

It was true. There was no one in front of the house, not even the elderly man from the *Coldsands and District Argus*. He could rely on her, everything she did for him worked.

'Well,' she said, 'you're home. And I'd better get back to London.'

'Why?' he said. 'Why not stay?'

'You're not pretending *this* is abroad?'

240

'Why do we have to wait for that?'

'Nothing ever stays the same. You can't expect it to.'

'So you feel differently. About me, I mean?'

'Yes,' she said. 'I think I love you.'

He felt a great wave of an unusual sensation he took for happiness. 'So you *will* stay?' he said.

'No. So I won't.'

'Why ever?'

'I used to say we'd done it in our heads, didn't I?' Her hands were caressing the steering-wheel and he dreaded what was to come. 'Well, now we've done so much more. So much has happened. Terrible things for you. Extraordinary things for me. After all that . . . Well, are you sure it's necessary? In that awful visiting-room I felt so close to you. Could we ever be closer than that?'

'Yes,' he said, 'now the screws aren't watching.'

'Get out now,' she said. 'Go back to your work. That's all you care about, isn't it?'

'No,' he said. 'You're all I care about. Some time, possibly . . . ?'

'Everything's possible.' She turned her face towards him, and he kissed her small lips, dry as insects' wings. Then she started the engine and he heard her drive away. He found the keys under a flowerpot where Mrs Ives had left them and opened the front door. No voice welcomed him. He felt completely alone.

He walked into his writing-room and it was as it had been on the day he first heard Gavin's voice on a tape. He looked down at his desk, at the pad of lined foolscap paper and the mug full of pens and pencils. He made sure that the metal duck full of paper-clips was directly in front of the clock presented to him by the public libraries of Sussex. He was about to straighten the glass paperweight with its view of the old Coldsands and then he caught sight of Chekhov. He felt ashamed of having borrowed the writer's name and, not being able to face him, put the photograph away in a drawer.

He had brought up a pile of letters which had grown by his front door. He looked at them without much interest but fished out an envelope marked OHMS and PROD. Placidity Jones had written again, standing in for Ken Savage who seemed to be permanently on holiday: 'Since we have had no reply to our previous letter we must ask for an immediate settlement of monies due for the maintenance of the child Ian Bowker . . .' Well, that was an easy one. When he got round to it, he would send Placidity a copy of the DNA reports and his responsibility for Miriam's child would be at an end for ever. Suddenly tired, he left the room to lie on his bed. There, curled up with the pillow round his ears, he fell into a deep sleep.

It was dark when he woke up, put on his glasses and went back to his workroom. He was waiting for the guilt about not writing to return. The room seemed stuffy so he went to the window and pushed it open; he looked out, listening to the perpetual, reassuring sound of the sea.

Then he saw on the pavement of the other side of the road, sitting on a bench under a street lamp, a familiar figure, waiting as though for a bus that never came.

At least it had stopped raining when Felix stood under the light and the small, serious boy in glasses looked up at him. 'Hullo, Dad,' Ian said.

Chapter Twenty-eight

'Teach the little buggers something about the countryside! Perhaps they'll get to know that eggs don't grow on trees, that bacon isn't made in plastic packages ready for the Tesco's freezer. Some of these mini-monsters have never seen grass, let alone a cow!' Bob Weaver of the Sleary Road Children's Home in South London was red-faced, explosive and tormented by conflicting emotions. He was genuinely concerned for the welfare of deprived and unfortunate children but, when it came to individual cases, children of all sorts irritated the hell out of him. They fell, in his experience, into two classes: the intolerably bumptious and the snivellingly self-pitying, and he was so torn between his duty to counsel and his longing to thump that he suffered permanent indigestion. His plan to get Miss O'Rourke to take these irritants off to visit the rural South Downs would get them out from under his feet.

'Am I to take Ian?' Miss O'Rourke spoke in a near whisper of plaintive compassion, which tempted Bob Weaver from time to time to thump her too. 'Watch out,' he reminded her. 'Ian has violence in his record.'

'Poor little lad,' Miss O'Rourke said. 'His mother's done a runner. Left him high and dry. Vanished off the face of the earth.'

Bob Weaver often wished that Ian would vanish also. Neither bumptious nor self-pitying, Ian Bowker had an unnerving way of staring at Mr Weaver, unblinking and for a long time, in an accusing sort of way. 'All right,' he said, 'take Ian. And there's no need to hurry back. Don't just let them taste the bloody countryside, give them a real dose of the stuff.' He planned to spend the afternoon in the Sleary Road Odeon where the latest American love story would blur his eyes with tears.

So Ian went on an expedition to the South Downs and stood in the ticket office of the nature reserve looking at the goods on sale. There were calendars, address books and knicker-bags decorated with badgers, baby deer and the occasional owl; dishcloths, egg cups and animal-covered aprons. Miss O'Rourke was struggling to keep the army of Sleary Road children from mutiny when the usually silent Ian approached her with a rabbit-decorated tissue-packet holder and asked if he could buy it for his mum. She was so astonished to hear Ian speak, and so touched by the boy's concern for a vanished mother, that she advanced him three pounds out of her float. She would charge it, she decided, to therapy.

Once out of the ticket office the children galloped into the woods, ignoring the carefully marked walkways. Soon Miss O'Rourke was alone, not knowing which way to turn, peering into the shadows under the dark trees from which golden leaves were still falling, calling, as her Irish mother used to call for her, 'Coo . . . eee . . . !' but answer came there none. It amazed her that so many children could disappear so swiftly and leave such a heavy silence behind them.

Ian had run as quickly as any of them, slithered down a precipice of wet leaves and stumbled over fallen branches. He felt the edge of a ploughed field sucking at his trainers until he reached the road. He hadn't bought a tissue-holder but still held the three, warm pound coins in his clenched fist. He would be able to pay for a bus if he could find one on the road he had seen signposted to Coldsands-on-Sea.

'I remembered where you live,' Ian said. 'I remember where Mum brought me. A long time ago.'

'Not so long.'

'Seems long to me.'

'Well, I suppose it does to me too.'

They were in Felix's kitchen eating fish and chips which they had bought opposite the pier. Ian still had change left from his bus fare and had offered a contribution which Felix refused. As he bit into a flabby chip, only made interesting by salt and vinegar, Felix remembered, for some reason, fish and chips with Ann on the night he brought her home after the theatre, when they talked about the ambiguity of art, and she made love to him with astonishing determination.

Ian said, 'Mum's not coming back.'

'How could you think that? Of course she is!'

'She wrote "I hope and pray it won't be long". But she took all her stuff. I don't think she'll be back.'

Felix thought of the varying appearances of Mirry, who had burst into his life and disappeared as suddenly because she had lied about a dead body. She might, indeed, stay away a long time.

'For good and all,' Ian said. 'I think she's gone for good.'

'Well, then.' Felix did his best to sound bright and encouraging. 'Is it all right where you are?'

'No.'

'What?'

'It's not all right.'

'Why not exactly?'

'With Mum it was a bit uncertain. I mean, you didn't quite

know what was going to happen next. And she wasn't all that good at keeping quiet. But in the children's home . . . I don't know. There are just too many people.'

'You don't like them?'

'Some of them are all right I suppose. But, well . . . We're not free. I just feel as if I've been captured.'

Unfortunately, Felix thought, I know what you mean.

'I don't want to stay there,' Ian said and selected another chip.

Then Felix didn't know what to say so, remembering his last conversation with Ian, he asked, 'Read any good books lately?'

'*The Dog's Dinner.*'

'Who's that by?'

'Nora Bone!'

Felix laughed; Ian looked solemn.

'Anything else?'

'*The Haunted House.*'

'Who wrote that, then?'

'Hugo First! You're not sending me back there, are you?'

'I suppose we'll have to ring up and explain. We can do that in the morning.'

'Explain what?'

'Well, where you are. Who I am. Why you came here.'

'I came here because I want you to look after me. That's all.'

'Me? Why do you think I'd look after you?' Felix was sorry when he'd said it. Ian looked suddenly lost, as though his last hope had gone. So they stared at each other, serious and solemn: the lonely man who had lived through a life he'd never thought to encounter, and the lonely boy who reminded him of himself.

'Because you're my dad. You are, aren't you?'

As though from a great distance away Felix heard himself saying, unaccountably, 'Yes.'

'This Miss O'Rourke's been quite helpful. Ian's going to come to me at weekends. Then he might be with me all the time. He could go to Coldsands High.'

It was strange but the sun always seemed to shine through the windows of the Evening Star Rest and Retirement Home. Felix's mother was looking straight up to the ceiling, smiling broadly.

'I knew it'd be a surprise to you to find out that you had a grandson you didn't know about. Well, to be honest with you, I didn't know about him either. But, well, Ian's got no one else to turn to now. You see, he's all alone. He's very quiet; a very quiet sort of boy. He enjoys jokes, you see, but in a quiet sort of way. When, well, when he's settled in, I might bring him to see you. You'd like that, wouldn't you?'

His mother turned her head slowly and looked at Felix. Then, as a cloud passed over the sun, her smile faded. He sat looking at her for a long time. Then he got up and went to find Miss Wellbeloved. Now Ian was his only living relative.

FOR THE BEST IN PAPERBACKS, LOOK FOR THE

In every corner of the world, on every subject under the sun, Penguin represents quality and variety—the very best in publishing today.

For complete information about books available from Penguin—including Puffins, Penguin Classics, and Arkana—and how to order them, write to us at the appropriate address below. Please note that for copyright reasons the selection of books varies from country to country.

In the United Kingdom: Please write to *Dept. JC, Penguin Books Ltd, FREEPOST, West Drayton, Middlesex UB7 0BR*.

If you have any difficulty in obtaining a title, please send your order with the correct money, plus ten percent for postage and packaging, to *P.O. Box No. 11, West Drayton, Middlesex UB7 0BR*

In the United States: Please write to *Consumer Sales, Penguin USA, P.O. Box 999, Dept. 17109, Bergenfield, New Jersey 07621-0120*. VISA and MasterCard holders call 1-800-253-6476 to order all Penguin titles

In Canada: Please write to *Penguin Books Canada Ltd, 10 Alcorn Avenue, Suite 300, Toronto, Ontario M4V 3B2*

In Australia: Please write to *Penguin Books Australia Ltd, P.O. Box 257, Ringwood, Victoria 3134*

In New Zealand: Please write to *Penguin Books (NZ) Ltd, Private Bag 102902, North Shore Mail Centre, Auckland 10*

In India: Please write to *Penguin Books India Pvt Ltd, 706 Eros Apartments, 56 Nehru Place, New Delhi 110 019*

In the Netherlands: Please write to *Penguin Books Netherlands bv, Postbus 3507, NL-1001 AH Amsterdam*

In Germany: Please write to *Penguin Books Deutschland GmbH, Metzlerstrasse 26, 60594 Frankfurt am Main*

In Spain: Please write to *Penguin Books S. A., Bravo Murillo 19, 1° B, 28015 Madrid*

In Italy: Please write to *Penguin Italia s.r.l., Via Felice Casati 20, I-20124 Milano*

In France: Please write to *Penguin France S. A., 17 rue Lejeune, F–31000 Toulouse*

In Japan: Please write to *Penguin Books Japan, Ishikiribashi Building, 2–5–4, Suido, Bunkyo-ku, Tokyo 112*

In Greece: Please write to *Penguin Hellas Ltd, Dimocritou 3, GR–106 71 Athens*

In South Africa: Please write to *Longman Penguin Southern Africa (Pty) Ltd, Private Bag X08, Bertsham 2013*